the cowboy says i do

DYLANN CRUSH

JOVE
New York

A JOVE BOOK
Published by Berkley
An imprint of Penguin Random House LLC
penguinrandomhouse.com

Copyright © 2020 by Dylann Crush
Excerpt from *Her Kind of Cowboy* © 2020 by Dylann Crush
Penguin Random House supports copyright. Copyright fuels creativity, encourages
diverse voices, promotes free speech, and creates a vibrant culture. Thank you for buying
an authorized edition of this book and for complying with copyright laws by not
reproducing, scanning, or distributing any part of it in any form without permission.
You are supporting writers and allowing Penguin Random House to continue to
publish books for every reader.

A JOVE BOOK, BERKLEY, and the BERKLEY & B colophon are
registered trademarks of Penguin Random House LLC.

ISBN: 9780593101643

First Edition: August 2020

Printed in the United States of America
1   3   5   7   9   10   8   6   4   2

Cover art: *couple* by Zaitsev Maksym / shutterstock;
puppy by Kerri Wile / Getty Images
Cover design by Ally Andryshak
Book design by Gaelyn Galbreath

To my mom, who instilled my fierce love of dogs,
especially those deemed the most unlovable,
and always made sure we had a four-legged
member of the family in the house.

one

⟡

"I do."

Lacey Cherish blinked multiple times, trying to see through the obnoxious fake eyelashes her assistant had talked her into wearing at the last minute. Her fingers fiddled with the microphone in front of her as she silently willed the reporter from the television station in Houston to give it a rest. Not even forty-eight hours into her term as the newly appointed mayor of the little town of Idont, Texas, and she already had a full-blown crisis on her hands.

The reporter didn't back down. Instead, she got up from the metal folding chair, causing the legs to scrape across the linoleum. Lacey squinted as she fought the urge to cover her ears. Her upper and lower eyelashes tangled together and she struggled to peer through the dark lines barring her vision.

"Let me rephrase that." The reporter cocked a hip while she consulted her notebook. "You expect us to believe you're going to find a way to put a positive spin on this?"

Lacey inhaled a deep breath through her nose in an

attempt to buy some time and answer with what might sound like a well-thought-out response. The problem was, she was winging this. No one had been more shocked than she was to find out the biggest business in town, Phillips Stationery and Imports, had closed their doors. The company had made their headquarters in Idont for over a hundred years, starting as a printing press then moving into manufacturing, and importing all kinds of novelties from overseas.

"I'm sure Mayor Cherish will have more to say as the situation unfolds." Leave it to Deputy Sheriff Bodie Phillips to bully everyone back into line. He was part of the problem. Granted, he wasn't the ogre who decided to shut down the warehouse, but he did share DNA with the two men in charge.

"I'll have a statement to the press by the end of the week," Lacey promised.

Her assistant stepped to the microphone as Lacey moved away. "Thanks, everyone, for coming. As Mayor Cherish said, she'll be prepared to address the closing by the end of the day on Friday."

"You okay?" Bodie appeared at her side. He angled his broad chest like a wall, as if trying to protect her from the prying eyes of the people who'd turned out for the press conference at city hall. All six of them.

"Yes. No thanks to you." She summoned her best scowl, ready to chastise him for interfering in her business. It didn't matter that much when they were kids, but he needed to see her in a different light now. She was the mayor, after all, not the same scrawny, bucktoothed little girl who used to follow him everywhere.

"I'm just as surprised as you." The look in his eyes proved he was telling the truth. She'd never seen that particular mixture of anger and frustration, and she was pretty sure she'd been exposed to all of his moods. "Dad didn't say a word to me about this and I spent the holidays over at their place, surrounded by the family."

"Well, you and your dad aren't exactly bosom buddies, now, are you?" She gathered her purse and shrugged on her jacket before heading down the hall to the back door of the building.

Bodie followed, taking one step to every three of hers. Damn heels. She would have been much more comfortable in a pair of ropers, but her new assistant never would have let her step in front of a microphone without looking the part of mayor. Which was precisely what Lacey paid her to do.

"Hey, you can't punish me for something my dad and my pops decided to do." Bodie stopped in front of her, his muscular frame blocking the door, his head nearly touching the low ceiling.

Lacey clamped a hand to her hip, ready for a throw-down. "I'm not trying to punish you. I just don't understand how all of a sudden, after a century in business, they decided they can't make a go of it anymore. And breaking the news right after the holidays?"

Bodie shrugged. "I don't know, Sweets."

"Stop calling me that. I'm the mayor now." She pursed her lips. Why couldn't he take her seriously? She'd figured the childhood nickname would have disappeared, along with her aggravating attraction to the man who'd been her big brother's best friend all her life. But here she was, back in Idont where nothing had changed, especially the way her traitorous body reacted to Bodie Phillips.

"Aw, come on, Lacey. You'll always be Sweets to me." He grinned, dazzling her with his million-dollar smile. Well, maybe not million-dollar, but she'd been there when he had to go through braces twice, so it had to be worth at least five or six grand.

She resisted the pull of his charm. He'd always been

able to tease her back into a good mood when hers had gone sour. But this was different. The only reason she'd run for mayor was because her dad had been forced out of office after a particularly embarrassing public incident. In which he drove a golf cart into a pond. A stolen golf cart. While drunk.

His stunt earned him his third DWI and twenty-four months of house arrest. During her tenure as mayor, she hoped she could polish off the tarnished family name and turn the tide of public opinion about the Cherish family. That, and she couldn't find a real job. Evidently a degree in communications wasn't worth much more than the paper her diploma was printed on.

"What am I going to do, Bodie?" She shook her head, her gaze drawn to a section of chipped linoleum on the floor. The whole town seemed to be falling apart.

"Maybe it's time to consider merging with Swynton."

Lacey jerked her head up, causing one of her fake eyelashes to flop up and down. "Please tell me you didn't just suggest we wave good-bye to our roots and hand our town over to that obnoxious man." She tried to reattach the line of lashes against her eyelid.

Bodie didn't bother to suppress his smile. "Come on, Lacey. You've got to admit, their economy could run circles around ours. I know you don't care for Buck, but he's doing something right over there."

She pressed her lips together. The only thing Mayor Buck Little was doing was turning the once-semicharming town of Swynton into a hot pocket of cheap housing and seedy businesses. "Have you seen how many building permits they've issued in the past three months? If he had it his way, we'd end up with empty strip malls and low-rent apartment buildings all over town."

"At least that would create jobs and give people some affordable housing options." Bodie leaned against the wall. "My family's business was our biggest employer."

"I know." Lacey gritted her teeth, wishing with all her heart she had someone to talk to about this. Someone who might be able to offer a realistic option, not just confirm everything she already knew about what a sorry situation they were in. "I need to think."

Bodie pushed open the door leading to the back parking lot and swept his arm forward, gesturing for her to go first. "You want to grab lunch over at the diner and talk?"

"I can't now. I'm late for my shift at the Burger Bonanza." She jammed her sunglasses on her face, crushing them against the stupid lashes as she brushed past him through the door into the sunny, but chilly, February day.

"When are you going to quit that job, Lacey Jane? The mayor shouldn't be flipping burgers and mixing milk shakes."

She turned, jabbing a finger into Bodie's chest. "I'll do what I have to do to pay the bills." She jabbed harder. "And I'll do what I have to do to keep this town afloat."

Despite her effort, the concrete plane of his pecs didn't budge. Damn him.

He grabbed her hand, twirling her around like they were doing a two-step instead of sparring about the future of their hometown. "That's one thing Idont has going for it that Swynton never will."

"What's that?" Lacey stumbled as he released her, not sure if she was dizzy from the spin or off-balance because of the way her hand had felt in his.

"You." Bodie tipped his cowboy hat at her as he walked away. "You're determined, I'll give you that, Mayor."

She adjusted her purse strap and tried to compose herself as he climbed into his pickup and drove away. Bodie wasn't one to dish out compliments, especially to a woman he'd considered a pesky nuisance most of his life. Either that was the nicest thing he'd ever said to her or he wanted something. Knowing him, it was the latter.

That would give her two things to think about while

she worked her shift at the Burger Bonanza . . . how to save the town of Idont, and why in the world Bodie was trying to butter her up like a fresh-baked biscuit.

"You're late." Jojo stood at the counter, loading her arms with blue plate specials. "Watch out for Helmut, he's on a bender."

"Thanks." Lacey slipped off her heels and slid her feet into her flats before tying an apron around her waist. "Where do you need me today?"

"Why don't you start on the floor and take over the grill when Helmut leaves?" Jojo had been waiting tables at the Burger Bonanza since she and Lacey started high school. If Helmut had taken the time to name a manager, Jojo would be the natural choice. But instead he paid her the same as the rest of the waitstaff and expected her to keep everyone in line.

"Sounds good." Lacey grabbed her order pad and made her way to the front of the restaurant.

"Table twelve just got seated." Jojo nodded toward the corner booth.

"Got it." Lacey headed that way, her eyes on her note-book. "Hey, can I get y'all something to drink?"

"Well, look who it is." The voice that had squashed a thousand of Lacey's childhood dreams drifted across the table.

Lacey lifted her gaze to stare right into the eyes of her high school nemesis—Adeline Monroe. "Oh, hi, Adeline. It's been a long time." And thank God for that. Adeline lived over in Swynton. It used to be the only reason she'd cross the river that divided the two towns was if she was on the hunt for some too-good-to-pass-up gossip. What was she after now?

"It sure has. And look at you. I heard you came back."

Adeline leaned over the table, lowering her voice, that familiar glint in her eye. "Is it true you got yourself elected mayor?"

Lacey nodded. "Yep, sure did. Now, what will it be? A round of Burger Bonanza Banzai Shakes? Or can I start you off with a basket of buffalo bites?" She tried to pull a smile from deep down, but it seemed to stick on the way to her face. Half of her mouth lifted, the other half slid down, probably making her look like an undecided clown, especially with the damn lashes still glued to her eyelids.

Adeline turned to the man next to her. A quick glance at the giant rock on her left hand confirmed he was probably her fiancé. What happened to the curse Lacey had cast at graduation? Adeline was supposed to be hairless and withered by now, or at least well on her way. Instead she looked like she'd just stepped out of a salon. Every highlighted hair was in place. Her eyebrows were plucked to perfection and there was no sign of premature aging.

"Lacey, I'd like you to meet my fiancé, Roman." Adeline put her hand on Roman's arm, obviously staking her claim. As if Lacey were going to try to hump the man right there at table twelve.

"Congratulations. Nice to meet you, Roman." She managed to correct her awkward expression and forced a smile. "Are you ready to order?"

Adeline's smirk faded. She ran a manicured nail down the side of the menu. "We'll take two Burger Bonanza baskets with fries. Diet for me."

"Do you have iced tea?" Roman asked.

Lacey nodded. She'd been afraid the man couldn't speak. She wouldn't have put it past Adeline to marry a man incapable of talking back to her. He probably didn't get a word in edgewise most of the time. "I'll be back in a minute with your drinks."

She tucked her order pad into the front of her apron.

First the news of the Phillips business closing, now an unexpected visit from Adeline. Bad news usually came in threes. What would happen next?

It took less than a minute to find out. As she approached the soda station to grab two cups, someone grabbed her arm.

Bodie.

"Mayor Cherish, you'll need to come with me." His voice was all business. The commanding tone sent a shiver straight through her. But his lips twitched. A hint of humor shone in those deep gray eyes. She'd spent way too much of her life thinking about what it would feel like to lose herself in those depths.

"What are you doing here? I've got a shift."

"I'm aware of that." His fingers closed around her elbow, eliminating any argument, propelling her toward the door. "But we've got a problem that needs your attention. Now."

two

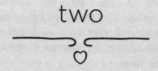

Bodie gripped Lacey's elbow a little tighter as he led her outside. He wouldn't admit it, but he kind of enjoyed spending time with Idont's new mayor—much more than he expected, and a lot more than he should.

"Stop, Bodie. I'm not taking another step until you tell me what's going on." Lacey planted her feet as she wrapped her arms around her middle. It was chilly, even for Texas. He should have grabbed her coat, but now he didn't want to take the time to go back inside.

"Here." He slid his jacket off then draped it over her shoulders.

"I don't want your jacket." She shrugged it off and tossed it back at him. "I want to know why you dragged me out here during my shift. Helmut's going to pop a blood vessel over this. What's so important?"

"There's a protest down at the warehouse. Seems Jonah Wylder has chained himself to the front doors. Says he's not leaving until someone gives him his job back."

"You've got to be kidding me." She tilted her head

back, giving him a full-on glimpse of the smooth ivory column of her neck.

When did the little girl who used to bug the hell out of him turn into such a beauty? Seemed like she'd always been underfoot as a kid. He and her big brother, Luke, couldn't go anywhere without her tagging along. Since she'd been back he hadn't paid much attention to her—he'd been too focused on trying to figure out a way to get out of Idont himself. But now with her taking on the doomed role of mayor, he started to wish he hadn't ignored her for so long.

"So what do we do?" Her jaw set, she leveled her gaze on him. "I suppose I need to try to talk some sense into him."

Bodie tried to suppress a smile. "Good luck with that. Jonah's not exactly known for keeping a level head."

"Let's go. I'll ride with you so we can talk on the way." She didn't give him much choice but to follow behind her as she crossed the parking lot to his truck.

Should he try to open the door for her or let her handle it on her own? He wavered as they got closer. He'd never treated Lacey as anything but a kid. But now, there was no trace of the freckle-faced teen. He increased his pace to make it to the passenger door before her.

"Thanks." She barely glanced at him as he held the door while she climbed into the truck.

While he waited for her to get settled, he couldn't help but notice the way her skirt rode up on her thighs. Rubbing a hand over the scruff on his chin, he chastised himself. This was Luke's sister he was undressing in his mind. He needed to shut that shit down. Fast. He closed the door and stomped around the truck to get behind the wheel.

They rode in silence for the first few minutes, giving him a chance to sort out his thoughts.

"So how do you suggest I handle Jonah?" Lacey swiveled in her seat to face Bodie.

"Let him sit out there and freeze his ass off." Bodie took a sip of water from his travel tumbler. "Jonah's a hothead. He'll make a scene but once everyone goes home and the excitement wears off he'll slink back to the rock he lives under."

"That's one of my constituents you're talking about." Lacey adjusted the vent on the dash.

"Yeah, I feel sorry for you about that. He was an ass-hole when he was younger and he's grown into an even bigger asshole now."

"Great. How long is my term again?" She twisted a strand of hair around her finger as she gazed out the front window.

"Four years. But as long as you don't get arrested, you'll probably get reelected." He meant that as a joke, a little bit of humor at her dad's expense, but Lacey didn't smile. Bodie glanced back and forth from the road in front of him to Lacey's profile. Her pulse ticked along her jaw as she drummed her fingers on her knee. "You know I didn't mean anything by that, right?"

Her breath came out on a long sigh. "I know. Wish I knew what Dad was thinking when he decided to go on a joyride."

"If it's any consolation"—Bodie gave her an apologetic grin—"I really didn't enjoy arresting your dad that day." Her dad had been more of a father figure to him growing up than his own flesh and blood.

"Nope." Her mouth quirked into a half smile. "That doesn't make me feel any better. I don't know why I thought it would be a good idea to run for mayor. What was I thinking?"

"You want me to answer that?" He could tell her if she really wanted to know. Lacey was a fixer. Always had been and always would be.

"No." She closed her eyes and let her head roll from

side to side, like she was trying to ease some tension. "I just wish I'd thought it through. Seemed like the thing to do when Dad had to step down."

"Idont is lucky you stepped up. If you hadn't, can you imagine where we'd be right now without a mayor?" He slowed the truck to make a right.

"Probably annexed into Swynton by now. I've heard Mayor Little works fast."

He'd heard that, too, and even experienced it firsthand. The mayor of Swynton had definite ideas about how things should be done. They'd had their fair share of run-ins during the few years he'd been working as deputy sheriff. Mayor Buck Little wasn't someone to cross.

"Have you had time to think about what you're going to do yet?" he asked.

"You mean in the fifteen minutes I had in between my dealings with you?" Lacey shook her head, sending her wavy, shoulder-length hair bouncing.

He caught a whiff of something flowery. Had to be her. Although he didn't recall her ever smelling like anything but horses when they were younger. Horses and the butterscotch candy she always seemed to have in her mouth. That's what earned her the nickname of Sweets in the first place. "You warm enough?"

"No." She clamped her arms around her middle. "But I'll be fine. What should we do with Jonah? A little 'good cop, bad cop' routine?"

"Sure, I'll rough him up then you sweet-talk him into going home." He slid his gaze her way to catch her reaction.

"Really? Does that kind of stuff work?"

"Only on TV."

She let out a groan. "Maybe I should just let you handle it, then. I can wait in the truck while you take care of Mr. Wylder."

"And miss out on the fun?" He'd known her all her life and had seen her in action time and again. She'd no more be able to step aside in a moment of crisis than he'd be able to ignore someone purposely breaking the law. The only difference was, he got paid to maintain law and order while she spent her life trying to fix things whether it fell under her job description or not.

"Yeah, I suppose I ought to at least try to talk to him."

"That's the spirit." Bodie pulled the truck into the long, tree-covered drive leading to the warehouse. Once, the land had belonged to the founder of the town, his great-great-great-great-great-grandfather. He'd built the giant Victorian house first. When he decided to become a printer, he put up an outbuilding just down the drive. Over the years the Phillips family had expanded until the outbuilding became the warehouse it was today.

"You mean him and the mob he's got with him?" Bodie asked.

"What?" Lacey turned toward him. "I can't imagine Jonah inciting a mob."

As he eased the truck to a stop, Bodie pointed through the windshield. "Okay, maybe not a mob, but he did bring some friends."

"Oh, come on. When am I going to catch a break?" She opened the door and climbed down, looking out of place in her slim skirt and blouse among the flannel-and-denim-clad crowd.

Bodie grabbed his hat, prepared to provide backup.

"Well, if it ain't our new mayor." Jonah sized her up as she approached. He stood at the front door of the building, layers of metal chains wrapped around his torso.

"What can I do for you, Mr. Wylder?" Lacey offered her hand but must have thought better of it when Jonah struggled to work his arm free to take it.

"For starters you can reopen the warehouse." His eyes narrowed. A chorus of encouraging "yeahs" and "that's rights" floated up from the small crowd. "And then you can give us all a nice, fat raise."

Lacey crossed her arms over her chest. "I'm afraid I can't make that happen."

"Then figure out a way." Jonah nodded, his head being the only part of his body that he seemed to be able to move.

"Look, Mr. Wylder—"

"Jonah," he insisted.

"Okay, Jonah. I'd love nothing more than to open up the warehouse, give all of you your jobs back, and double your pay. But we both know that's not going to happen."

"Then I'll just stay here until you find a way." Jonah shrugged, making the chains clink together.

Bodie shifted his weight from one foot to the other, waiting to see how the situation would play out. Lacey looked like she was about to cry. Her bottom lip trembled and she tightened her grip around her middle. He couldn't let them get the best of her, not on her second day on the job.

"You're just going to stay out here all night, then?" Bodie asked.

Jonah nodded. "If that's what it takes."

"And I suppose you've got a permit for that?" He took a step toward Lacey, sensing her focus shift from Jonah to him.

Jonah glanced to one of his buddies. "I don't need a permit to stay out here."

"This land is private property. If you want to hold a demonstration or a public gathering, based on city code, you need to ask for permission from the owners first." Bodie shrugged his shoulders "Unless you'd rather I arrest you and take you in."

"What are you doing?" Lacey whispered. "I'm handling this."

Bodie put a hand out, gesturing for her to be quiet. "Your call, Jonah, but I bet your wife will be real pissed if you end up with another offense."

Jonah gritted his teeth, then muttered something under his breath.

Lacey glared at Bodie. "I said I've got this."

"Fine." Jonah shook his head, the fight draining from him. "Boys, get me out of here. We'll have to find another way to settle our differences."

One of Jonah's friends fumbled with a set of keys. While he waited for the men to disperse, Bodie turned to Lacey, pretty damn pleased at the way he'd managed to break things up. No one got hurt, Lacey saved face, and it was a win-win all around.

But the look she gave him wasn't full of the thanks he expected—the thanks he deserved.

"What?" He held his hands out, wondering what he'd done to incite such an angry response. "You're welcome. Aren't you going to say something?"

Fire blazed in those bright baby blues, burning hot and icy cold at the same time. "Oh, I'm going to say something, all right."

three

"You're welcome? You expect me to thank you for that stunt?" Lacey bit her tongue to keep from yelling a string of obscenities at the dense deputy. How could he possibly think he'd been helping?

"I got Jonah to leave, didn't I?" Bodie gave her one of his most patronizing looks, the one that drove her absolutely bonkers, like she was too stupid to even realize what a savior move he'd pulled.

"We resolved nothing. I had a chance to make some headway with those men and you blew it for me." She glanced skyward, trying to shake off the urge to throttle the man. As she looked up, the damn eyelash fluttered into her eye. "Oh hell."

"What's wrong?" Bodie put his hand on her back as she doubled over, trying to get her fingers on the fuzzy black strip.

"These stupid eyelashes. I don't know why I let Chelsea talk me into them. She said I needed to glam it up for my first time on camera." Lacey rubbed at her eyelid, not caring anymore if she ended up with mascara and eye-liner all over her cheek. She needed to get the damn fuzzy caterpillars off her face.

"Let me see." Bodie batted her hands away. "Close your eyes and hold still."

She did. His fingers gently fluttered across her cheek. "Be careful."

He stepped close, close enough that an intoxicating scent of woodsy, earthy male washed over her. She breathed him in, hyperaware of his proximity. He had to be close, almost touching. The thought almost sent her into a full-blown panic attack. But then his fingers brushed back her hair.

"Got it." His words came out on a breath, warming her cheek.

She opened her eyes and stared directly into his. A crackle of awareness zipped through her. Unable to move, she waited, all sense of time and space suspended. Bodie's mouth couldn't have been more than a few inches from hers. Did he feel something, too?

Click. Click. The unmistakable sound of a camera shutter snapped her out of her trance.

Bodie startled, stepping back, taking his warmth with him. Lacey ran a hand over her face to make sure her extended lashes weren't stuck to her forehead, then took in her surroundings. Jonah and his band of misfits had loaded up and were leaving. But Cyrus Beasely, the photographer from the local paper, stood about fifty yards away, snapping pictures of the warehouse, the hand-printed CLOSED sign stuck to the front door, and them.

"What do you think you're doing?" She sprang into offense mode.

Cyrus kept snapping pictures as she approached. "Mayor Cherish, care to comment on the protest here today?"

"What protest?" She swiveled her head from side to side. "You need to leave. The warehouse and the grounds are closed to the public."

"Care to comment on your association with Deputy Sheriff Phillips, then?" Cyrus let the camera settle against his chest while he pulled a notebook out of his bag.

"Excuse me? My what?" Lacey stalked toward him, ready to rip the camera off his neck and smash it to smithereens against the pavement.

Bodie stepped into her path, wrapped an arm around her, and prevented her from taking another step. "Hey, settle down, Lacey."

"You." She whirled out of his grasp, landing a pointer finger on his chest. Ouch. When would she learn that Bodie's pecs were just a slab of granite in disguise? "You stay out of this."

"That's okay, I've got all I need." Cyrus lifted his camera, zoomed in on her, and snapped one more shot before racing back to his car.

Lacey stopped, took in a deep breath, and tried to center herself. She focused on her breathing—in and out—trying to prevent herself from slumping into a heap at Bodie's feet.

"What the hell was that?" Bodie's voice popped the imaginary bubble she'd created to protect herself.

"I don't know. He must have caught wind something was going down out here." She shook her head.

Bodie stopped right in front of her, obscuring her view of the parking lot. "Not him. You. What the hell are you doing, Sweets?"

Forehead scrunched, she gazed up at him. Past the scruff on his chin, over the disappointed scowl on his lips, settling on the hard glint in his eyes. "What do you mean? Cyrus had no right to take photos of me. Of us."

"You're living in the public eye now. Cyrus is just doing his job."

Her stomach knotted into a giant mess, bigger and tighter than the tangle of yarn she'd created when she tried to learn how to crochet. "Oh no, do you think he thinks . . ." The idea was too horrifying to even say out loud.

"Thinks what?" Bodie glared down at her.

Lacey covered her mouth with her hand. "The eyelashes. And you were close, so close. What if he thinks there's something going on between us?"

"Between you and me?" Bodie's eyebrows lifted, almost disappearing under the brim of his hat. "Don't be ridiculous."

"Never mind." Was the idea so out of line he couldn't even consider it?

Lips quirked up in a smirk, Bodie clasped a hand to her shoulder. "You're an elected official now. Get used to it. People are going to be following you around, waiting for you to mess up. Don't you remember what it was like when your dad was mayor?"

"I wasn't here much." Lacey shrugged, warmth radiating down from her shoulder where Bodie's hand still rested. "He didn't take office until I was off at college, and then I only came home on holidays. It didn't really affect me."

"I suppose." Bodie jerked his thumb toward the truck. "Can we get out of here? I've got a meeting back at the office in a bit."

"Yeah." Lacey swept her gaze around the area. The warehouse sat undisturbed. Off in the distance she could see the turret of the main house. What was going to happen to this space now that the Phillips family had shut everything down? With a sinking feeling settling in her gut, she followed Bodie to the truck.

four

"I'm home." Lacey let the front door slam behind her.

"Did you bring dinner?" Her dad sat in his favorite recliner, the arms worn from years of use.

"Yes." She set the bag of takeout on the table in the front hall while she shrugged out of her jacket. "Burgers again. Is that okay?"

"Beggars can't be choosers, now, can they?" The resignation in his tone made her glance up.

"I wouldn't exactly call you a beggar." She carried the bag into the living room, the smell of grease making her stomach twinge.

He reached for the bag. "Thanks for taking care of your dear old dad, honey."

She released the bag into his hands, glancing at the collection of empty beer cans on the side table as she did. "You get anything done today?"

The bag crinkled as he pulled a double-decker Bonanza Burger from the sack. "Sure. I went into the office, chatted up the city council, and made plans to reopen the warehouse that just closed down."

Lacey sighed. The "poor, pitiful me" routine her dad had been pulling for the past few months was getting old. It was his own fault he ended up on house arrest. Why did he make it out to seem like he was the victim? "Very funny. I thought you were going to talk to that college buddy of yours about doing some consulting."

"They don't need me anymore. Although they did manage to hire someone else to help them with their new campaign." He nibbled on a fry.

"I'm sure something else will turn up." She put a hand on his shoulder and squeezed. The longer he sat here, un-engaged and uninterested in anything going on around him, the longer she'd have to stay. She'd given up her place in town when he got sentenced to house arrest. At the time it made sense. Paying for rent on her small studio apartment seemed like an unnecessary expense when she'd be spending so much time at her dad's place. Besides, now she could use what she'd pay in rent to afford her assistant.

"Saw you on the news this afternoon." Dad spread the paper wrapper out on his stomach. "You handled that reporter from Houston pretty well, just like a pro."

"Until Bodie butted in." Lacey scowled. "He thinks I need his help. Which I don't."

Dad laughed, making his burger bounce up and down on his belly. "Bodie has a mind of his own, sweetheart."

"You know, maybe you can help me. I need to figure out what to do now that the Phillips family is closing down their business." Her dad had years of experience dealing with the inner workings of Idont. He might not be able to leave the house, but he could still help her navigate the muddy water she'd suddenly found herself drowning in.

"I was pretty surprised when I heard." He took a bite

of burger. She waited while he swallowed. "Seems to me like they'd want to stay on the good side of the town."

"Why's that?" Lacey sat down on the edge of the couch and eased her shoes off. Her feet ached from the short stint in heels this morning. She either needed to practice wearing them more or better yet, give them up for good.

"The town owns the land out there. Phillips defaulted on the payments about eighteen months ago when I was still in office. Their business isn't doing as well as they'd like people to think."

"What does that mean?" Lacey asked.

"Means whatever they left on the town's property ought to belong to the town. Have you looked inside?" He reached for one of the beer cans on the table next to him, then drained it. "Hey, sweetheart, can you bring me another beer?"

She got up, padding to the kitchen on bare feet. While she filled a glass with water from the dispenser on the fridge, she thought about what her dad said. If the town owned the warehouse and everything in it, maybe they could sell the inventory to raise some money. But that still didn't fix the fact that dozens of people were without jobs.

"What's that?" her dad asked as she set the water next to him and gathered the beer cans.

"Why don't you try to stay hydrated?" She turned, taking the cans to the recycle bin. Seeing her dad fall into the deep, dark hole he preferred to reside in had bothered her most of her life. Once upon a time he'd been full of smiles and laughs. Back when her mom was still alive. Lacey dumped the beer cans, grateful her mom wasn't around to see how her dad was doing. Mom had been the love of his life, and when she passed away it was like a light inside of him had shut off. No matter what she did, Lacey couldn't seem to get it lit again.

"I'm going to take a bath." The need to wash away the

failure of the day overwhelmed her. A nice warm bath and a glass of wine would do the trick.

"Thanks for dinner, honey."

"You're welcome." She shuffled back to her bedroom to change into her robe before pouring herself a glass of wine from the box she kept hidden in her closet. It wouldn't do any good for her dad to find her stash. He'd blow through that, too. If she could only get the local beer barn to stop delivering to him, maybe then he'd stop wallowing in self-pity.

Ten minutes later she settled into the tub, her glass of wine perched on the edge. Relaxing into the lavender-scented bubbles, she let out a deep breath. Being mayor wasn't what she expected. Granted, she was only two days in, but it was supposed to be somewhat of an honorary title. It wasn't even a part-time job. And now she had a whole town to save and a rekindled attraction to Bodie that needed to be stifled.

She opened her eyes, looking for something to distract her. A rack of magazines sat a few feet away. Lacey hadn't flipped through those in years. Afraid she might come across one of Luke's rags full of half-naked women, she settled on the one at the front. A photo of a summer bride decorated the front cover.

Lacey sighed as she gazed at the bouquets of lilacs and white roses. She'd dreamed of having a wedding like that one day. Back when she was a kid she'd even made lists of what they'd eat, what kind of flowers they'd have, and what kind of gifts she'd get for her twelve bridesmaids. A soft laugh escaped her lips. Twelve bridesmaids. She'd had big dreams back then. If she got married tomorrow she'd have only one person she was close enough with to invite to be in her wedding—her best friend, Zina.

It hadn't been Zina's choice to come back to Idont either, but at least they still had each other. Although, as the director of For Pitties' Sake, the local pit bull rescue, Zina had even less free time than Lacey did.

Her mind wandered farther down the path of her childhood dreams. The groom. Her cheeks tingled. She'd almost forgotten. Every time she'd imagined getting married, she'd pretended the groom was Bodie. She sat up in the tub, causing water to splash over the side. Of course she'd pictured him. He was the only boy besides her brother who'd ever bothered to say anything nice to her. She shrugged away the thought that it might mean something and flipped the magazine open.

She skimmed the first few pages, passing over ads for cosmetics, promises of how she could make any man fall in love with her, and a quiz that would tell her which fairy-tale hero would be her Mr. Right. The next page flipped open, showcasing the same bride from the front cover. It was an article about how to plan the most romantic wedding. Lacey vaguely remembered reading the article years ago. She'd even circled some of the tips with her favorite purple pen.

As she devoured the single-spaced pages, including a whole section of wedding themes, an idea started to form. Idont needed a new source of income. People needed jobs. She needed a way to restore her family's name. What if she could take care of all three things at once?

five

⌒⌒
♡

Bodie sat at his desk, draining his coffee mug. He'd been working up the nerve to head over to his folks' place and start asking questions. He could guess all he wanted, but the only way to find out for sure why his family decided to close the warehouse was to come right out and ask. As he got up from his chair, determined to go through with his plan, he noticed her in the doorway.

Lacey. She had on tight jeans, the kind that didn't leave much to the imagination, and a pair of well-worn boots. She must have come from riding since she wore her dad's old canvas jacket over a flannel button-down shirt. He swallowed, his mouth suddenly feeling rather dry. She'd never looked so appealing.

"Bodie." She met him on his way to the door. "We need to talk."

He looked around the office. The sheriff's secretary eyed them over her cup of tea. "I'm heading out to run an errand. Why don't you come with me and we can talk on the way?"

She grabbed his arm. Heat seemed to scorch his skin, even through the heavy jacket he'd shrugged on. "I have an idea, a good one. A way to save the town, put people back to work, and—"

"Let's go." He pulled his arm out of her grasp and put his hand on her shoulder, steering her toward the exit.

Once they made it through the door and into the parking lot, she rounded on him. "What the heck? I come in trying to talk to you about my idea—my great idea—and you can't even bother to give me a minute or two of your time?"

"Sorry, I didn't want anyone to overhear. Tell me, what's the big idea?"

Her cheeks pinked with excitement, her enthusiasm almost contagious.

"Weddings." She climbed into the truck, bouncing onto the seat next to him. "They're big business. Huge. In fact, the wedding industry pulls in over fifty billion dollars a year."

"Weddings? What do weddings have to do with Idont?" Bodie backed out of his spot and pulled onto the road. "We don't even have a hall big enough to host a reception."

Her eyebrows lifted, and her lips curved into a smile.

"Wait." Bodie eased the truck to a stop on the side of the road, then shifted in his seat, twisting to face her. "What's going on in that head of yours?"

"It's the perfect solution. I stayed up last night working out the details." She reached into her purse, feeling around for something. A notebook. She leaned close. Close enough that he could catch a whiff of the sweet smell of hay and horses. "Here you go."

He glanced at the notebook she'd set on the seat between them. Line after line of Lacey's curly script covered the page. "Can you give me the condensed version?"

She huffed out a breath. "Fine. Did you know the average wedding costs thirty-nine thousand dollars? And about eighty-five percent of that goes toward the reception?"

"Those are great stats. But I still don't see what that has to do with Idont. We're not exactly wedding central around here." He picked up the notebook and handed it back to her.

"That's just it." Next to him, Lacey practically vibrated with excitement. "Idont isn't. But what if we change the town name to Ido? We could position the town as a major wedding destination. Ido, Texas. Has a certain ring to it, don't you think?"

He stared at her—the way her eyes shone with enthusiasm, the way her mouth curved into a smile. And then he laughed. A full-on, doubled-over, deep-from-the-belly laugh.

Her palms pushed at his arm. "It's not funny."

"Sorry, Lacey." He put up his hands in an attempt to protect himself. "It *is* funny. It's hysterical." He tried to catch his breath, but every time he came close he thought of his dad or pops dressed up in penguin suits, ushering in another wedding party. "Who's going to do the food? I guess you could serve Banzai Burgers. Maybe you can offer Jonah a job as master of ceremonies. The man does have a way with words."

She gave up on pushing his arm, deciding to whack him over the head with her notebook instead. "I never should have told you. All you ever do is make me feel stupid."

"Hey." He caught her hands, his heart squeezing into a tight knot at the sound of heartbreak in her voice. "I don't think you're stupid."

She pulled her hands away, turning to face the window. "Can you take me back to my truck now?"

"Lacey." He reached out, brushing the hair from her shoulder. It was soft, softer than he imagined when he thought of holding her head in his hands, tilting her face at just the right angle so he could kiss her. "I'm sorry. I never want to make you feel less than you are."

"Doesn't matter what you think." Her voice came out soft, low, full of hurt. "You go on, move to Swynton with your dad and your pops. I'll figure this out on my own."

He pinched the bridge of his nose as he let out a groan. "I never said I was moving to Swynton."

"You never said you weren't."

It was like arguing with the ten-year-old version of Lacey all over again. But they weren't talking about which flavor of Airheads was the most sour. This was serious stuff. "I'm not going anywhere." At least not yet. Not until he made sure she was safe and figured out what his dad and pops were up to.

"Wouldn't matter to me either way." Her shoulders curled forward, like she was trying to shield herself from him.

He swallowed the bitter taste in his mouth as he maneuvered the truck into a wide U-turn in the middle of the road. "Fine. Why don't we try talking about this again later?"

"Fine." She crossed her arms across her middle. "But I need you to do something for me."

Lacey wasn't one to ask for favors. But he owed it to Luke to look after her while he was overseas, fighting a much bigger enemy than they'd ever face in their tiny corner of Texas. "Name it."

She leaned against the door, adjusting her body to face his. "I need you to back the hell off."

"Come again?" Did she seriously just tell him to leave her alone?

"I mean it. No one is going to take me seriously or listen to a word I say if you're standing in front of me, trying to fight my battles the whole time."

He draped one hand over the steering wheel. "Look, if it's about Jonah—"

"It's not just about Jonah." She shook her head. "It's

about everything. First you interrupted my press conference—"

"You answered three questions. I'd hardly call that a—"

"Doesn't matter what you'd call it. That's my point." Her chin jutted into the air. "I don't want you calling anything. If we're going to survive each other, I need you to butt out of my business."

He chewed on the inside of his cheek to keep from saying something he might regret. "You about done?"

"Maybe." She sulked, leaning against the door.

Bodie almost laughed. Her attitude reminded him so much of when they were kids. When she didn't get her way she'd pout, sticking that lower lip out just about as far as it would go. "You're the mayor, Lacey."

"I know that. The headache I've been dealing with for the past two days has been a constant reminder." She put her hand to her temple as she gazed out the window.

"That means I can't stay out of your business. The sheriff's office works pretty damn close with the mayor's office. I'd even go so far as to say your business *is* my business."

"What's that?" She reached over and put her hand on his leg. Dammit. His foot flew off the brake, and his hips almost bucked up at her touch.

"What the hell?" He regained control of his hormones as he swiveled to face her. For a moment Bodie forgot he was sitting in his truck with his buddy's little sister. He was just a man and she was just a woman, and . . .

"Over there. Watch out!" Lacey pointed at something ahead.

Bodie slammed on the brakes, but not in time to avoid crashing into the trash cans at the edge of the sheriff's parking lot. The truck came to a stop and he'd barely shoved it into park before he jumped out to take a look at his front bumper.

Lacey caught up to him. "Any damage?"

He straightened. "Nothing major." Just another little dent in the bumper.

"Oh no." Lacey turned to point at something behind the trash cans. "Not another one."

"What?" He followed her finger, his breath hitching in his chest as he spotted the frightened dog. "Hell. You want to make a difference as mayor, figure out a way to catch the assholes who keep dumping their dogs out here."

The animal stood shivering by a strand of scrubby bushes, its mouth bound closed by duct tape.

"That poor thing." Lacey stepped next to him.

Bodie inched toward the animal. The dog didn't move, just kept a wary eye on him. "I'm not going to hurt you, sweetheart."

The dog glanced between him and Lacey, its tail starting to wag, just a tiny bit.

"Give me your belt, Lacey," Bodie mumbled.

"I can't do that, my jeans will fall off." She clamped her hand on his arm, sending a pulse of awareness through him.

"It's either that or it might run." He rummaged in his pocket for something to offer as a bribe. The dog couldn't be much older than a year or so. Baggy skin hung from its frame. Based on the size of its paws, it still had lots of growing left to do.

"Fine." Lacey handed over her belt. "But if I end up mooning everyone in town, it'll be all your fault."

He cracked a grin at the thought of getting a glimpse at Lacey's behind. "I'll take full responsibility." Arranging the belt into a loop, he took a few more steps closer to the dog. "Are you hungry, bud?" He held out a piece of venison jerky he found at the bottom of his pocket.

The dog sniffed the air and inched closer. Dried blood covered the poor thing's muzzle. Bodie's stomach clenched. He'd seen more than his fair share of evil in the way men treated each other. But there was no excuse for mishandling an animal.

"There you go." With the dog sniffing the piece of jerky, Bodie slipped the belt around its neck. "We're going to get you taken care of."

He stood, walking the few feet back to Lacey with the dog on the makeshift leash.

"Poor thing. Who did this to you?" Lacey dropped down, her hands immediately going to the dog's head. "We've got to get this tape off of him."

"Her." Bodie pointed to the pup's underside. "You've definitely got a little girl on your hands there. Hold on to her for a sec? I've got a first aid kit in the truck."

Lacey took the belt, but it didn't seem like she'd need to hold on too hard. The pup nudged her nose into her cheek, her tail wagging like crazy. Looked like they'd both found a friend.

By the time Bodie got the scissors and cut the tape holding the pup's mouth shut, Lacey had given the animal a complete once-over. She'd also taken it upon herself to snag Bodie's huge water bottle and let the dog take a drink. He cringed as the dog covered the mouth of his stainless steel tumbler with quick, sloppy laps.

"We've got to get her to Zina's. She can see if she has a chip and check her over." Lacey stood from where she'd been running a hand over the dog's side. "Looks like she's in pretty good shape besides the obvious."

"You're in charge, Mayor Cherish." He picked up his water bottle and pointed to the truck. "Should I assume she's riding shotgun with you?"

"Absolutely." The smile she gave him was worth having to sanitize his water bottle when he got home.

"Let's go." The dog didn't have any problem hopping up into the cab. Once Lacey got settled, the pup climbed onto her lap and covered her face with kisses.

"Hey, cut that out." She ran her hand over the dog's head. "Where do you think she came from?"

Bodie's heart constricted. That was the million-dollar question. Ever since For Pitties' Sake rescue had opened up outside of town a few years ago, they'd been inundated with stray dogs. And not just any kind of dogs. Pit bulls. "I wish I knew. Best guess is someone decided she was getting too big and wanted to find a place to dump her."

"But why tape her mouth shut? That's inhumane." The dog nudged her head under Lacey's hand in a demand for more attention.

Bodie swept his palm over the dog's side, earning him a couple of licks. "I agree. Just once I'd like to get my hands on one of the bastards."

"What would you do if you caught one?" She cocked her head, evaluating him with those big blue eyes.

The way she stared up at him, her eyes full of sass, made him wish he and Luke weren't such good friends. There was no excuse for the kind of thoughts he was having about his best friend's little sister. "Things I don't feel comfortable describing in present company."

"You think I can't handle it?" She let out a huffy breath. "After all the time we've known each other, you still think of me as a weak little girl, don't you?"

"What?" He scoffed. It would be best if he let her think that. Nothing good would come out of telling her how he really felt. He hadn't thought of her as a little girl since she came back to town. Still, he kept trying to remind himself that the bombshell sitting next to him was off-limits. That she was the same annoying kid he'd been forced to tolerate while he hung out with her brother. Even if the sight of her made his pulse ratchet up and his palms sweat.

"I'm all grown up now, Bodie, and I don't need you looking out for me."

He pulled into the parking lot of the dog rescue and brought the truck to an abrupt halt. "I'm well aware of the fact you've grown." Did she have to keep drawing his attention to that? How could he not notice the way her lanky limbs had given way to curves that didn't end? Her smile had changed from a loopy, toothy girl's to a seductive grin that was most definitely all woman.

"Well, fine, then." She led the dog from the truck.

Bodie caught up in time to open the door for her.

"I can open my own doors, you know."

"Be my guest." He let go of the handle. The door closed.

She let out an exasperated groan as she reached for the handle.

"What? Do you or do you not want me to open the door for you?" She was sending enough mixed signals that he'd never find his way out of the tiff they'd started.

As they stood arguing on the concrete pad in front of the building, a guy came up behind them. "Can I get the door for you?" He reached in front of Lacey and grabbed the handle.

"Thank you." The smile she gave the stranger overflowed with charm.

Bodie groaned as he followed her into the building. One thing was certain. He was going to have his hands full with Lacey, even if he didn't get to experience the pleasure of actually touching her.

six

Lacey hiked her jeans up as she held tight to the pup's leash. She couldn't help but be acutely aware of Bodie's presence behind her. Why was he irritating her so much lately? Maybe it was the way he seemed to want to man-handle her, to poke his nose into places it didn't belong. Or maybe it was because since she'd been back in town she couldn't help but look at him in a new light. As she waited for Zina to come to the front desk, she let herself consider that possibility.

For as long as she could remember, Bodie had been a part of her life. Like a second big brother. He and Luke spent all their time together. Especially after her mom passed away and the structure and routine seeped out of their days. If someone wanted to find Luke, all they had to do was locate Bodie. And vice versa. Most of the time she trailed behind them, a little lost while her dad worked all day and stayed out all night drowning his sorrows at the local watering hole.

While Dad was away it was up to Luke to keep an eye

on her. She'd never been much for causing trouble, but she didn't like to be home alone in their house out in the country, which was why she so often found herself trailing behind the two boys. But when Bodie left for college and Luke reported for basic training she was on her own. By the time Bodie came back to work for the sheriff's department, she'd been on her way to San Antonio to earn her degree. It had been over eight years since she'd spent any amount of time around him.

That's probably all it was. They just needed to get used to each other again. Bodie had always been a bit of a bully, but Luke had been there like a buffer between them. Without her brother in the middle, Lacey would have to manage Bodie on her own.

Before she could give it much more thought, Zina came through the door leading to the back of the building. "Hey, what are you doing here, Mayor Cherish? Don't you have a town to save?"

Lacey rolled her eyes. "Not you, too?" She and Zina had been friends since middle school. Right about the time Luke and Bodie had left town, Zina moved in, finally giving her the friend she'd so desperately wanted.

"Saw you on the noon news yesterday. You looked really good. Now, where did this gorgeous girl come from?"

"We found her in the parking lot of Bodie's office." Lacey shot a side glance to Bodie. "Our deputy sheriff almost hit her."

"Hey"—Bodie's hands went out, palms facing outward—"that was just as much your fault as mine."

Arms crossed over her chest, Lacey glared at him. "How do you figure that exactly?"

"While you two sort out your story, I'm going to take her back for a quick exam. Do you want to wait here or should I call you when I'm done?"

"I've got to get home. Can I follow up with you later?" Lacey asked.

"Sure thing." Zina ran a hand over the dog's back. "We'll get her all checked out. I think with a little love she's going to be just fine."

"Do you have a leash you can use? Bodie thought my belt would make a good substitute but I need it back if I want to keep my pants on."

"You sure are a hot mess today." Zina slipped a nylon leash over the dog's head before handing Lacey her belt.

"That's an understatement." She slid her belt through her belt loops while Bodie said good-bye to the dog.

"What will you do with her?" Bodie asked.

Lacey glanced over at him, wondering if he really was capable of having a soft spot for another living creature. In her experience he'd always been a love-'em-and-leave-'em kind of guy. She mentally chastised herself. That wasn't fair. She had no idea what kind of a guy he was now. Too much time had gone by for her to pass judgment.

"We'll get her checked over and make sure she doesn't have anything going on besides the superficial injuries. Then we'll test her for temperament." Zina leaned over, earning a sloppy kiss from the dog. "Based on initial observation, I think she'll be eligible for adoption. She's a cutie."

"Keep us posted, will you?" Bodie scratched the dog behind the ears.

"Sure will. By the way, if she doesn't have a chip, what do you think we should call her?"

Bodie cocked his head and looked to Lacey. "She sure enjoyed riding in the front seat. I say you call her Shotgun."

"All right. Shotgun it is. I'll give you a call later." Zina disappeared through the door, taking Shotgun with her. The poor pup looked back, reluctant to follow.

"She likes you." Lacey nodded toward the dog. "Not sure why."

"I'm a likable guy." Bodie gestured for her to go ahead

of him. "It wasn't that long ago you might have said the same thing."

"Why, because you and Luke tolerated me?" She pushed the door open then held it for him as he followed.

He gave his head a slight shake as he passed. "Can you answer one question for me, Lacey?"

Shrugging her shoulders, she shot him some major side-eye as they made their way back to his truck. "Shoot."

He stopped as they reached the bumper. "Just how big is that stick you've got up your ass?"

Her jaw dropped. Her eyes popped. Her hands clenched into fists. "Excuse me?"

"You've done nothing but bust my chops since you've been back. I'd like to know how much longer I can expect that to last."

"You can't talk to me like that." Heat flooded her face. She wanted to hobble him with a scathing comeback, wanted to slap him upside the head, wanted to knee him in the groin and leave him writhing on the ground. But under all of that animosity, another kind of desire simmered. She wanted to kiss him. And that scared her the most.

"I know things aren't going like you planned." Bodie leaned against the back panel of his truck. "You thought you'd take over as mayor, spit shine the family name, and add a nice bullet point to your résumé."

The glare she gave him should have curdled his stomach and wiped that smug grin off his face. Instead, he kept going. His words pinned her to the pavement.

"I'm sorry it's not working out like you wanted. But if we're going to figure out how to save Idont, we're going to have to work together in some capacity." He nodded, finally meeting her gaze. "And I'd rather we keep things civil."

Civil. She could do civil. She'd be so freaking civil he'd be wishing and hoping for something to break up the sheer politeness of her properness.

She swallowed the urge to spite him, nodding instead. "That sounds great, just great." She even thrust her hand out, figuring they'd officially seal the deal.

He hesitated, probably figuring she was going to try to undermine him in some way, before reaching for her hand. "All right, then. Can I give you a ride back to your truck?"

"Yes, please." She squeezed his hand as hard as she could. His expression didn't change. He probably couldn't even feel it. But she sure could. A sizzling awareness zinged through her, snapping along every nerve ending from the tip of her toes to the ends of her hair. For all she knew her wavy locks might possibly be standing on end."

Bodie released his grip. "Let's go." He rounded the bumper, leaving her standing in place.

Smoothing her hands over her hair, she forced herself to move to the cab. She didn't have time to think about Bodie Phillips in any capacity other than someone who could help her find a way out of the quicksand sucking her down. And before he'd even be willing to do that she had to figure out what kind of stick she had up her butt and how the heck she was going to remove it.

They drove in silence the rest of the way back to the sheriff's office. He pulled into the spot next to her truck, expecting her to jump out before he even stopped moving. But she sat there instead, her back to him.

"Lacey?" He reached out to touch her shoulder then thought better of it. "You okay?"

"I'm fine." She nodded as she turned to stare straight ahead. "I am going to find a way to save this town though."

He rested a hand on top of the steering wheel. "I have no doubt you will."

"With or without your help." Her eyebrows lifted, like she'd asked a question she wanted him to answer.

His jaw set, his pulse ticking away at the base of his

throat. When he didn't respond, she opened her door and climbed out of the truck. He waited for the door to close behind her before he let out the breath he'd been holding.

He knew Lacey would do whatever she had to do to fix things in Idont. The only time he'd ever seen her give up at anything was during a heated game of Monopoly. She must have been about eleven years old. When the game stretched into the early-morning hours, Lacey had wanted to take a break and pick up again the next day. He and Luke had pushed and pushed, telling her if she went to bed she'd lose. Finally, she dozed off, her face landing in the pile of Free Parking money in the center of the table. While Luke had danced around the kitchen table, celebrating, Bodie had carried her out to the couch in the living room and covered her with a homemade quilt.

Reconciling the determined-but-vulnerable eleven-year-old Lacey with the strong, grown-up version had him reeling. He'd always held a soft spot in his heart for her, thinking of her like the little sister he'd never had. But recently the kind of thoughts he'd been having about her were anything but brotherly.

In fact, they might be the most polar opposite kind of thoughts he could possibly have. Thoughts that included running his hands over those filled-out curves, nipping his teeth along the column of her neck, and, God help him, getting to know the grown-up Lacey in the most primal way known to man.

Yeah, Luke would kick his ass to next Tuesday if he had even an inkling of the kind of ideas Bodie had been entertaining about Lacey. Once he got this whole warehouse business sorted, he'd be doing them all a favor if he started seriously looking for a deputy job in a bigger county. Maybe even a different state.

Before the whole day got away from him, he ought to try to do something productive. He snagged his phone and pulled up his dad's number.

"Hello, Son." His dad's deep, rough voice came across the line.

"You around? I'd like to stop by." The sooner, the better, too.

"How about tomorrow morning?" A horn honked. The sound of passing traffic served as background noise.

"Where are you?" Dad couldn't be in town. Idont had one stoplight and even then, it worked only about 25 percent of the time.

"Working a deal over in Houston but I'll be back tonight. Stop by tomorrow morning and we'll have ourselves a nice, long chat."

"Yeah, okay." Bodie didn't particularly care if it was nice or long, but they'd be chatting, all right. And he wouldn't give up until he had the answers he needed.

"See you tomorrow." Dad disconnected.

Bodie stared at his phone for a long moment. He'd chat with his dad, settle things with Lacey, and put together an action plan of steps he needed to take to get serious about finding a new job.

He'd become complacent. This latest stunt from his dad and pops was just another sign that he needed to separate himself from their unsavory way of doing business.

Before it was too late.

seven

The next day Bodie wiped his boots on the outdoor rug before knocking on the door and entering his dad's office.

"Son, glad you could stop by." His dad sat behind a massive desk, a cigar on the edge of the ashtray in front of him. Mom wouldn't let him smoke in their showplace of a house, so Dad spent the majority of his time in the office he'd had built onto the side of the family home.

"You said it was important." Bodie crossed the Mexican tile to where the desk sat, centered between two giant picture windows overlooking the three hundred acres they'd had in the family for generations.

Dad gestured to one of the leather chairs. "Take a seat. Your pops and I want to talk to you about something."

"Oh yeah?" Bodie settled in the chair. "Like how the two of you decided to shut down the warehouse without even mentioning it to me?"

"Bygones." Dad picked up the cigar, taking a few brisk puffs. "You said you weren't interested in the family business, remember?"

Yeah, he remembered. He'd always dreamed of carrying on the family name. For a brief period of time he'd considered following in the footsteps of his dad and his pops. But then he found out some of their business practices leaned toward the dark gray side of his black-and-white world. He couldn't embrace the way they followed the laws that benefited the business and found a work-around for the ones that didn't.

"That doesn't mean I don't want to know when you're making decisions that affect the town. People depend on you for jobs, to feed their families." Bodie's pulse ratcheted up at the thought of all of their employees going without a paycheck.

Dad returned his cigar to the ashtray, blowing a cloud of smoke into the air above them. "Relax, it's a temporary thing."

"What do you mean?" He leaned forward, his forearms resting on his thighs. If his dad planned on reopening the warehouse, that would solve a lot of his problems. Like having to work so closely with Lacey.

"Pops!" Dad called out over his shoulder. "Care to join us for this part of the conversation?"

Bodie's grandfather ambled from the back room over to the desk. "I can't figure out twenty-seven across. Four-letter word for *appealing*."

"Sexy." The word left Bodie's mouth before he had a chance to stop it. Damn, that's what thinking about Lacey did to him.

Pops scratched his pencil against the page. "That works, thanks." He held out a hand to Bodie. "Glad you could join us."

Bodie stood and took his hand, not resisting the half hug his grandfather pulled him into. "What's up, Pops?"

"We've got a situation." Pops took the seat next to Bodie.

"What's that?" Bodie asked.

"A business opportunity presented itself. We took it. But now we have a few, let's say, loose ends, we need to wrap up." Dad leaned back in his chair, folding his hands over the impressive belly he'd earned by eating too many tamales.

"Why did y'all shut the warehouse?" Bodie asked. "I still don't understand what prompted that decision."

Pops leaned a sinewy forearm onto the desk. He might be getting up in years but he still had the hard-earned physique of a man who'd worked the land for a large portion of his life. "We need you to drop the deputy title for this conversation. Think you can do that?"

Bodie glanced back and forth between his dad and his pops. "What the hell did the two of you do?"

"Are we having a family conversation here, Son?" Dad asked.

"Sure." Bodie settled against the back of his chair and drew in a long breath. His dad's mantra of "family first" had been drilled into him his entire life. But he was getting tired of being guilted into looking the other way. "Tell me what's going on."

"Buck Little made us an offer we couldn't refuse." Dad's chair creaked under his weight. "Simple as that."

"What kind of offer?" Bodie's stomach tightened. He had a feeling the kind of offer Buck made wasn't exactly above the law.

"He wants us to move our operation over to Swynton." Pops lifted his foot, placing his custom-made alligator boot on top of his knee. "Like your dad said, it was an offer we couldn't refuse."

"But Idont needs the business. How can you turn your back? Our family settled this town, it's in our blood—"

"Business is business. Sales have been down. Buck is giving us some tax breaks we don't get here," Dad said.

"And free rent." Pops rubbed his hand along the white

whiskers on his chin. "We gave up the land the business sits on years ago."

"What?" Bodie's gaze bounced between the two men. "What do you mean?"

"The land belongs to the town," Dad said. "We've been leasing it back from them for over a decade. With sales taking a dip, we haven't made a payment for a while. When Buck offered us a break, we decided to take it."

"Sounds like you've got it all worked out, then." Bodie stood, eager for a breath of fresh air.

"Wait a minute." Dad pointed to the chair. "Like we said, we have a few loose ends to tie up."

Bodie slumped back into his chair. "I don't understand what this has to do with me."

"We should have cleared out the inventory before we made the announcement to shut down." Pops glared across the desk. "Your dad got a little trigger-happy spreading the word."

"And?" Bodie had lost just about all the patience he possessed. "I still don't get what you want me to do about it."

"Well, since we aren't current on our rent, the town considers us in default. Now they've told us they're going to seize our assets to pay off the debt. We need to get our stuff out of there so we can move it over to the new place in Swynton. Figure out a way to make it happen."

"Hold up. How exactly am I supposed to do that? You want me to help you break into the warehouse and steal back all of your stuff?" Bodie stood again. He didn't have time to listen to their harebrained ideas.

"Of course, we wouldn't ask you to help unless there was something in it for you." Dad pointed to the seat Bodie had vacated.

"I'll stand." He crossed his arms over his chest. What could they possibly offer him that would make him consider breaking the law he'd sworn to uphold?

"Suit yourself." Dad shrugged. "But Buck is willing to guarantee you the sheriff's position in the next election if you help us out."

His eyes narrowed. "Why would he want to do that?"

"Buck knows how things work around here. He scratches our back, we scratch his."

"He must want one hell of a back scratch in return for rigging an election." Of course, it had been done in the past. Rumor had it Lacey's dad hadn't won the mayor's seat fair and square when he'd been elected. But to so blatantly be offered the bribe . . . Something didn't add up.

Pops grunted. "You don't need to worry about that part of the negotiations. Just figure out a way to get in and grab our stuff and you'll get yourself a promotion. Why the hell you want to work in law enforcement boggles my mind, but isn't that your dream job? Sheriff?"

Bodie had enjoyed learning the ropes in the tiny town of Idont, but his career aspirations didn't stop at playing deputy sheriff for the rest of his life. Sure, he wanted to move up. Even more than that, he wanted to move out. He'd always had his eyes set on a bigger town. One that would get him far out from under the thumb of his meddling family, making it impossible to get himself wedged into a situation just like this.

"I don't know, Pops. Who else knows about this?" Bodie scrubbed his hands over his cheeks.

"You, me, Buck, your dad. Probably whoever takes care of payments down at city hall. But we don't want to cause a scene. Just get our stuff moved over to the new place in Swynton before anyone notices it's gone. Should be easy enough."

"I'm gonna have to think about this." He should leave his dad's office and head straight to the sheriff. But was he willing to rat out his family and sever those ties once and for all? His dad and granddad had caused a stink over the years but they'd always managed to find a way to come up smelling like the aromatic gardenias his mom had planted around the pool out back.

"We don't have a hell of a lot of time, Son." Dad grunted as he levered himself out of his chair. "We'll need an answer soon."

"Give me until the weekend?" Three days. They could give him three damn days to think about whether or not he wanted to risk career suicide.

"You got it." Pops stood, too, then lifted his arm so his hand stuck out in front of him. "Family handshake?"

Dad put his hand on top of Pops's. Both men looked to Bodie. Hell, why not? He put his hand on top of theirs, then the three of them lowered and raised their hands.

Bodie shook his head as he stepped back from the desk. "Do you promise not to do anything until I have a chance to think this through?"

Dad bent over to pick up his cigar. "You have our word."

Even though he knew their word wasn't worth any more than the smoke-choked air he breathed in, Bodie nodded. "I'll be in touch."

"See you, Son." Dad plugged his mouth with the cigar while Pops lifted a hand in a wave.

Bodie retraced his steps to the door of the office, the pit in the bottom of his stomach growing. Something else was going on besides just needing their stuff out of the warehouse. Why hadn't he heard about them not owning the land before?

He'd always known the Victorian house his ancestors lived in had been donated to the town years before he'd ever been born. The town officials decorated it for the holidays and used it as a meeting place every once in a while. But this was the first he'd heard that his family no longer owned the land the warehouse sat on. When had they given that up?

His dad and pops might be a stone-cold wall of silence

on the subject but he had other ways of finding out. Ways that unfortunately involved crossing paths with Lacey again. And it would have to be sooner rather than later. He didn't have much time.

As he climbed into his truck, the sound of his phone demanded his attention. He jerked it to his ear without checking the number. "Phillips here."

"Bodie, hey, it's Zina over at For Pitties' Sake."

"Oh, hey. How's Shotgun doing?" Something about that poor dog got to him yesterday. He couldn't stand to see an animal in pain, especially when it was intentionally caused by some asswipe of a human.

"That's why I'm calling. She checked out just fine. She's underweight and will need someone to work with her to reestablish trust."

Relief coursed through him. "That's great. Thanks for letting me know."

"You're welcome. I have a favor to ask though."

"What's that?"

Zina cleared her throat. "We're full here at the shelter. The two of you seemed to bond, and I was wondering if you could take her for a couple of days."

"My place is pretty tight." No. He couldn't take on the care of a dog, not with everything going down with the business and Lacey.

"I wouldn't ask if I didn't need the help. I really think she'd do much better in a home than at the shelter right now. She's in a vulnerable place."

Vulnerable. Why'd she have to use that word? An image of Lacey smiling as she held Shotgun on her lap floated through his head. "Just a couple of days?"

"A week at most," Zina said. "She's had a bath and I can send her home with supplies so you don't have to buy anything."

Bodie rubbed a hand along the back of his neck. "Fine. When do you need me to come get her?"

"Now? Think you could swing by in the next hour or so? I've got to head out for a bit and I want to be here when you get here so I can go over how to tend to the sores on her muzzle."

"Yeah, sure. I'll head over in a few."

"You're a good guy, Bodie."

"Thanks." Now, if she could just convince Lacey of that, he'd be in good shape.

eight

Lacey cleared her throat before stepping in front of the podium. She'd promised to have a statement to the press about the closing of the Phillips business by the end of the week. At four thirty on Friday afternoon she was cutting it pretty close. The crowd had multiplied since her initial press conference on Monday. The citizens of Idont were concerned. She and Chelsea had been fielding their calls, e-mails, texts, and unannounced visits all week. She'd even been accosted at the Burger Bonanza while she tried to finish up the lunch shift yesterday. Everyone wanted to know . . . What was she going to do about it?

Thankfully, she had a plan. Despite Bodie's doubts, the more she researched the idea of positioning Idont as Ido, the perfect wedding destination, the more excited she got. Now she just needed to convince everyone else.

"Thank you for your patience while we sorted through the announcement that the Phillips family decided to shut their doors." She glanced down at her notes, worried she'd forget a main point or two. "After consulting with the city management we've decided to repurpose the Phillips House into an event center."

A hand shot into the air—the same reporter from Houston who'd given her a hard time at the press conference earlier in the week.

"Yes?" While she waited for the reporter to check her notes, Lacey sought out the friendly faces in the crowd. Zina smiled at her, giving a slight nod of encouragement. Lacey had filled in her best friend on her idea over a pitcher of margaritas last night. For someone who didn't consider herself much of a romantic, Zina was on board. If she believed in the idea, the good folks of the newly christened Ido would come around, too.

"Mayor Cherish, what kind of events do you envision the Phillips House hosting? You're hardly a hotbed of tourist activity around here." Soft laughter bubbled up from the crowd.

Lacey pasted on a patient smile. "We're already working on a plan. Of course we'll continue to host the annual events we always do, like the Crawfish Craze and Pitty Parade. But extensive research shows that our best bet is to focus on the happily-ever-after variety of events."

"Such as?" the reporter asked, her pen poised to capture whatever words of wisdom Lacey shared.

"Weddings. The wedding industry is booming and we're in a great spot to cash in on some of that billion-dollar industry. In fact, I'm proposing we even change the name of our town to Ido to cement our place in the destination-wedding market." Half a dozen hands shot into the air. "I imagine you all have a bunch of questions. As we work out the details we'll be sure to keep you informed. In the meantime, any employees of Phillips Stationery and Imports are welcome to fill out an application to help with repurposing the house."

"Mayor Cherish—"

Lacey didn't stick around to face the crowd. She ducked

out the back door of the hall and click-clacked across the pavement as fast as she could. She'd no sooner pulled the heavy door of her truck closed behind her than someone knocked on the passenger window. She let out a shriek.

Bodie.

He motioned for her to roll down the window. "You're really going through with this, huh?" he asked.

Lacey cranked up the heat, hoping to eliminate the chill in the air, even if it seemed to be coming mostly from Bodie. "You have a better idea?"

"Maybe I can arrange a meeting with Dad and Pops. There are a couple of things they'd like to talk to you about."

"I bet." She shook her head. "They jumped the gun, didn't they?"

Bodie arched a brow, making him look all brooding, reminding her of the picture of a rugged cowboy she'd stared at in that magazine the other night. "What do you mean?"

"The inventory. You can't tell me they planned on leaving all of their inventory behind."

Bodie tapped a finger on the doorframe. "How to handle the inventory would definitely be an item on the agenda."

Lacey wanted to laugh at the way he tried to play it cool. Had he forgotten she knew all of his telltale signs? From the time he and Luke taught her how to play Texas Hold'em she'd always been able to tell when he was holding something back. He was hiding something and knowing his dad and pops, it had to be something big. "I'm sure they've told you by now they've been in default on their payments for months."

He nodded as he turned to face the western horizon. The sun had started its descent, framing Bodie's profile in breathtaking shades of orange and red. His chin jutted out slightly, his jaw clenched tight. For a moment she wondered what it might feel like to brush her hand against his cheek, or run her fingers through that unruly head of hair. Her breath caught as he turned, meeting her gaze.

"I'm in a pickle here, Lacey." Gray eyes, the color of the sky just before a summer storm, begged for some level of understanding. But if he felt like he was in a pickle, she was squeezed into a full jar of them.

"Then I suggest you snag a sandwich and some chips and settle in for a nice, long snack." She wasn't ready to forgive and forget. Not yet. Maybe not ever. His family had been in control long enough. It was time the good people of Idont reclaimed their town. Although, she'd better start thinking of the town as Ido. She'd been given the green light to go ahead with the name change. The vote would just be a formality. No matter what they named the town, they were better off without the Phillips family running the show.

Bodie let out a huff, obviously not pleased with her response. "Will you at least meet with them?" He cocked his head to the left, then bent down to mumble something.

Lacey lifted herself up to peer out the window. "What have you got down there?"

He opened the door to her truck and a dog clambered into the passenger seat. A huge wet tongue swiped across her chin.

"That's not Shotgun, is it?" Her hand smoothed down the short hair on the dog's back. There was no way this squirming bundle of energy could be the same dog they'd dropped off at Zina's the other day.

Bodie cracked a grin. "Sure is. She cleaned up nice, didn't she?" He filled the open doorway of the truck as he reached over to ruffle the hair behind the dog's ears.

"Hi there, girl. Don't you look gorgeous?" Lacey laughed as the dog jumped across the center console to land in her lap. "Zina said you agreed to take her for a while."

"A few days." Bodie leaned farther into the truck, his

hand wrapped around a teal nylon leash with pink hearts on it.

"That was awfully nice of you."

"Yeah, well, she needs a friend right now." His gaze met Lacey's. "And I guess I do, too."

The shell around her heart cracked at the forlorn look in his eyes. She'd been the pesky sidekick to her brother and Bodie when they were kids. They tolerated her for the most part and often left her behind. But she'd spent enough time around Bodie to know that his family played some pretty sick mind games with him. As the only child of the empire his pops and dad had built, they'd expected him to follow in their footsteps and take the business to the next level. When he didn't fall into line there had been some words exchanged. From what Luke told her—and she'd had to beg for the little bit of info he'd shared—Bodie held his ground about following his dreams. But something had changed. He always had a cloud of sadness hovering around him when it came to discussing his family.

"Fine. Tell your dad and pops that I'd be willing to chat with them."

He let out a long, drawn-out sigh. "I wouldn't ask if I didn't think you'd both have something to gain."

"I know." Her hand passed over his as she gave Shotgun a scratch under the chin. The dog burrowed closer, finally turning circles then settling into her lap. "What are you going to do with her?"

"I don't know. I'm not sure how she'd do home alone so I've been taking her with me everywhere. Someone must have worked with her at some point. She knows some basic commands."

"Did Zina say when she'd be ready for adoption?"

"Nah. She wants to see how she does first. Somebody did wrong by her. I noticed she gets a little nervous around men."

"But not you," Lacey said.

"Just when I surprise her."

"I guess she can tell you wouldn't hurt a fly."

Bodie's chest puffed out. "What are you talking about? I'm in charge of intimidating bad guys."

"When's the last time you had to catch a bad guy around here?"

His mouth screwed up. "Does Kirby Ketchum count?"

Lacey let out a laugh. "No, Kirby doesn't count. He's more of a nuisance than a bad guy." In the few short days she'd been working as mayor, she'd already fielded a couple of complaints about the man. He had an address out west of town—a mobile home that sat in the middle of ten acres of dry land. But he seemed to spend most of his time poking around the center of town.

"Well, I'd catch a bad guy if we had any."

Lacey caught the way his mouth drew into a line. Would his vow hold if it was one of his kin that turned out to be the bad guy? She'd like to think that Bodie's sense of honor and duty would win over any family ties, but that was the thing about family. Oftentimes that was the only time exceptions were made to the rules.

"So when will this showdown take place?" she asked.

"Aw, come on, Sweets. It's not like you're going into a cage match with them."

"I'd never agree to that. Your pops might be older than the hills but he'd be able to take down a man twice his size and a quarter of his age."

That statement earned her a laugh from Bodie. He held out a fist and bumped knuckles with her. "That's the honest truth. They just want to chat. Maybe over a nice, cold glass of lemonade. Nothing to be afraid of."

"Fine. They can come to the house."

"Your place? I figured you'd want a neutral location."

"You'll have your family in tow, I want to have some backup of my own."

"Your dad?"

She shrugged. "I'd prefer to have Luke in my corner but his leave isn't coming up for another few months."

"How long has it been since you've seen him?"

"Too long." She lifted her gaze to meet Bodie's. Talk of her older brother was one of the few things that could make her tear up. Didn't matter that the thought of seeing Luke again made her heart warm. She wouldn't believe he was okay until she got to wrap her arms around him in a hug. He'd been out of the picture when everything went down with her dad so she'd had to handle it all on her own. Sure, they'd video-chat every once in a while but it wasn't the same as knowing the one person who'd always had her back would be next to her.

"Can't wait to see him for myself." Bodie peered through the fogged-up windshield. "Never did understand why he felt like he had to become such a hero."

Lacey almost pointed out to him that he'd done the same thing, just stateside instead of overseas. "How about tomorrow afternoon? I'll make up a pitcher of that strawberry lemonade you like."

"Might snow tomorrow."

"You're kidding." Even in February, temps never fell below freezing. "Maybe hot cocoa instead?"

"Come on, Shotgun." Bodie tugged on the leash. "We've got to make a pit stop at the feed store and pick up a new leash for you."

"Not a fan of the hearts?" Lacey asked.

"Hearts are fine for her. But I wouldn't mind something a little less, well, a little less pink."

"There's nothing wrong with pink. And you'd better get used to it. I read that it's one of the most popular wedding colors this year." She put her hands on either side of Shotgun's muzzle, careful to avoid the sores left from the tape.

"You're really going to pursue this, aren't you?"

"Of course I am. The town's even going to change its name from Idont to Ido. It's on the agenda for the next council meeting. Don't you think that will go along better with the whole wedding thing?"

Bodie snorted. "You're really something, Mayor Cherish. Come on, Shotgun."

The dog gave Lacey a final look, her big brown eyes staring deep into her soul. Then her tongue swept over her face. Lacey couldn't help but let out a laugh. "She's a kissing monster."

"Nah, she just knows you like getting a face full of tongue." With a gentle tug on the leash, Bodie helped Shotgun scramble out of the truck. "Three o'clock tomorrow sound good?"

Lacey used her sleeve to wipe the remaining doggie spit off her cheeks. "Yeah. I'll see you then."

Bodie shut the door, then lingered in the open window. "So . . ."

"Yeah?"

"Thanks. I appreciate you doing this." The edges of his eyes crinkled, making her wonder how long it had been since he'd offered her a genuine smile.

She smiled back, glad she could help. Maybe she could work something out with the Phillips family. "I'm the mayor, it's my job to try to work out any kinks with my constituents." She owed it to herself and Bodie to try.

nine

Kinks. Why'd she have to say "kinks" out loud? This business of having to work with Lacey made his stomach churn, made his pants feel a little too tight as well. Up until about a year ago he hadn't thought of her as anything but the toothy tagalong sister of his best friend. She'd annoyed him, just like she bugged the hell out of her brother growing up. But they'd had some fun times, too.

Luke was a great shot, loved to camp, and could win any kind of race whether on foot or on four wheels. But Lacey was the one who'd engaged Bodie in long conversations. Usually while they sat on the dock of Pappy's Pond, fishing poles in hand. Luke wasn't patient enough to wait for the fish to bite. He'd hand his pole over, then spend the rest of the afternoon swinging off the thick rope left over from other kids who'd visited the swimming hole long before them. But Bodie and Lacey would sit for hours with nothing but the sound of crickets and locusts between them. Every once in a while they'd pick up a string of conversation. But comfortable silence worked, too.

He'd never felt awkward like he needed to fill the long stretches between them.

But he'd also never thought of her as a girl. Not when she'd dig around in the dirt for night crawlers to use as bait. Not when she'd chase snakes with them. And definitely not when she'd jump in the pond in her T-shirt and shorts, her chest flatter than the boards of the dock they'd sit on to dry off.

When he'd left for college she'd still been in braces. But now, there was no escaping the fact that Lacey Cherish had morphed from the gangly girl he used to know into a confident, good-looking woman.

But business was business. The sooner he figured out a way to salvage the family fortune without rocking the boat, the sooner he could start looking for a job far from the family who always seemed to wedge him in between a rock and a hard place. And far from the woman who could single-handedly ruin him.

He reached over to give Shotgun a pat on the head. At least he had company tonight. With nothing stretching ahead of him but another lonely Friday evening, it would be nice to have a warm body to share the couch with. Even if it was only a dog. For a moment Bodie let himself imagine what it would feel like to curl himself around someone of the two-legged variety. Someone like Lacey Cherish.

"Dammit." He slapped a palm on the dash before he cranked up the volume on his radio.

Shotgun let out a bark as she wagged her tail.

"That's right. Time to change the subject. How about we stop in for some takeout on the way home?"

A giant tongue doused his cheek in doggie saliva, signaling Shotgun was most likely on board with that decision.

Fifteen minutes later Bodie sat on a stool at the counter while Jojo raced around the restaurant. "Don't you have any help tonight?"

"Nope. Lacey was scheduled but she called in a bit

ago." Jojo clipped two order tickets to the window between the kitchen and the dining room. "I think that press conference about did her in."

"You two are close, aren't you?"

"If by 'close' you mean we can carry on a conversation about something beyond what the daily special is, then yeah, I suppose so." She paused next to him, clamping her hands to her hips. "Why?"

Bodie swiveled on the stool to face her. "Just curious. She's had a rough first week on the job. I hope it's not getting to her."

"Lacey?" Jojo waved a hand. "That girl's not made out of sugar, spice, and everything nice. She's got ice running through those veins of hers. I've never seen someone able to stay so cool and collected. And let me tell ya, working around Helmut"—she nudged her chin toward the grill—"that's really saying something."

"Good. I'd hate to think this thing with the import business had her rattled."

"If you don't mind me saying so, it's probably about time your dad and pops found someplace else to settle down." She leaned closer, whispering into the narrow space between them. "Lots of folks aren't so happy with the way your family's been doing business around here lately."

Bodie backed away, evaluating her expression to gauge how serious she was.

Jojo's brow drew down, causing her forehead to crease. "I didn't say nothin', okay?"

"Nothin'," Bodie agreed.

The bell dinged and Jojo whirled around, snagging a brown paper bag from the window. "Here you go. Double Banzai burger loaded and two patties on the side." She passed the bag to him, but didn't let go as his hand wrapped around the top. "You're not doing one of those weird high-protein diets, are you?"

"No. The extra patties are for the dog."

"You got yourself a dog?" Jojo let go of the bag and tucked her arms under her chest. "What did you get, a pup, or what?"

"It's a rescue from For Pitties' Sake. Lacey and I found it in a parking lot the other day."

Jojo's jaw clenched. "Those poor animals. Someone's got to figure out where they're coming from."

"I'm working on that." Bodie stood, taking the bag with him. "Have a good night now."

"You, too, Deputy Phillips."

He pushed through the door, smiling as he caught sight of Shotgun standing behind the wheel on the seat of his truck. As he approached, the dog's backside wiggled faster and faster.

"Brought you something." Bodie reached into the bag, pulling out one of the plain hamburger patties. Zina had sent him home from the rescue center with a whole bag of dry kibble. Based on the way Shotgun reacted to the scent of fresh-fried ground beef, she much preferred something hot off the grill as opposed to kibble straight out of the bag.

The dog gulped down the burger patty in one big bite. Then sat down on the passenger seat, wagging her tail in anticipation.

"We're saving the other one till we get home."

Shotgun must have sensed she wasn't going to get another treat. She curled up as best she could into a ball and lay down. Her legs hung over the edge. She was going to be big, that was obvious from the size of her paws. Bodie figured he wouldn't be able to keep the dog much longer. But he'd enjoy the company while he could.

"Let's go, girl." He laid a hand on Shotgun's head and pulled out of the parking lot. He had a long night ahead of him if he wanted to figure out how to handle the meeting between Lacey and his family tomorrow with minimal collateral damage.

ten

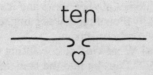

"Excuse me?" Lacey tried to summon a polite smile. However, present company made the task so much more difficult. "You want to do what?"

Mr. Phillips leaned across the kitchen table and wrapped his fingers around the handle of the coffee mug she'd set in front of him over an hour ago. "No harm, no foul. You let us take back our stuff and we'll get out of your hair and not put up a stink about your new plans for the house."

Did he really think he actually had the right to put up any kind of stink? She leaned against the back of her chair, trying to size up Bodie's dad. "You realize you defaulted on the agreement you had. So legally everything in that warehouse is now the property of the town. Including all of the inventory."

Bodie's granddad reached for one of the cookies she'd set out. On her mama's fine china, no less. "These cookies are really good. You make them yourself?"

"Yes—well, no. Actually, Dad made them." Lacey

glanced at her dad, who'd remained silent throughout the interaction.

The senior Phillips let out a chuckle. "So that's what you're doing with your spare time now, Wyatt?"

Dad's face reddened but he didn't say anything.

"My father's very busy. He's working as a consultant." How dare they come into her home and insult her dad. If the Phillips family thought that was going to work in their favor they were sorely mistaken.

"Is that right? What kind of consulting are you doing now, Mr. Mayor?" Pops bit into the homemade chocolate chip cookie then wiped the bit of melted chocolate from his lip.

"Pops"—Bodie tilted his head in Lacey's direction— "Lacey's mayor now. Mr. Cherish is retired."

Of course his pops already knew that. The slight was just another barb in his attempt to undermine her authority. He'd been taking potshots ever since they arrived.

"Oh, I know. Just trying to be respectful."

Lacey bit back her response. This conversation wasn't going anywhere. At least nowhere productive. "Maybe we ought to wrap up for today and give things more thought." At that point all she wanted was to get the Phillips men out of her house. All three of them.

"Lacey honey . . ." Bodie's dad leaned forward, his elbows on the table. "What's it going to take to get you to see things our way?"

Prickles raised the hair on her arms. "You can start by leaving all that 'honey' bullshit at the door. Which, as you'll recall, is right this way." She stood, her chair scraping across the hardwood floor. "This meeting is over."

"Look"—Bodie put his palms out—"can we all just take a deep breath?"

"That's a great idea, Deputy Phillips. Why don't you, your dad, and your pops go do some calm breathing exercises? When you're ready to be reasonable, I'd be more than happy to get together again." Her own breath came shallow and short.

"This has been a waste of time." Bodie's dad got up from his chair. "Wyatt, it was good to see you. We miss you down at the club. Hope you'll be back to manning your barstool again soon."

"Dad." Bodie popped up and muttered something into his dad's ear. His pops just sat at the table, his cool blue eyes never leaving Lacey's face.

She wouldn't have felt more exposed if he'd been trying to look at her under a microscope. What was it about the Phillips family that made them think they were better than everyone else? Her dad had gotten into multiple rows over the years with them. Evidently it was part of the mayor's job. From what she could tell, they fought dirty and weren't above doing what it took to get whatever they wanted.

That would stop with her. They might be able to push other folks around, but when she'd taken her vow to work for the good people of Ido, she'd taken it seriously. No matter what they threw at her, she'd be up for facing it.

"You coming, Pops?" Bodie asked.

The older man's eyes sparkled as he reached out and took two more cookies. "Yeah. But this conversation isn't over. We all want the same thing, don't we?"

Lacey's hands clamped to her hips. "I don't really see us working toward the same goals, Mr. Phillips."

"Call me Monty, will you?" He put his cowboy hat back on his head and tipped it toward her. "Think about it, girl. We all want a fresh start. You give us our inventory so we can strike out new and you'll have a clear way to start over with your harebrained scheme right here in town."

"You can call me Mayor Cherish, Monty." Lacey narrowed her eyes at him. "And based on the way y'all handled things here, I don't think you deserve a fresh start."

"Dad, Pops, let's go." Bodie herded his dad and grandfather toward the front door.

Lacey followed, more to make sure they actually left than to extend any additional hospitality. Once the front door shut behind them, she whirled around and leaned against the door.

"Dad, why didn't you say anything?"

Her dad made his way from the kitchen to the front room, shaking his head. "I didn't realize how bad this was. Just give them what they want and be done with it, honey."

"What do you mean?" She'd never seen her dad look so defeated, so shaken. "They're trying to bully me into letting them have something that doesn't even belong to them."

Her dad wrapped his hands around her upper arms and peered straight into her eyes. "Trust me, you don't want to get involved in a standoff with the Phillips family."

"What are you talking about?" Her heart stuttered at the fear in his eyes. He was scared. The man she'd looked up to most of her life was basically telling her to sell out.

"They have deep pockets and hands that can reach down to the bottom and beyond." His mouth set in a grim line; his face was devoid of any hint of humor.

"You're serious."

"I am. And you'd better start taking them seriously, too. They're not the kind of people you want to piss off."

"Wait, what happened?"

Her dad moved past her to clear the mugs off the table. "Just let them go about their business and be done with them."

She let him walk away, deciding not to pursue the conversation for the time being. But her dad's reaction made her more determined than ever to stand her ground against the Phillips family. Someone had to. The only thing that gave her pause was wondering which side Bodie would end up on.

eleven

"Dammit. Think you could have handled that any worse?" Bodie slammed the door to his truck behind him. Pops had climbed in the backseat while his dad took up more than half of the front.

"It'll work out the way it's supposed to, you'll see. I know you've got a soft spot for those folks. Talk some sense into that filly before she goes and gets in over her head, will you?" His dad pulled one of his cigars from his front pocket.

"I don't know what you've got planned, but Lacey Cherish is off-limits, you understand?" He shot a glance at his dad. "And put that thing away. You're not smoking in my truck."

His dad ignored him, lighting up the cigar with the custom filigreed lighter he picked up in Mexico. "I knew I shouldn't have let you spend so much time at their place when you were a kid. Luke was all right but their dad's got a soft head on his shoulders. And now his daughter's following in his footsteps. She'd best mind her own business and work out her little wedding plans without mucking up what we've got going on."

"Dad, you understand it's my job to uphold the law, right?"

"Of course. You don't know how proud it makes me to be able to say my son is a member of Idont's finest."

Bodie shook his head. "You know Lacey's changing the name of the town. Better start referring to it as Ido. And can you please put that thing out?"

His dad rolled the window down an inch. "Nonsense. Don't you go getting all soft on me, too."

A firm hand clamped on to his shoulder. Pops leaned forward, between the bucket seats. "Family comes first. Bodie knows that."

Bodie met his grandfather's gaze in the rearview mirror. Pops's blue eyes stuck out against his weathered, leathery skin. Yeah, family did come first. That fact had been drilled into him since he was a kid. But he'd recently noticed his dad and his pops seemed to adhere to their personal mantra only when it suited them.

"You got time for supper at the house tonight?" Dad asked. "Your mother's been cookin' up a storm. I think she even asked Maria to make some of those tamales you like."

Bodie's stomach gurgled at the thought of Maria's tamales. She'd been best friends with his mom since grade school. The two of them rarely spent time in the kitchen anymore, but when they did . . . he'd gone into a food coma multiple times after indulging in Maria's homemade family recipes.

"I could stick around for a bit."

"Good. Gotta have something to wash away the taste of mediocrity." Pops let out a gruff laugh.

There had never been good vibes between his family and the Cherish family. At least not where the older generation was concerned. But Bodie and Luke had forged a fast friendship their first day of kindergarten and as much as his dad tried to encourage him to find someone else to hang out with beyond the Cherish family, Bodie held his ground. It finally got to the point where his dad gave up. He didn't like to involve himself in the child-rearing part of parenting, preferring to focus on his business and leave the day-to-day stuff to his wife.

Bodie had never quite figured out what caused the tension between his dad and Mr. Cherish but he and Luke had been gloriously ignorant of the details. For some reason, now it seemed like his dad had it out for the Cherish family. Mr. Cherish could hold his own, but Bodie wouldn't have Lacey get caught in the crosshairs. Not on his watch.

He'd spent most of his childhood looking out for Luke's younger sister, so the sense of protectiveness didn't surprise him. But the intensity of his need to keep her from harm did. He shook it off, leaving those thoughts for another day, as he pulled into the long drive leading to his parents' house.

A decked-out dually truck sat on the concrete pad next to the garage.

"You expecting company?" Bodie asked.

His dad flicked his cigar ash out the window as they came to a stop. "Just a little supper between friends. Come on in. Those tamales are waiting."

Pops scrambled out of the backseat like a man a third his age. What did the two of them have planned? Reluctantly, Bodie shifted the truck into park and followed the two men into the house.

"Phillips!" A booming voice echoed across the tile floors, bouncing off the adobe walls of his childhood home. Mayor Buck Little of Swynton took long strides across the foyer to wrap Bodie's dad in a half-hug handshake.

"Sorry we're a little late. We had some business to take care of with our illustrious mayor." Bodie's dad grinned— a kind of cat-devoured-the-canary type—as he nodded toward Bodie. "You remember my son? Deputy Sheriff Phillips?"

"Of course." Buck released his grip and stepped back, sizing Bodie up with deep-set beady eyes. "How are you, Son?"

Bodie cringed at the familiarity. He didn't want any link between him and Mayor Little. "Just fine. How about you, Mayor?"

They shook hands, Bodie adding a little extra squeeze.

"Oh, I'm fine, just fine. And I'll be even better once we get the particulars figured out." He winked.

Bodie backed away, feeling the need to take a nice, hot shower to rid himself of the heebie-jeebies that seemed to ooze out of Buck Little and taint anyone within a five-foot radius. He left his dad and pops to the mayor and moved toward the kitchen, where the smell of cumin and cilantro called.

"Hey, Mom." He stopped behind where his mother stood at the counter, a glass of white wine in hand.

"Well, hello, sweetheart. What a nice surprise." She tilted her head up. The smell of expensive perfume hit his nose as he pressed an obligatory kiss to her cheek.

"Dad said Maria was here with tamales." He lifted his brows as he stalked toward where Maria stood, folding husks together to form her mouthwatering tamales.

"Your mom didn't tell me you were coming." She turned, giving him a hug, being careful to hold her hands out since they were covered in cornmeal.

"I didn't know I was coming either until Dad mentioned your tamales." He pulled her in close. Auntie Ria had been a fixture in his life for years. She and her husband had never had kids so she used to spoil him rotten when he was younger.

"How long has it been?" She turned back to the task at hand.

Bodie settled half his butt on a kitchen stool and watched

her scoop, roll, and tie the tamales into neatly bound pack-ages of deliciousness. "Been too long. You need to move back closer where we can see you more often."

She and her husband had moved to Austin years ago. Bodie couldn't remember the last time he'd had one of her home-cooked dinners.

"Why don't you help set the table, sweetheart?" His mom took a sip of her wine.

"Who else is coming?" Bodie asked, already heading for the cabinet where they stored the hand-thrown ceramic plates.

"Who knows? This is your father's deal." She set her glass down on the counter and reached for the silverware drawer.

Bodie nodded. His mom had always steered clear of his dad's business dealings. He didn't blame her. Igno-rance was bliss. Or at least ignorance didn't keep her up at night, wondering what kind of business her husband was dealing in. He wished he could look the other way like she seemed to be able to do. But it took more than shopping trips to Dallas or cruises to the French Riviera to distract him. His mom might be willing to embrace the oblivion, but Bodie had a moral obligation to keep his family on the straight and narrow.

By the time dinner was ready they'd been joined by Mayor Little's second-in-command along with his wife and son. Bodie felt for the ten-year-old kid. He'd probably much rather be home playing video games or out with his friends.

As the older men covered safe topics like the price of oil and whether or not the Cowboys had been cheated out of a Super Bowl run, Bodie kept his head down, listening to the conversation and enjoying every single bite. By the time his mom pulled out the flan, he'd stuffed himself so full he couldn't possibly eat anything else.

"We're heading over to the office to talk shop." His dad rose from the table. "Gentlemen?"

Although the meal had been one he'd remember for a long time, Bodie had no intention of getting caught up in conversation with his dad and Mayor Little.

"Wish I could stick around but I've got to go." He gave his mom a peck on the cheek, hugged Maria, and offered his hand to his dad.

"Buck wants to have a little chat with you, Son." His dad leaned in, his beer breath brushing against Bodie's ear.

"Not tonight. I've got a prior commitment." He pulled his hand away and took long strides toward the foyer.

His dad followed. "It would be in your best interest to join us for a cigar and a whiskey." With his thumbs tucked into the belt loops of his jeans, he leveled a penetrating gaze at Bodie.

"Like I said, wish I could." Bodie grabbed his cowboy hat off the hook by the front door. "Maybe another time."

He left the house, pulling the huge hand-carved door closed behind him. As he walked down the path to his truck, he let out a breath. His dad was getting too close to Mayor Little. Something was going on and he'd better figure it out before Lacey did. If she caught wind of something unsavory taking place she'd latch on like a dog with a soup bone. He couldn't let that happen.

twelve

"I can't believe all the stuff they left behind." Lacey opened up another cardboard box. She'd conned Zina into helping her sort through some of the stuff left in the warehouse. Shelves filled with boxes lined the walls. Valentine's decorations mixed in with birthday party paper supplies. They'd even come across an entire pallet full of garden gnomes.

"They had a very eclectic assortment." Zina held up a figurine. "Why in the world would they carry something like this? I don't even know what it is."

Lacey paused sorting through a carton of novelty pencil toppers. "Maybe they had an order to supply the high school mascot. Or one of their retailers could be big into beavers."

Zina snorted. "Big into beavers or into big beavers?"

The beaver's tail seemed disproportionately large based on the smaller size of its body. "Either way, they sure have a lot of beavers."

"Who's got a lot of beavers?" Bodie rounded a tall shelving unit.

Lacey's face heated. "What are you doing here?"

"Saw your truck parked out front and wanted to make sure everything was okay." He had on a pair of jeans and a button-down flannel plaid shirt. It was nice to see him outside of his usual deputy uniform. Reminded her of when they used to just be friends, not grown-ups trying to navigate a new professional relationship.

"I meant to lock the door. Zina and I are just taking a look at the inventory. Your family sure has some interesting tastes." She took the ceramic beaver from Zina's hands. "Any idea why they'd have hundreds of breakable beavers?"

Now Bodie's cheeks tinged pink. "No idea. They're the high school's mascot, right? Maybe they ordered them or they're for a festival or something."

"The breakable beaver festival?" Zina asked.

Lacey stifled a laugh. Bodie reached for the ceramic figurine. "Who knows? If there was a market for it, I'm sure my dad had a good reason."

"How's Shotgun doing?" Zina asked.

Bodie's eyes lit up as he set the beaver down on the shelf. "She's doing great. I've actually got her out in the truck if you want to say hi."

"I'd love that. Y'all carry on, I'm going to go give her a treat." Lacey loved the fact that her friend didn't go anywhere without a pocketful of dog treats. Zina made her way down the long aisle of shelves and disappeared into the front office.

"So how's it going? Find anything interesting?" Bodie asked.

"Not really. Tons of Valentine's decor and a bunch of weird stuff."

"Like cases of beavers?" His lips split into a teasing grin.

"Yes, exactly like that," she agreed. "Are your dad and pops still trying to get all of this precious stuff back? There's a lot of it but I can't imagine it's worth much."

"What are you planning on doing with it?"

"Well, some of it we can probably use." Lacey fingered a bolt of white tulle netting. "I'm thinking of liquidating the rest so we can finance the project. If your family wants it back bad enough I suppose they can buy it from us."

Bodie's long fingers traced the rim of his hat. "Sounds fair enough. How quick are you looking to move on it?"

"Quick. Adeline heard what we're doing and wants to be our first client so she moved her wedding from September to May." She closed the box she'd been checking. "That's good timing anyway since most weddings take place from June to October."

"You sure are becoming quite the expert on the subject." Surprisingly, his tone held no judgment.

"It's kind of fun. A nice break from slinging burgers."

"I bet." He glanced toward his boots and shuffled his feet around. "Hey, as long as we have a second . . ."

Lacey looked up. Those gorgeous gray eyes focused in on her, making it impossible to look away. He bit his lip. If she didn't know him any better she might think he was nervous. But Bodie Phillips didn't get nervous. He didn't get flustered, either—at least not unless he found himself holding a breakable beaver.

"What's up?"

He shifted his weight, finally releasing her from that penetrating gaze. "I wanted to apologize for yesterday. The way my dad and pops acted over at your place. It was—"

"It was fine." Lacey took a step toward him. "Obviously they're upset. I would be, too, if I dropped the ball and cost myself a mint."

"The stuff they said though. I just want you to know that I don't feel the same way they do."

Lacey gulped in a breath. It wasn't like Bodie to talk about feelings. He kept things lighthearted. Even when her mom passed, Bodie was the one who made her laugh again, who reminded her how to have fun. "How exactly do you feel?"

She'd reached him by then, stood next to where he leaned against a shelf full of cherub-shaped tumblers. "That's just it. I don't know. My gut tells me something's going down with the family business. Dad's been talking to Buck Little a lot."

"Yeah, he said he's moving his operation to Swynton for some big tax cut." Lacey scoffed. "My dad said they had that conversation many times over the years."

"Be careful."

She eyed him through lowered lids. "Careful of what?"

"I don't know. It's just a feeling. Something's off."

"You aren't responsible for the actions of your dad and your pops, you know." Her breath caught in her chest as he lifted his gaze to meet hers.

His fingers brushed hers. "I know. There's still no excuse for it though, and I don't want you to get mixed up in it."

"What *do* you want, Bodie?" Silence pressed down around them. Her heartbeat thundered in her ears as his gaze flickered to her mouth.

He took a step even closer, invading her personal bubble of space. "I want . . ."

She wet her lips with her tongue, uncomfortably aware of the ball of warmth gathering in her core. "Yes?"

He leaned down, his gaze searching hers.

Lacey's heart dipped, flipped, and tripped around in her chest. Just like the time she tried to boogie-board down in Galveston and got swept up in a wave then tossed and tumbled to shore, not knowing which way was up.

He lowered his head, his mouth moving closer to hers.

The realization that he was about to kiss her engulfed her, flooding all other thoughts out of her head.

She fisted one hand in the front of his shirt and held on to his shoulder with the other. As her knees gave out he gathered her against him, his strong arms pulling her tight to his chest. Her breath caught in her throat as she focused on the midpoint of his bottom lip, so eager to feel his mouth on hers. She let her eyes drift closed then waited, the anticipation almost too much to bear.

A loud crash came from the front-office area. Bodie pulled back, his eyes unfocused like he'd just been pulled out of a dream.

Shotgun bounded through the warehouse, headed straight for them. When she reached them the dog jumped to her hind legs and bounced up and down, trying to lick Bodie's face.

"I'm okay," Zina yelled from the front room.

"What happened?" Lacey shouted.

Zina joined them, holding a frayed piece of leash. "She looked so sad in the truck I wanted to bring her in. I didn't realize she'd chewed halfway through her leash though."

As the shock wore off, Lacey stepped back, unsure about meeting Bodie's gaze. "You've got your hands full."

"She's keeping me on my toes." Bodie barely looked at her as he rubbed his hands over Shotgun's head. "I'd better get home. You'll let me know when you decide to hold the sale?"

"Absolutely." She touched a finger to her lips.

Bodie picked up the ceramic beaver. "Yeah, there are some real finds here. Make sure you lock up if you're here by yourself."

"Aw, isn't that sweet? You looking out for her like that?" Zina landed a playful swat on Bodie's arm. "Seems like old times."

"Right." But the look he gave Lacey didn't seem like

old times at all. There was something new simmering in the depths of his eyes. She wasn't sure what to call it, but it made her feel exposed. It made her feel vulnerable. It made her feel like tucking tail and running as far and as fast as she could.

"Well, that was fun," Zina commented once Bodie left. "What do you think he really wanted?"

"What do you mean? He said he saw my truck and wanted to make sure all was okay." Lacey shrugged, not wanting to talk about the almost-kiss until she'd had a chance to mull it over on her own. "What's so weird about that?"

Zina lifted a small box from a lower shelf and began to cut the tape holding it closed. "Personal safety checks from the deputy sheriff? Is that typical?"

Lacey cleared her throat. "I don't know why not. Based on the way the employees feel about the warehouse closing, I suppose someone could come by and start some trouble."

"Mmm-hmm." Zina turned to face her, a ring of fake flowers resting on top of her thick, black hair. "Am I ready for the Renaissance festival?"

Grateful for the change of subject, Lacey grinned. "You know what would be fun?"

"What?" Zina picked up a lacy fan and fluttered it against her chest.

"What if we use some of this stuff for theme weddings?" She fingered the edge of Zina's flowery headband. "So far we've got typical wedding decor, cherubs, Renaissance stuff . . . we could come up with some fun themed decor from stuff we already have right here."

"You know what? I think you're onto something." Zina smiled.

"Really?"

"Sure. What bride wouldn't want her guest tables decorated with unicorn poop?" She opened the top of the box in front of her and lifted a bundle of rainbow-colored streamers.

"I'm serious." Lacey swatted at the ribbons.

"Oh, I've no doubt you are." Zina took off the flowery headband. "Just let me know how I can help."

"Really?" Lacey turned toward her friend.

"I know I'm going to get roped into this one way or another. I guess I'd rather go willingly."

"That's the spirit." Lacey glanced around at all of the boxes they hadn't checked yet. "I wonder what kind of wedding Adeline wants."

"Knowing her, nothing but the best. Are you really going to let her be your first client?"

"Someone's got to be first. May as well be her. You know she'll get the word out."

Zina shook her head. "She's never had a problem with being the center of attention."

"You know . . ." Lacey tapped a finger to her lip. "You're right about that."

"Uh-oh. I know that look. What are you thinking?" Zina asked.

"What if we use Adeline's wedding as a publicity move? I could see if I can get a magazine or newspaper or something interested in doing a piece about it."

"That might actually work."

"Really?" Zina usually shot down Lacey's ideas before they fully formed, so the fact she supported this one made it seem almost too good to be true.

"Sure, why not? Adeline would be thrilled, you'd get some free publicity"—she shrugged her shoulders—"What have you got to lose?"

"All right. Let's do it." Lacey nodded. "I'll start looking into places to contact tomorrow."

"Who's going to coordinate with the bride-to-be?" Zina's brow arched.

Lacey's stomach pitched at the thought of spending

time with the woman who'd made her high school years such a living hell. "You said you'd help, right?"

"Oh hell to the no on that. I can't stand to be within five miles of that woman."

"Then I think it's going to have to be me. Until we have a chance to get things set and have enough funds to hire someone to manage things, this will probably be a volunteer effort."

"On top of working at the Burger Bonanza and being mayor?" Zina continued to stare at Lacey, her brow lifted into a perfect arch.

"It's not like I have much of a social life. It'll be good to stay busy. Besides, the town needs this."

"The town needs this, or you need this?" Zina's gaze bored into hers. "I know you feel like you've got to polish off the Cherish name after your dad—"

"It's not about that." Lacey nodded, trying to convince herself that Zina hadn't hit the nail square on the head. "If I'm going to be mayor, I've got to look out for the whole town. That means the economy, the people—"

"And if you do enough good maybe people will forget about how your dad's term ended?" Zina pressed.

Lacey let out a gruff breath. "Fine. If that's a side benefit, I'm not going to complain."

"So when is this big sale happening?"

"How long do you think it's going to take us to go through the rest of these boxes?"

Zina's gaze drifted around the room. "You buying pizza tonight?"

"Sure."

"Then let's get a move on."

Lacey grinned. It was good to be back in a place where she had friends who would go the extra mile for her, where people had her back, where she felt like she might be able to make a difference. Even if it did mean fighting off the feelings for Bodie she'd hauled around with her for as long as she could remember.

He might believe in putting family first, but she believed in putting the town first. Forging attachments would only slow her down and hurt her in the long run.

thirteen

Bodie stopped his truck on the side of the road. It had been almost two weeks since he'd been out at the warehouse checking on Lacey. Now the parking lot overflowed and people had left their vehicles in a hodgepodge dotting the drive to the Phillips House and warehouse. When Lacey called earlier in the week to let him know about the sale, she told him she expected a large turnout over the weekend. But the number of people drifting toward the warehouse doors made it look like attendance might even exceed her expectations. He passed a giant sign advertising the sale as he let the crowd sweep him inside.

"Welcome." Zina thrust a piece of paper into his hands. "Here's a map of the warehouse. We've got items separated by theme and everything's marked."

"So Lacey pressed you into service?" he asked.

"Me and everyone else who's ever owed her a favor." Zina continued to hand sheets out to the people coming in behind him.

"Looks like a success so far. Have you sold much?"

"We just opened a half hour ago but there are a ton of people in there." She nodded toward the door leading into the warehouse. "Lacey's back by the checkout table if you want to find her."

"Thanks. I think I'll go track her down." He hadn't seen her since that awkward almost-kiss. Even thinking about his lack of control made his cheeks burn with embarrassment. But they were both adults. They could put it behind them and keep things professional.

He was about to bypass the line of people snaking into the warehouse when a scuffle outside the front door diverted his attention. His dad and pops pushed ahead of everyone else to enter the office area.

"What's all this?" Dad asked.

Bodie stepped out of the line to stop his dad before he passed into the warehouse. "It's the sale I told you about."

"You said if we showed up today we could get some of our stuff back."

"No. I told you Lacey organized a fund-raiser."

His dad snagged the sheet of paper from Bodie's hands. "What the hell has she gone and done?"

"Looks like she's organized a pretty successful sale," Bodie commented. "I was about to go find her and see how business has been."

His pops scanned the sheet of paper. "Where are the tchotchkes?"

"The what?" Bodie squinted at the map.

"The damn decoration stuff. The breakables." Pops ran a finger over the paper, scanning the print.

"I'm not sure. You want to come with me to find Lacey?"

His dad growled as someone bumped into him from behind. "Watch yourself."

"Come on." Bodie led the way, entering the warehouse. Lacey must have rearranged things. Industrial shelving lined the perimeter of the area. Boxes stacked high into the air. They passed a section of toys, crafts, kitchenware, and gardening supplies before he noticed the checkout tables set up against the far wall.

"This isn't right," Pops muttered. "We should have had a chance to get in here before she turned it into a damn circus."

"No offense, Pops, but if you'd handled things the right way, you wouldn't be trying to buy back your old property in the first place." He didn't like the way his dad and pops seemed to feel entitled to what wasn't legally theirs anymore. They still hadn't given him any more information on what might really be going down. But his suspicions hadn't been cleared up so he was still keeping an eye out for signs.

"Don't talk to your grandfather like that," his dad ground out. "If you'd been able to get our property out of here we wouldn't be trying to buy back something we already own."

Bodie clenched his jaw. It wasn't worth it to argue with either one of them. He'd learned that long ago.

The sight of Lacey bending over a long table brightened his mood. She'd piled her hair up on top of her head. A pencil stuck through it, holding it in place. She had on a fitted long-sleeve shirt under a thermal vest. She looked good in pink. Maybe he'd get up the nerve to tell her that one day. *Keep it professional*, he reminded himself.

"Mayor Cherish." His dad reached the table first and thrust his hand toward Lacey.

She looked up, her gaze bouncing from his dad to his pops to him. "Hi there. Glad you could make it. Line starts over there." She nudged her chin toward a long line of people waiting to check out.

"We're not in line." Pops put his palms on the table and leaned toward her. "We're looking for something in particular and I'm wondering if you can tell us where it is."

"Oh?" Lacey regarded his granddad with indifference, most likely not an attitude Pops was used to feeling. She picked up a sheet of paper from the table and handed it across the table. "We made up a map."

Pops crumpled the page into a ball as Lacey's eyes widened. "I don't need a map. I need to know where you put the figurines."

Her forehead creased. "Mr. Phillips, half of the inventory could be considered figurines. Can you be more specific?"

Pops looked like he wanted to leap over the table. He'd never been the patient type.

"I'll handle this, Dad." Bodie's dad stepped forward, drawing Lacey's attention. "We're looking for something specific. I believe we ordered a pallet full of the high school mascot." A grin spread across his face. "Beavers, actually."

"Oh, the beavers, right." Lacey grinned. "The beavers aren't for sale."

"Not for sale?" Pops shifted his weight forward, knocking into the table.

Lacey either didn't notice or decided to ignore it. "That's right, Mr. Phillips. With the beavers being the high school mascot we figured we'd have plenty of opportunity to use them as centerpieces, or—"

"They're not meant for centerpieces," Pops grunted.

Dad shot Pops a look. Bodie couldn't see his dad's face from where he stood slightly behind him, but it was enough to get Pops to clamp his mouth shut and spin away from the table.

"That's right. The beaver's a popular critter around here, that's for sure." Dad let out a bark of laughter. "That's why we ordered them. Folks around here can't get enough. It's been one of our top sellers."

"Well, you'll have to order more. Like I said, the beavers aren't for sale." Lacey gave them another long look. Someone called her from a few tables away. "If you gentlemen will excuse me, I've got work to do."

Bodie watched her walk away. The way her jeans hugged

her ass made something twinge deep in his chest. Dammit. It was Lacey, the gal he used to tease by launching spit wads into her hair. Although, there'd been nothing girlish about the way she'd responded to him a couple of weeks ago, a fact he still hadn't taken the time to acknowledge.

"Well, there you have it. No beavers." Bodie gestured toward the door. "If that's all y'all were after—"

"Not so fast," Dad said. "We've got to get those beavers back one way or another. Did you think about Buck's little proposition?"

Bodie leaned close. "I'm not jeopardizing my career to get your case of ceramic doodads back. Just order more and be done with it if they're so important."

"Supplier's out. Can't get more." Pops ground his molars together. "See if you can sweet-talk your girlfriend." Then he turned on his heel and headed toward the door.

"Do what your granddad says." His dad made a fist and gave Bodie a playful punch on the arm. "Sheriff Phillips . . . can't you hear it now?"

Bodie took in a deep breath through his nose, trying to refill his patience with air. "She's not my girlfriend."

"Maybe if she was, you'd be able to do what we need you to do. The family's counting on you, Son." His dad fake-punched him on the arm then followed in Pops's footsteps, disappearing out into the drizzly gray morning.

He was tired of the family counting on him, tired of being made to feel solely responsible for cleaning up their messes. He'd looked the other way when his dad was accused of blackmailing the drugstore owner to stop carrying party supplies. There hadn't been physical proof, although Bodie knew in his heart his dad had something to do with it. And when he got a call that Pops had gotten pissed off and shot up the jukebox down at Ortega's, Bodie had smoothed things over, allowing Pops to avoid an arrest. He hadn't gone into law enforcement to give his family a free pass.

The weather fit his mood today: bleak, gloomy, and

somewhat hopeless. Bodie located Lacey, who stood behind one of the long tables, bagging up someone's purchases. He didn't want to get in the way so he decided to take a closer look at the kind of things they had for sale. Rows and rows of miscellaneous party and paper supplies lined the warehouse floor. He'd never been directly involved in the import business, preferring to try to keep a little separation between family and his career. But he knew business hadn't been so great over the past several years. What would cause his dad and Pops to bother with moving a failing operation all the way across the river?

As he contemplated potential motives, he walked back through to the office area. Zina stood on one side of the room, her hand tangled in a clump of leashes. Dogs in various colors and sizes gathered around her legs.

"What's going on?" he asked.

She turned around, almost knocking herself over. "Oh, hey. Lacey suggested I bring some of the dogs over. May as well see if we can find any of them a good home while we have so many people moving through."

"Good idea." He bent to scratch between the ears of a gray-and-white pit bull. It licked his hand in thanks.

"With any luck I'll have room for you to bring Shotgun back next week." Zina separated the dogs, leading them into a series of makeshift pens.

Bodie's heart squeezed. "No rush." She'd told him it would only be for a few days at first but kept asking if Shotgun could stay longer. He'd enjoyed having the company of the four-legged beast. They'd always had a variety of dogs around the ranch while he was growing up. Since he'd been out on his own he hadn't had reason to care for anyone or anything else. But now with Shotgun around he found he liked sharing space, especially with a living being who didn't try to tell him what to do all the time.

"How's her muzzle healing?" Zina continued to separate the dogs and steer them into the pens.

"Great. She's coming around, too. Not nearly as shy as she was the day we found her."

"Good. She's a keeper. She'll make a great family pet for someone." Zina got the last dog settled then turned to face him. "Want to help me get the paperwork together?"

Bodie glanced around. He didn't have plans today. Nothing on his agenda except maybe hitting up the bar with a few friends later. He could spare an hour or two to pitch in. "Sure. Just show me what I need to do."

Zina dragged two chairs over and slid them behind a long table. "I'll handle the questions if you handle the dogs. If people want to see a particular animal, just get it out of the pen so they can do a meet and greet. All of the info is on the notecard taped to the front of their crate."

Sounded easy enough. Bodie leaned down to check out the notecard taped to the first pen. *Bella—great with kids, doesn't like cats, relinquished by her owners because she had too much energy.* Poor dog. He dangled his fingers in front of Bella's nose so she could sniff him. Satisfied he wasn't a threat or withholding some kind of treat, she licked his palm. Seemed like a sweet girl. She nudged his hand with her nose, trying to get her block-sized head under his fingers.

"You angling for a rub?" he asked.

A couple stopped to chat with Zina at the table. Bodie waited to see if they'd want to meet one of the dogs. His gaze swept the office area of the space. Standard cubicles lined the area in rows, except for the spot they occupied, that had been separated from the rest of the office area by a counter-height wall. What exactly did Lacey have in mind? Whatever it was, he couldn't see it. But he'd make damn sure that no one messed with her while she tried to carry out her vision, however crazy it might be.

fourteen

"Over there. Yeah, just a few feet to the left, I think."
Lacey clamped her hands to her hips as she directed the
sign installer. Not everyone in town seemed all in on her
idea to transform the Phillips property into wedding central, but regardless, she had a plan and she was sticking to
it. They'd either succeed and blow away everyone's expectations or go down in a plume of tulle, glitter, and fake
rose petals.

The woodworking company in town had come through,
creating a beautiful handcrafted sign that lit up from
within. Lacey grinned as the guys attached it to the base
they'd set in concrete last week.

Satisfied they didn't need her help anymore, she turned
to head inside the house. That's where the majority of
their time and budget would go. With only a few months
before Adeline's wedding, they'd need every spare second
to transform the house into an event space. She paused on
the wraparound front porch. She'd been to events at the
Phillips House over the years but it hadn't been the show-

piece she'd envisioned. The city had transformed the gorgeous interior into more of a functional space. Now it was up to her and the team of volunteers to restore it to its original glory and make it the kind of wedding venue that brides couldn't pass up.

She turned the handle on the original mahogany door and stepped into the massive front foyer. Instead of hearing the buzz of the sanding machine from the vendor who was supposed to be refinishing all of the hardwood floors, a high-pitched shriek filled her ears.

Lacey turned around just in time to collide with Adeline. Papers flew everywhere. Adeline barreled past her, through the front door, and didn't stop until she'd hit the middle of the front sidewalk.

"What the heck was that?" Lacey muttered as she bent down to pick up the paper explosion.

"Rats." Roman walked toward her from the doorway leading to the kitchen.

"It's okay, I've got it." Lacey gathered the papers from the floor.

Roman squatted next to her. "I mean, you've got rats. Adeline wanted to take a closer look at the space and we came across a baby rat in the kitchen."

Lacey's pulse thundered in her ears. "Rats? Are you sure you saw a rat?"

"Pretty sure. Either that or you've got a mouse on steroids." He pointed toward the front door that stood wide open. "Did she go out?"

"Um, yeah. She's out on the lawn." Lacey swept the papers into her hands then handed them to Roman as she stood. "Here, she dropped these on her way out."

"Thanks." He took the stack of papers then left.

Rats. Could they really have a rat problem? Weren't rats more likely to make their home somewhere dark and dank? Like the New York subway system? She took cautious steps toward the doorway to the kitchen, hoping that

Adeline and Roman were wrong. Maybe they saw a family
of kittens. Or if it had to be wild animals, maybe somehow
a mama bunny had found her way into the building and
made a burrow. It didn't matter that it was only March and
most baby bunnies weren't born until spring. Trying to
convince herself that surely they'd been mistaken, she
crept closer to the kitchen. Maybe the mama bunny had
gotten herself in a family way and taken refuge against the
cooler temps inside the house. And maybe she had a few
friends who'd done the same. For all she knew, the Phillips
House had become a home for single bunny mamas. Word
could be on the street. That's probably all it was.

Bunnies were cute and helpless. Adeline wasn't the
outdoorsy type. It would be easy to confuse a baby bunny
with a . . . rat! Lacey jumped onto a built-in barstool as
she entered the kitchen. A giant creature, more than double the size of a baby bunny, scrambled past where she
clung to the stool.

"Mayor Cherish." The guy who was supposed to be
returning the hardwood floors to their former glory tipped
his baseball cap at her. "We've got a problem."

Lacey folded her arms across her chest as Bodie taped the
sign to the front window of the house. "How long until we
can get back in there?"

"Depends on the contractor. Did you call the guy I told
you to?"

"Yeah. He said he can come out on Thursday to take a
look." She shifted positions and shoved her hands in the
pockets of her jacket. "But we're on a tight deadline.
Every single day matters."

Bodie shrugged. "Then work on the exterior for now.
You've got landscaping, painting, tuck-pointing . . . there
are all kinds of things you can do until your problem is
taken care of."

Lacey knew that, of course she did, she was the one who came up with the project plan in the first place. But she didn't like being put off schedule. "How could Adeline mix up an armadillo with a rat?"

"I'm sure she didn't stick around to take a real close look." He took out his phone and pulled up a picture he'd snapped. "Besides, if she just caught a glimpse of the tail, she probably thought it was a rat."

"Have you ever heard of an armadillo infestation?" Lacey examined the picture of the strange creature on the screen. The only time she'd seen armadillos in the wild were on the side of the road, usually with a tire mark down the middle. They weren't known for being the smartest animals.

Bodie tucked his phone away. "We had a few out at the ranch but the dogs tended to keep them away. Maybe we need to bring Shotgun over to run armadillo prevention."

"No. I'll let the wildlife expert do his thing." It was too bad she couldn't get him out here until Thursday though.

"Expecting someone?" Bodie nodded toward a van coming down the long drive.

"What?" Lacey swiveled around, her mind already racing with ways to adjust her to-do list. "No, I told everyone to head to lunch until we figure out where to go from here."

"We?" Bodie tipped his head down, meeting her gaze with those big, gray eyes.

"Yes, we. We're in this together, remember? You're the one who said the mayor and the sheriff's office share the same business."

"And who's that?" Bodie nudged his chin toward the small parking area where a woman climbed out of the passenger side of the van.

She wore a cropped black leather jacket over a tight pencil skirt. Long blond hair flowed over her shoulders in perfect waves. She paused to pull a tube of lipstick out of her bag then angled the side mirror so she could see to apply it.

Lacey's phone vibrated in her back pocket, trilling the annoying sound bite she'd chosen for her alarm. The alarm she'd set to remind her of the appointment she had today.

"Oh no. It's the reporter from *Texas Times*."

"How the hell do you know that?" Bodie asked.

Lacey reached behind him to rip the freshly taped notice from the front door. "Because we have an appointment today. I sent out press releases to try to get some interest from the media in our renovation. She's the only one who got back to me."

A guy holding a large camera rounded the van. Lacey's vision fuzzed at the edges.

"Hey, you can't remove that notice." Bodie clamped a hand around her wrist. "It's legal."

"Legal schmegal. If the one media outlet that took any interest in our project finds out we've got an armadillo problem, our venture will be sunk before it even begins." She crumpled up the paper and shoved it in her pocket. "If you'll excuse me for a moment."

Bodie didn't follow her down the steps to the sidewalk. Thank goodness. They might be in this together but she didn't need him literally following in her footsteps and blocking her at every turn.

As she approached the van the woman looked up and smiled. Lacey held out a hand. "Hi, I'm Lacey Cherish. You must be from the *Texas Times*."

"I'm Samantha Cross and this is my cameraman, Jay. Thanks for making time for us today." Her slim fingers gripped Lacey's in a firm grip.

"Thanks for coming. I do have some bad news though."

"Oh?" Samantha cocked her head. "Is now a bad time?"

"We're in the middle of renovations and the team refinishing the flooring just put a topcoat on the hardwoods." Lacey screwed her lips into a frown. "I was really hoping to show you the inside today. I even asked them to hold off, but you know how it is when you're working with a bunch of contractors."

Jay swung the camera down from his shoulder. "Well, that's a waste of time. We drove all the way out here from Beaumont to do this piece."

"Hi, I'm Deputy Sheriff Bodie Phillips." Leave it to Bodie to step in. "As Mayor Cherish mentioned, the interior is off-limits. Those guys would gnaw us to pieces if we messed with their floors. But how about taking a look at the exterior? This place was in my family for generations. I can give you some backstory if you'd like."

Samantha turned toward Bodie, a huge smile on her face, basically giving Lacey a cold shoulder.

Lacey wanted to wrap her hands around Bodie's neck and squeeze. Instead she managed to summon a grin. "That would be great, Bodie. Maybe you can start with why your family business decided to go under after so long. If Samantha really wants to get the history of the place down, she probably wants to hear the whole story."

"I'd love that." Samantha reached into her bag and pulled out her phone. "You don't mind if I record the conversation, do you? I find it's easier than trying to keep up taking notes."

"Not at all." Bodie gave Lacey a strained smile. "Why don't we start at the beginning? Follow me."

fifteen

By the time he was done giving the reporter and her side-kick a personal tour of the exterior of the Phillips House, including a guided walk around the grounds and the wild raspberry patch that always made him break out in hives, Bodie was out of patience.

He stood on the gravel next to Lacey, waving as Jay and Samantha backed down the drive.

Lacey's smile faded as soon as the van disappeared around a curve. "I asked you to stop butting into my business."

"What?" Bodie glared at her. "You've got to be kidding me. I saved your ass."

"No. You made a bad situation worse. I had it under control. You've got to stop stepping in." She whirled around, her boots crunching on the gravel as she stomped toward the house.

Bodie caught up to her in just a few steps. He wrapped a hand around her arm, causing her to stop. "Look, Sweets, if I hadn't stepped in, you would have been screwed. That reporter would have left, pissed off that she'd wasted an entire morning driving out here for nothing."

Lacey turned on him, spitfire sparking in her eyes. "Do you think maybe I had an idea? One that didn't involve you divulging your entire family history?"

"Really?" Bodie let go of her arm, stepping back and crossing his arms over his chest. Damn if she wasn't even more attractive when she had a little fire in her belly. "Enlighten me, please."

"Forget it, it's too late."

"Oh no, you don't. You want to rip me a new one because I intervened to help, you're going to tell me how you planned to save the day."

"Fine. I was going to talk to her about Adeline. How she's practically Swynton royalty and how she really wants to be the first one to get married in our new venue."

Bodie shook his head from side to side. "No way Adeline's story trumps mine. I even showed her where my relatives used to hide their moonshine during Prohibition."

"I appreciate your help, but we've got to stop thinking about this place as a piece of the Phillips family history and start trying to position it as a charming location that's exclusive to Ido."

"But it is a part of Phillips history. And it always will be, even if you'd rather take a big eraser and wipe my family out of the town's history. Just like you're changing the name. Like it or not, they helped found this place."

"And if we're not careful, they'll be the ones who destroy it forever."

They stood facing each other, locked in a standoff for what felt like forever. Bodie was too stubborn to admit she was right.

Finally, Lacey shifted her gaze to the parking area. "I've got to find Adeline before she tells everyone the whole place is infested with rats."

Bodie wanted to ease her worries. The slump of Lacey's shoulders made it look like she had the weight of the world resting on her slim frame. "Want me to come with you?"

Her palm pressed on his chest. A field of warmth radiated out from where she touched him. "You've done enough for today. Don't you have official sheriff business to attend to?"

Nothing pressing unless he wanted to follow up on another random lead about a potential dogfighting ring. The sheriff's office had been hearing rumors of a mobile dogfighting circuit for years. Trouble was, as soon as they got wind that someone was onto them, the whole operation would pick up and move, making it impossible to catch them in the act.

Bodie grabbed her hand, giving her fingers a squeeze. "Be careful, okay?"

"You afraid Adeline is going to take desperate measures?"

"That woman's capable of things I wouldn't put past even some of the most hardened criminals I've worked with."

Lacey laughed off his concern. "Don't worry about me. I'm sure we can work something out. I'll just tell her she saw someone's pet or something."

"You really think she's going to buy that?"

"Maybe not, but what's the alternative? Tell her that she'll need to invest in traps so we can make sure a giant mammal doesn't take off with her wedding cake?"

"Good luck. Let me know how it goes."

"You'll be my first call." She rolled her eyes. "Now, don't you have something better to do?"

Bodie reluctantly withdrew his hand. The promise he'd made to keep an eye on Lacey was turning into a bit of a chore. Not because he resented having to follow her around, but for reasons exactly the opposite. The more time he spent trying to keep Lacey out of trouble, the more time he spent with her. The more time he spent with her, the more he enjoyed her company. The more he enjoyed her company, the more he could picture her flush against his chest, his arms wrapped around her, her lips tangled with his . . .

"Bodie?" Her forehead creased. "You okay?"

"Yeah, um, see you later." His face flushed with heat. It wouldn't do anyone any good for him to voice the kind of thoughts he'd been having about Lacey. He waited until she made it to her truck. Then he climbed into his own pickup. Thanks to her ruining his notice, he'd have to head back to the office and print off another one before he could do much else. Maybe he'd stop by the house on his way. Shotgun had been cooped up in her kennel all morning. It would do the dog some good to get some fresh air.

As he climbed into the truck, his stomach grumbling in anticipation of his lunch, his cell rang.

Pops. Dammit. Why did his family seem to have the worst timing in the world?

"What's up, Pops?"

"It's your dad. He's in the hospital over in Swynton."

Bodie's lungs seized then squeezed together. He tried to take in a breath around the giant lump forming in his chest. "What's wrong?"

"Somebody sent him a message. Get your ass over there, we've got to figure this out."

"Is he okay?"

"He will be. Not much more hurt than his pride. This time." The line went dead.

Pops had never been a fan of long conversations or conversations in general. With hope for a quiet afternoon shattered, Bodie turned his truck toward Swynton—the last place he wanted to go.

sixteen

———◦♡◦———

"Just a temporary setback." Lacey took in a deep breath through her nose as she faced Adeline. She'd finally tracked her down at work. Someone somewhere seemed to think having no heart made Adeline the perfect choice for being a pediatric nurse at the local urgent care clinic.

Adeline pointed a bright pink fingernail at Lacey. "You sure there wasn't more than just one? I think you're trying to pull a fast one over on me."

"What good would it do me to do that?" Lacey wrapped her hand around the warm cup of coffee she'd bought from the gas station/bait shop across the street, wishing she had something a little stronger at her disposal. "We're in this together. You get the wedding of your dreams and we get the publicity we need to kick off our project. How would me lying about an armadillo infestation be in my best interest?" As the word *infestation* fell from her lips, Lacey said a silent prayer that it wouldn't come to that.

"So you really think it was just one armadillo? Who

was it you said used to work out there?" Adeline wanted to believe her, Lacey could tell.

"The grounds manager. He used to live in the caretaker shed on the edge of the property. His pet armadillo went missing one day while he was checking the building. It's got to be"—she scrambled to think of a name to give the fictional pet—"Moses. He used to make the rounds with the guy."

"So are you returning the armadillo to this caretaker?" Adeline squinted.

Moses was a bad name. Who would believe there was a pet armadillo named Moses on the loose? "Well, we tried. But he's moved away. I have no idea how to contact him. But don't worry, we'll catch Moses and then we can get back to planning the perfect ceremony and reception for you and Roman."

Adeline tapped her fingernails on the wooden laminate tabletop. The click-click-clicking made Lacey want to smack her hand down on the table. "I don't know . . ."

Desperate times called for desperate measures. "Hey, remember the picture you showed me of that Cinderella-style carriage? What if we throw that into your wedding package for free?"

Adeline stopped clacking her nails and drew a heart on the tabletop with her pointer finger. "With the twinkle lights and tulle netting?"

Lacey squelched the panic rising from her gut. "Of course."

"Deal." Adeline shoved her hand out to shake. "But I'm not going back in that building until you catch Moses."

Lacey wrapped her hand around Adeline's, wondering how in the world she was going to come up with a Cinderella carriage. "I understand. They've got to get the floors redone anyway so the building won't be accessible for a few weeks. By then we'll have Moses contained and everything will be under control." She hoped. She prayed. She tried to make a deal with God that all would go well. Not only her future, but the future of the whole town depended on it.

"As long as you're here, do you want to talk about a few other details?"

"Sure. What do you have in mind?" Lacey clasped her hands on the table in front of her. They had only about two months. Not a lot of time to plan for what would hopefully be their catalyst event.

"Just a few ideas." Adeline reached into her bag and pulled out a thick binder. "I've been imagining this day since I was a little girl. It's got to be perfect."

Lacey swallowed. Hard. She could picture Adeline as a little girl, orchestrating play weddings with her stuffed animals or dolls. That had never been Lacey's style. When she was little and thought about what it would be like to grow up and get married she always pictured her and Bodie, standing under a wooden arbor on the edge of a field of wildflowers. No need for china, crystal, or towering tiered cakes. She laughed to herself at the image of Bodie in a tux. She'd most likely pictured him as her groom since he was the only boy who'd been halfway nice to her as a girl. Didn't have anything to do with the way he made her insides warm and gooey like a brownie fresh from the oven.

"Should we start with the invitations?" Adeline flipped the binder open.

"Haven't you already made arrangements for those?" Lacey gazed at the samples Adeline had stuffed into the bulging sheet protector.

"I'd planned on going through Phillips. But with them closing their doors, I need a plan B."

Lacey nodded. Plan B would be up to her. "Okay, let's break this down." The magazine article she'd read talked about establishing a theme for the wedding. After that, the theme would guide the rest of the decisions. "Have you thought about a theme?"

"Oooh, like we had for prom? A Night Under the Stars? Under the Sea?"

A groan escaped Lacey's lips. "Not exactly like that." She racked her brain trying to remember the most popular themes they'd listed in the article. Granted, it was from over a decade ago, but the wedding business couldn't have changed that much. Love was love. Getting hitched meant the same thing no matter what year it was. "I mean more like a fairy-tale wedding, or a simple country get-together."

"Fairy tale for sure. If we have Cinderella's carriage we definitely have to do that. Although, Roman really likes to watch rugby. I want the wedding to reflect what he wants, too. Can we somehow work rugby into the equation?"

Cinderella meets the rugby player of her dreams? Lacey screwed her lips into a frown. How would that go over? "Are you planning on a groom's cake? We could definitely work that in somehow."

"Yes." Adeline clapped her hands together. "Let's do a groom's cake in the shape of a rugby field."

"Um, okay." It didn't matter that Lacey had no idea who would be making any kind of cakes, much less a rugby-themed groom's cake. But she had one goal for this meeting today: keep Adeline as their client. No matter what ridiculous ideas she came up with, Lacey would figure out a way to make them work. She had to.

"You have a dress, right?" Lacey asked. Surely Adeline had already figured that piece out.

"Well, since I wasn't planning on getting married until the fall, I haven't made a final decision. My bridesmaids and I are planning on going to Dallas next weekend to take one last look."

"Okay." Lacey nodded. "It can take several weeks if you need alterations so that should be priority number one."

"Oh my gosh." Adeline grabbed Lacey's hands. "You should come with us!"

She needed an excuse. A good excuse. Like now. "Um, I don't think I can get the time off work. Helmut's down a waitress right now, and—"

"You just let me take care of that part. I'll have a talk with him. It would mean a lot to me if you'd come. Now that we've got a theme and all, I want to make sure it's all going to work together."

"I don't know." Lacey hemmed and hawed. She hadn't seen this new development coming. She'd planned on re-vamping the event space and providing a new industry for her hometown. Becoming a wedding planner hadn't factored into her goals at all. Not one tiny bit. Especially for Adeline, who'd made her high school life such a living hell.

"Are you sure you want me there? Isn't this a time for you and your closest friends to get together?"

"It's my wedding and you're my wedding planner. You've got to coordinate everything so it all works together. I simply won't take no for an answer. It's settled. We're going on Friday. We'll leave early in the morning so we can fit in a few stops on Friday afternoon. This is going to be so much fun."

"Yeah." Lacey nodded. "Fun."

"I've got to get back. Thanks for stopping by. I really appreciate you settling my nerves." She stood from the table and pushed her chair in. "You'll let me know when they catch Moses, right?"

Moses . . . Lacey's mind had gone blank.

"The armadillo." Adeline narrowed her eyes. "Are you feeling okay? You look a little pale."

Shaking her head, Lacey stood. "Yeah, I'm fine." Or at least she would be when she had a moment to compose herself and evaluate the situation.

"Great. See you Friday." Adeline turned and walked away, a bounce in her step that hadn't been there before.

Lacey figured she was one for two. She'd succeeded in keeping Adeline from freaking out, but now she found herself even more ingrained in the wedding-planning process.

Frustrated and with one person to blame, she pulled up Bodie's number. If she had to go to Dallas to shop for wedding dresses all weekend, he'd have to pick up the slack around town.

seventeen

Bodie cringed as the overpowering scent of antiseptic enveloped him. He hated going to the hospital. It was bad enough when he had to interview a victim or follow up with a suspect. But having to visit his dad in the hospital was ten times worse, especially since Pops had been less than helpful on the phone.

With the help of a nurse, two volunteers, and a doctor who looked like he'd just rolled off a twenty-four-hour shift, Bodie located his dad. He was in the emergency room, bellowing orders from his bed. Bodie pushed back the curtain and did a double take.

"Dad?" Clearly the man in the flimsy hospital gown was his dad. But a giant bandage covered half his head, including his right eye. "What the hell?"

"Just a little accident." Pops stood and pulled the curtain closed.

"Are you going to be okay? What happened?" For someone trained in crisis management and critical situations, Bodie's natural instincts took over. "Who did this to you?"

Pops shot him a silencing glare. "Like I said, just a little accident. He'll be good as new by Friday."

Bodie's gaze drifted over his dad's face. The bandage covered most of his right cheek, stretching up to his eyebrow. A purple-bluish tinge spread from under the edges. "*Good as new by Friday*" seemed very optimistic. "But you said someone sent him a—"

"Shh." Pops's eyebrows drew down into a fierce line. "We can talk about that later."

Dad waved off the nurse messing with his IV. "I'll be fine. I don't know why your grandfather called you to begin with."

"What happened?" Based on Pops's reaction, Bodie hoped they'd fill him in later.

"Tried two-stepping with a two-by-four," Dad joked. "The board won."

Bodie shook his head as he stepped closer to the bed. "I'm glad to know you'll be all right. Pops could have mentioned that on the phone so I didn't race over here wondering if you were about to take your last breath."

Pops shrugged. He was never one to waste unnecessary words. Bodie should be used to that by now.

"Looks like I'll live to tell." Dad lowered his voice. "At least for another day or two."

He and Pops were tighter than two ticks on a coonhound. But until they felt like bringing Bodie into the circle of trust, it wouldn't do any good to pry.

"Can I do anything for you? When are they going to let you out of here?" Based on what he saw, his dad wasn't in any danger. At least nothing more than the danger of having a bad headache and a face that might frighten small children away for the next couple of weeks.

Pops slumped into the vinyl recliner next to the bed. "I'll make sure he gets home okay. But we need to talk about this."

Nodding, Bodie agreed. "Yeah, you two need to tell me what's going on."

"Stop by tomorrow afternoon," Pops said. "We'll chat then."

Bodie stepped closer to the bed. "Let me know if you need anything." He reached out to put his hand on his dad's, then thought better of it and pulled back.

"You know what we need," Dad grunted. "Did you make arrangements yet?"

Bodie's heart squeezed. Dad was talking about Lacey. What was it with those damn beavers anyway? "No."

Dad's fist came down on the thin hospital mattress with a whomp. "Dammit, we don't have forever."

"What's going on?" Bodie asked. It wasn't like his dad to get worked up over something so weird. Wasn't like his dad to get worked up over something, period.

"I said we'll talk about it later," Pops ground out. "We'll see you tomorrow."

"Yeah, okay. Tomorrow." Bodie parted the curtain and moved down the hall. Whatever his dad and pops were up to appeared to be getting out of hand. Before he had much time to think about it, his phone rang.

The sight of Lacey's number surprised him. He figured she needed longer than a couple of hours to cool off after he'd shut down the Phillips House.

"Did you call to apologize?" Bodie asked.

"Absolutely not. I called to let you know that I'm going to be shopping for wedding dresses in Dallas this weekend so you'll have to hold down the fort here in town."

"Who's the lucky guy? Do I know him?" He assumed she was joking, but his heart pinched the tiniest bit at the thought of Lacey getting married. Whomever she chose as her groom would be one lucky bastard.

"Very funny. I caught up to Adeline and convinced her not to cancel."

"Good job. How did you do that?" For a moment his heart swelled. Lacey could do just about anything she set her mind to. Hopefully he'd figure out his dad's secret before she got a whiff of something rotten going on there.

"I told her the armadillo used to be the caretaker's pet."

"Armadillo? From what I heard you've got *armadillos*, a total infestation. They wouldn't close you down for a single armadillo."

"I know. But she bought it and that's all that matters." A low groan came through the phone. "Now somehow she's convinced that I need to go to Dallas with her to shop for the perfect dress."

He couldn't stop the deep chuckle from escaping. "So a girls' weekend with one of your favorite home gals, huh?"

"It's not funny. I need to be here, planning for the opening, taking care of our rogue-pet issue, and making sure everyone stays on task."

"One weekend in Dallas isn't going to derail you."

"That's what you think. You're not spending two days with Adeline."

"True. What's that saying about something not killing you makes you better?"

"What doesn't kill us makes us stronger."

"That's right. Just think of Adeline as your personal strength coach."

Lacey sighed. "This had better work."

"The weekend in Dallas?"

"Not just that. Restoring the house, my proposal to re-name the town, all of it. If it doesn't, I don't know—"

"It will." The uncertainty in her voice pulled at him. He'd say anything in that moment to ease her worry, even though he had no idea whether she was right about her plans for the town or not.

"Thanks, Bodie." The waver in her voice did funny things to his stomach. Made it flip over on itself, kind of like how he felt the first time he caught a snake—a little uncomfortable but pretty proud of himself all at once.

"So when do you leave?" he asked, trying to shake off the weird sensation.

"Sometime on Friday. Any words of advice?"

"You're on your own with this one."

"Gee, thanks. And here I thought we were in this together."

Together. Another wave of flip-flopping hit his gut. She didn't mean anything by it. But he still couldn't shake the sliver of unease sliding around in his belly. "I've got your back. If anything goes wrong, just give me a call, okay?"

"And you'll race up to Dallas and save me?"

"Hopefully it won't be anything that drastic. But if Adeline gives you trouble, I'm only a phone call away."

"Got it. I'll make a list of things going on this weekend so you know what to check on. Do you want me to text it or e-mail?"

"Are you going to be at the warehouse at all in the next day or two?"

"Sure am. Since I can't work on the house right now I figured I'd get a few more things organized over there. Why?"

"Why don't you jot it down and I'll swing by to pick it up next time you're over there." Maybe he'd have a chance to snoop around and find the box of beavers. For some reason his dad and his pops were desperate to get their hands on them. There had to be a reason why.

"You sure you don't want me to just text you?"

"Nah, that's okay. I think I might have dropped something while I was over there for the sale. It'll give me a chance to look for it."

"Okay. I'll be there tomorrow after my shift. Probably after eight."

"I'll stop by then."

"Sounds good."

He waited until the call disconnected then dropped his phone into his pocket. Tomorrow night. His pulse sped up when he thought about seeing Lacey again. Either something was wrong with him or after the past few weeks he'd developed some sort of unnatural feelings for his gorgeous new mayor. He put his hands to his head. No, his best friend's little sister. He kept trying, but he couldn't seem to think of Lacey as the tagalong tween he'd known all those years ago anymore.

Now when he thought of her, which was way too often, he saw the swell of her breasts, the curve of her hips, and the fullness of that bottom lip she always seemed to have captured between her teeth.

The more he tried to not think of her as a woman, the more his brain latched on to visions of her wrapped in his arms, her tongue tangled in his. Only one way to chase the impossible images out of his head. He needed to run.

He climbed into his truck, hell-bent on getting home, changing into his running gear, and hitting the road to pound out a few miles. Hopefully Shotgun was up for it. Because if he didn't get his run in before he met up with Lacey again, he might be running into a hell of a lot more than he bargained for.

eighteen

With the new key she'd had made, Lacey unlocked the front door leading into the office. She'd typically not worry about rekeying the locks, but with the onslaught of interest in the warehouse event space, the continued obsession of Bodie's family with the beavers, and the pressure she'd been feeling from the past employees, playing it safe was better than playing it sorry.

Once inside, she flipped the lights and let the door close behind her. A quick glance around the front office assured her everything was in its proper place. What could Bodie be looking for? He'd helped out with the pet-rescue portion of the sale so if he dropped something it had to be in the front area.

She leaned down, searching under desks and chairs. Apart from a few dust bunnies that might be mistaken for tumbleweeds, nothing stood out. Bodie didn't seem like the kind of man who needed a ploy. But she couldn't help but wonder why he didn't just have her text him the information. Oh well. At least she'd have a chance to see him before she left town.

That intimate moment they'd shared a few weeks ago had left her reeling. She needed to set eyes on him and prove to herself that he was still the annoying bully he'd been since she moved back to town. Anything else might get in the way of her focusing all of her attention on transforming the Phillips House and she couldn't have that. With so little time left before their first event, she still couldn't believe she'd let Adeline talk her into going wedding dress shopping.

But she'd do just about anything to hold on to the hope that Ido would someday be a destination wedding site. It would work. It had to.

As she took a final look around, headlights swept through the window. Bodie.

His footsteps crunched on the gravel outside and she heard him coming long before he knocked at the door.

"Hey." She pushed open the door to the outside, then stepped back when she realized whom he'd brought with him. "Shotgun! Hey, girl."

The pup danced on her hind legs, trying to jump up and smother Lacey's face with kisses.

"Down." At Bodie's command, Shotgun stood on all fours, her tail wagging so hard the back half of her body whipped back and forth like a rag doll. "We're working on manners."

"I'm impressed." Lacey looked up at Bodie as she leaned down to pet the dog. "She seems to be doing great."

Shotgun jumped up, cracking the top of her head against Lacey's chin. Lacey stumbled back but a strong hand caught her before her tailbone hit the ground.

"You okay?" Bodie's hands gripped her arms and pulled her back to a standing position. "Sorry about that. She's a work in progress."

"Aren't we all?" Lacey grinned even though the area

under her chin throbbed from the impact. "Shotgun, your head seems to be as hard as a rock."

Bodie put a hand on either side of Lacey's face and tipped her head back. Tiny pinpricks of awareness swept over her cheeks. "She got you good. You want me to grab some ice?"

Lacey stepped back, more worried about the feel of Bodie's fingertips on her skin than any bruising that might be forming on her face. "No, I'm fine."

Shotgun stood in front of her, minus a bit of her previous enthusiasm, her tail no longer thrashing the air. She cocked her head one way, then tilted it the other.

"That's the universal way of saying *I'm sorry* in dog talk." Bodie reached down to ruffle the dog's ears. "She also says maybe I should have named her Bonehead instead."

Lacey let out a laugh as she arched a brow. "I had no idea you could communicate with animals like that."

"It's a newly developed talent." Bodie shrugged. "Just one of my superpowers, I guess."

Bodie was big enough to be a superhero. Her inner teenager had always considered his mere presence a superpower in and of itself. The way he could make her laugh no matter what kind of mood she was in, the way he'd resort to desperate and embarrassing lengths to coax a smile. Lacey peered up at him as she squatted next to Shotgun. Yeah, Bodie was all of her favorite superheroes combined.

Her breath caught in her chest, making her cough on her own inhale. When did she become such a sap? She shook all cheesy thoughts of Bodie out of her head.

"So you want that checklist?" She gave Shotgun a final pat then stood, brushing stray dog hair off her shirt.

"Yeah, that would be great. What's on it?"

She pulled a piece of paper out of her pocket and unfolded it as she stepped close to the counter. "Not too much."

His finger grazed hers as he pointed to the first item on

the list. Her breath hitched. Since when did being around Bodie incite choking on air? Since he'd stopped looking at her like a bug he'd like to squash and started looking at her as someone he might want to . . . what? As he ran his finger over the paper, she wondered what might happen if she pressed her hand onto his.

"Moses removal?" His finger stopped on item number three. "Who's Moses?"

She jerked her finger back as hot prickles raced across her cheeks. What had gotten into her lately?

"Lacey?" Bodie poked her in the arm. The kind of poke he might have given to her twelve-year-old self. The kind intended for someone he didn't think of as more than an annoying little sister.

"Moses. Yeah, that's the armadillo Adeline saw."

"You named him after a biblical figure?"

Her shoulders shook as a shiver raced through her. "It was the best I could do at the time."

"Fill in holes in the yard? Don't you think we should wait until item one is taken care of to do that?"

"It looks like a fairy garden graveyard out there. Can't we fill in some of them so people don't wonder why there are holes all over the place?"

"A fairy garden graveyard?" Bodie's head dipped. Then it shook from side to side like he'd never heard anything so stupid. But she knew for a fact he had. He and Luke used to make stuff up all the time. They once told her that an old tree in the backyard came alive at night. She was terrified to go in the backyard alone for months.

"Just deal with the armadillos, okay? Everything else can wait until I get back."

"We'll have to set live traps. Do you have a budget for that?"

"I don't have a budget for any of this. We've got a little bit left from the warehouse sale." She noticed the way his shoulders hunched when she mentioned it. "Other than that we've almost maxed out the maintenance budget set aside for the house and property."

"I'll see what I can do." He folded up the paper and shoved it in his pocket. "Now, do you mind if I look around? I'm pretty sure I dropped my mini flashlight while I was here for the sale."

"Go ahead. I didn't see anything up here in the office so it must be in back." She gestured toward the door to the warehouse.

"Thanks. You want me to take Shotgun with me or leave her out here with you?"

"I have to come back anyway to sort through some more boxes. We can all head out back." Did Bodie really wince or did she imagine it?

"All right. Lead the way." He held the door open, letting her pass through first. Shotgun bounded after her, dragging her new green-and-brown-camouflage-print leash behind her.

"I'll be over here sorting through fake flowers. Let me know if you need anything." She turned left to head down one aisle while Bodie went to the opposite side of the warehouse.

While she sorted through boxes and bins of silk flowers, garlands, and greenery, she couldn't help but think about the predicament she'd stuck herself in. If she didn't come through for Adeline's wedding, she might as well kiss any hope of success good-bye. Adeline wasn't the kind of woman who believed in doling out second chances. She expected 120 percent effort all the time. If a single thing went wrong, no matter how well the rest of the event went, it would shroud the evening in failure. Lacey took in a gulp of air and forced it down, past the tightness in her chest.

As she opened another box, a crash sounded from the other side of the warehouse. "Bodie? Are you okay?"

Shotgun barked. Bodie yelled something she couldn't make out, and Lacey took off in that direction.

She rounded a set of shelves to find Shotgun and Bodie engaged in a game of tug-of-war. Bodie crouched down, his hands wrapped around something Shotgun held in her mouth.

"What's going on?"

Bodie looked up, letting go of his grip. "Damn dog knocked over a box of breakables."

Lacey's gaze passed over the chunks of white ceramic scattered all over the floor. "What was it?"

"It was a box of beavers." He stretched his hands to the sides, nodding toward the mix of cardboard and packing peanuts spilling over the floor in front of him. "Shotgun wouldn't leave it alone. She jumped up and knocked it off the shelf."

Lacey nudged the mess with the toe of her boot. "Are they all broken?"

Bodie knelt down and sifted through the packing material. "What the hell?"

"What?" Lacey squatted next to him.

He lifted up the remains of a bucktoothed beaver figurine. Something long and brown stuck up from the center. "Well, I'll be damned."

Lacey squinted, trying to see what Bodie must be seeing. "What is it?"

"I think we just figured out why my dad and pops were so eager to get their hands on your beavers."

"Excuse me?"

Bodie made eye contact, looking like he'd just realized where they were and who squatted down next to him. "Sorry, I mean the beaver figurines. Do you know what this is?"

Lacey squinted again as she shook her head. "No. Are you going to tell me?"

He let the beaver's bottom drop to the floor and held the bundle in front of her. "This makes so much sense now."

Impatience was getting the best of her. She clamped

her hands to her hips as she stood. "I'm glad you've figured out what's going on. Now, do you want to enlighten me? Please?"

Still squatting, he had to look up to meet her eyes. "Have you ever seen my dad without a cigar in his mouth?"

She nibbled on her lower lip as she considered the question. "No, I can't say that I have."

As Bodie stood, he handed her the bundle. "Any idea what kind of cigars my dad likes to smoke?" At her blank stare, he rolled his eyes. "Cubans."

Lacey shrugged. "So?"

She still didn't get it. Bodie wanted to grab her by the shoulders and shake some sense into her. Not in a creepy way. In a "come on girl, get with the program" way. "It's illegal to import Cuban cigars into the States for commercial purposes, Mayor Cherish."

Finally, a hint of understanding lit her gaze. "You mean your dad and pops were using the import business as a front to illegally import them?"

"I don't know, but I'd say we've got some irrefutable evidence here." He leaned over, digging through the box of broken beavers. Every single one of them had a bundle of cigars tucked inside. "How many boxes of beavers do you have?"

She looked up at the shelf towering above her. "All the boxes on this shelving unit. Plus some more against the wall over there."

Bodie put his hand to his temple as he shook his head. "No wonder they wanted them back. There's got to be thousands of dollars' worth of cigars here."

"So what are you waiting for?" Lacey tossed another bundle onto the heap.

"What do you mean?"

Her gaze shifted to where Shotgun lay on the ground,

chewing up a piece of cardboard. "If what you said is true, they're breaking the law. Aren't you going to arrest them?"

"Not without a little more investigating." Bodie grimaced. "I need to figure out what they wanted to do with them, where they were getting them . . . letting them know we're onto them wouldn't help the case at this point."

She clamped her arms to her waist, her brow furrowed. "So you're not going to say anything about this?"

"No"—he put his hand on her shoulder—"and you can't, either."

Lacey's gaze traveled to where his palm rested, making him acutely aware of the heat generated by his touch. "And why not?"

"Because if they know we know something they'll be liable to destroy the evidence." That would set him back, putting him even farther away from learning what his dad and pops were up to.

"You think your dad's going to smoke them all?" Her lips quirked up at the edges like she wanted to laugh at the ridiculousness of the idea.

"Just promise me you won't say anything for a few days?"

nineteen

Bodie's stomach clenched as he waited for her response. In his experience, Lacey could be unpredictable. At least she had been when she was younger. She'd promise to stay behind so he and Luke could meet up with friends then always show up where she knew they'd be. Hopefully she placed more value on her word than she had when she was ten. He studied her, trying to figure out if she'd be on board.

"Fine."

He exhaled, his breath seeping out like a deflating balloon. "Thank you."

"I'm not doing it for you." Her lashes fluttered as she blinked her eyes, drawing his gaze to the light smattering of freckles that still danced across her nose. "I'm doing it for everyone else. The town deserves to know what's going on and if holding off gives you a better chance to uncover the whole story . . ."

"It will. I promise." He squeezed her shoulder then let his hand fall to his side. Knowing Lacey wouldn't spill the beans took care of one issue. Now he had to deal with the more dangerous one—confronting his family. He didn't know much about cigars beyond the fact his dad always seemed to have one clenched between his teeth, but if what they were doing was illegal . . .

"I'm going to go grab a broom and sweep up this mess." Lacey used her foot to nudge the broken pieces into a pile. "Hey, where did Shotgun go?"

Bodie glanced to where the dog had been shredding the cardboard just moments before. "I don't know. Shotgun!"

When the dog didn't come right away, Lacey moved toward the end of the aisle. "Shotgun, come here, girl."

"You go left, I'll go right?" Bodie asked, already heading in the opposite direction.

Lacey nodded before she disappeared around the corner. Bodie turned the other way, peering down the aisles as he went. Where could the dog go? It's not like she would have sniffed out anything edible in the mix of decorations and figurines.

"Found her." Lacey's voice came from a few rows over.

Bodie followed, rounding the corner to see Lacey crouched over the poor mutt. Shotgun lay on her side, her tongue lolling out of her mouth.

"What happened?" Bodie squatted down next to her, not liking the way the dog didn't make any kind of effort to get up. His stomach churned as he ran a hand behind her ears. "Come on, girl."

"I think she ate your evidence." Lacey pointed to what was left of a chewed-up bundle of cigars. "Do you think the tobacco made her sick?"

"I don't know, but we'd better get her to the vet." He scooped Shotgun up in his arms. A giant pink tongue lapped at his cheek. Once. Twice. Then Shotgun panted as Bodie tried to get a better grip. "Do you want to try Zina or should we find an emergency vet?"

Lacey must have already dialed. She held her phone to her ear. "She's not picking up."

"To the vet, then. Can you try to find the nearest one?" He pushed through the front door, Shotgun still in his arms.

Lacey climbed into his truck first then he laid Shotgun in her lap. "Hurry, Lacey."

Her fingers tapped on her phone. "There's one about forty-five minutes away. Just east of Swynton."

"You going with me?"

"Of course."

"All right, then." He turned the key and threw the truck into drive. The beavers would have to wait. He'd become more attached than he thought he would to the pup Lacey held in her arms. More than he should have.

Lacey ran her hand over Shotgun's side. "You'll be okay, hon."

Bodie reached over to rub Shotgun's belly, his hand nudging Lacey's. She looked up and his heart bounced around in his chest.

"She's going to be okay, isn't she?" Lacey asked.

"Of course. They'll probably just make her throw up. She'll be back to her bad manners in no time." To further prove his point, he covered Lacey's hand with his and gave it a squeeze.

Lacey nodded then turned her head toward the window. She held tight to his hand though, making him all too aware of how fragile she suddenly seemed. She'd lost someone close to her already. Although, comparing the loss of her mom to her fear of losing Shotgun didn't seem fair. With luck and hopefully a talented vet at the emergency center, she wouldn't have to go through losing anyone else. Not if he had anything to say about it.

By the time they pulled into the clinic, Shotgun had begun to shake. Bodie scooped her off Lacey's lap and raced into the clinic. Since they'd called ahead, someone met him at the door and ushered him back to a room right away. Lacey followed, her face reflecting his own fear. After everything the dog had been through, he wouldn't be able to live with himself if something bad happened and he hadn't been able to prevent it.

The vet tech got Shotgun settled on the table as the vet came into the room.

"Hi, I'm Dr. Yang." She shook both of their hands then quickly got to work examining Shotgun. "Can you tell me what happened?"

Bodie glanced to Lacey, then spoke up. "We think she ate a number of cigars."

"What do you mean by 'a number'?" Dr. Yang pressed a stethoscope against the dog's chest then moved it around.

"I'm not sure. A handful of them. Maybe three to five?" Bodie shrugged. "Is she going to be okay?"

"Nicotine is very dangerous for dogs, especially smaller breeds. But even a dog her size can be affected. How long ago did this happen?"

"About an hour," Lacey said.

The vet nodded. "We're going to give her something to make her throw up then probably start an IV to help flush out her system. We'll be moving her to one of the back rooms so if you want to head out to the waiting room, I'll let you know when we have more information."

"Okay." Bodie ran a hand down Shotgun's side. The dog looked up at him. "You're going to be okay, girl."

Lacey rubbed Shotgun's head. "We'll be right outside."

Bodie reached for Lacey's hand, twining his fingers with hers as the vet tech picked up Shotgun and carried her out of the room.

"She's going to be okay, isn't she?" Lacey turned her gaze to him, her lower lip trembling.

"I'm sure they're doing everything they can." Bodie wanted more than anything to reassure her, to tell her that everything would be just fine. But he didn't want to be a liar. He rubbed his thumb over her knuckles. "Hey, why didn't you ever get a dog or a cat when you were growing up?"

She glanced at him then dropped her gaze to where his hand wrapped around hers. "We had a cat, remember?"

All of a sudden, an image of a tiny orange-and-white tabby formed. Shortly after her mom died, Lacey found a stray kitten. She'd cared for that little cat like her life depended on it. Looking back, it probably had. He'd been so busy then trying to be there for Luke while he grieved. Neither one of them paid much attention to Lacey and her crusade to save the kitten. She ended up losing it. The cat was too young.

"That's right. You had that kitten for a little while." He leaned forward, resting his elbow on his knee.

"Not long enough." She reached up and swiped at her cheek.

Dammit, was she crying?

"Hey." He let go of her hand and wrapped an arm around her shoulder instead. Pulling her close, he nestled her against his chest in an awkward, side-by-side hug. "It's okay. Shotgun's going to be fine."

It was over almost as soon as it started. She sat up, sniffled, wiped the back of her hand across her cheek, and cleared her throat. "We never got another pet because . . ."

He waited for her to finish the thought. The way she was with Shotgun, hell, the way she was with people, he couldn't understand how she'd never owned a cat or dog. Lacey was a fixer. She took care of people. He'd seen her go out of her way to help anyone in need. It didn't make sense that she'd never turned that toward a pet. "Because why?"

"Because pets die." She looked up at him again. "They leave you and there's nothing you can do about it."

Bodie thought about his own childhood pets: the coonhound who had a horrible sense of smell, the barn cat who was afraid of flies, and the various other small critters he'd kept. "You're right. They don't always live as long as we'd like. But when they're around, it's worth it, isn't it?"

She stood. "I don't know. Sometimes I think it's better not to even put forth the effort if I'm only going to have my heart broken in the end."

The harsh fluorescent overhead light cast half her face in shadow. "Lacey . . ."

"I'm going to wait outside."

He made a move to stand, wanting nothing more than to hug her tight until all of her fear seeped out of her. That wasn't a way to live—constantly fearing the loss of someone you loved.

"Can I just have a few minutes by myself?"

"Sure." He sat back down, watching her disappear through the sliding glass doors, wishing he could do something to ease her heartache, and wondering how he'd manage his own if he suddenly found himself to blame for causing Lacey any pain.

twenty

Lacey grabbed the hanger and pulled another dress out of her closet. She'd been trying to pack for the last hour but couldn't find a single thing that screamed *reluctant wedding dress shopper*. It was pointless. Adeline wouldn't care what she had on as long as it wasn't flashier, prettier, or sexier than what the bride-to-be would be wearing. She'd said as much in the text she'd sent.

Even though nothing would make her happier than to call the whole thing off, Lacey had to see the weekend through. After the fiasco with Shotgun the other night, she'd been tempted to cancel. But then Bodie called and said the dog would be fine. Thank goodness. She'd all but forgotten what it was like to put her heart on the line. Almost having it crushed was a good reminder. She'd keep hers right where it belonged—safe and sound tucked behind her uncompromising set of rules. Rule number one: don't risk your heart.

She envied Bodie sometimes. He'd never lost anyone or anything close to him. Lucky for him he'd never had to go through the gut-wrenching heartbreak that followed. Although, if his suspicions were right and his dad and grandfather were involved in some unsavory business practices, he might have to be the one to bring them down. That would put a serious damper on family get-togethers. What would that do to him?

Shrugging the dress on over her head, she thought about the way Bodie had pulled her into him. The way she burrowed into his chest. The way she'd felt protected, safe, secure in his arms. He'd always made her feel that way. When her mom died it wasn't her dad who comforted her. It wasn't her brother, either. It was Bodie. She shivered as she remembered. With both her and Bodie being back in town, memories were bound to surface. She'd just have to find a way to hold them at bay. Wouldn't do any good to get attached.

She turned to face herself in the mirror. Adeline had said to bring her favorite LBD. Lacey had to Google the term to see what it meant. At least she had one, even if it probably didn't bend to the convention of current fashion styles. It was a little low across the bust and hugged her ass a tad too tightly. But there was no way she'd head to Dallas without the required LBD, so it would have to do.

By the time she'd changed back into her jeans, stuffed her makeup in a case, and zipped up her bag, someone knocked on the front door.

"I'll get it, Dad." She didn't want Adeline getting an eyeful of her dad serving his house arrest. Rumors were already bad enough without adding Adeline's brand of fuel onto the fire.

A man in a dark suit stood at the door. "Lacey Cherish?"

"Yes." She peered past him to see the stretch limo parked at the curb.

Adeline popped up through the sunroof, a tiara on her head, waving a bottle of champagne. "The girls surprised me with a bachelorette weekend. We'll shop for dresses by day and party at night! Isn't that perfect?"

Perfect? A perfect disaster. Lacey had been dreading the shopping enough. But now she'd be expected to paste on a smile while Adeline waded through miles of tulle and lace and also hold it together for two nights of hard-core partying? Her temple pulsed with the promise of an oncoming headache.

"Can I take your bag, ma'am?" The driver reached for her suitcase.

Ma'am? Did he just call her ma'am? "Sure, go ahead."

He reached behind her and grabbed her overnight bag.

"I'll be back on Sunday," she called into the house. No telling where her dad was, but she was grateful he wasn't there to witness her departure.

As she walked toward the limo, music began to pour through the open windows. The bass thumped so loud she could feel it in her chest. The driver opened the door and Lacey climbed in. She squat-walked to the front since every other seat had been claimed.

Adeline ducked back through the window and grabbed Lacey in an awkward hug. "I'm so glad you could come. We're going to have a blast."

Lacey nodded, smiling at the other women as she un-tangled herself from Adeline's grasp. She hadn't quite gotten used to the idea of them trying to be actual friends.

"Everyone, this is Lacey. And Lacey, this is everyone." Adeline swept her arm wide, knocking over the bottle of champagne she'd set down on the floor. "Ooops."

Great, just great. If the rocky start was any indication of how the weekend might go, Lacey was screwed. She didn't have time or patience to babysit a bunch of bache-lorettes in the big city. While Adeline's gal pals cleaned up the spill, the driver pulled away from the curb. One of the other women handed Lacey a glass of bubbly, and she accepted. Why not join in the festivities? It was already— she checked her watch—nine thirty in the morning. Had to be after five o'clock somewhere. Wherever it was,

Lacey wished with all her might she'd be magically transported there. Far away from bridezilla and her minions.

No such luck. The drive to Dallas passed by in a hazy blend of loud music, popping champagne corks, and drinking games. By the time they stopped in front of the first bridal shop on the itinerary, Lacey was so ready to stretch her legs she bounded past the other women to be the first one out of the limo.

Stumbling to the sidewalk, she inhaled a breath of fresh air. Her headache had worsened but she'd managed to hold a full-blown migraine at bay with a front line of ibuprofen. As she stood and faced the entrance to Bride World, she worried she'd need to bring in backup pain-med resources if she wanted to win the battle. Tall double doors stood in front of her, the only barrier between her and an afternoon of hell.

"Let's go, girls." Adeline had pulled herself together and projected the perfect blend of calm, cool, and collected.

Lacey filed into line behind two of the bridesmaids. These must be Adeline's friends from college or her sorority sisters. She didn't recognize a single one. They all seemed to be clones of their leader.

A saleswoman met them at the door, although she insisted on calling herself a bridal style concierge. She ushered Adeline's posse into a large private dressing room where a tray of champagne glasses sat on a low coffee table. Lacey perched on the edge of a chair. She'd prefer to slump against the cushions on one of the love seats but if she had, she might not ever get up. The combination of headache threat and defeat had her ready to throw in the towel.

"So how do you know the bride?" One of the other women took the chair next to Lacey and reached for a glass.

"Um, she's having her wedding at the Phillips House."

Lacey summoned a smile, hoping it looked better than it felt.

"You're the wedding planner. She's told us all about you." The woman thrust her hand toward Lacey. "I'm Celeste, one of her bridesmaids. She's so excited about having her wedding at your new place."

"We're so excited she's chosen to be the first." Lacey reached for a glass of champagne. She might need it.

The bridal style concierge clapped her hands together, drawing everyone's attention. "Ladies, let me present, dress one. It's a delectable confection of layered netting. This is truly the princess look."

Adeline stepped out of the dressing room, her torso sticking up from the center of a massive ring of netting. If she chose that dress Roman wouldn't be able to get within five feet of her. The posse mobilized, surrounding her with shrieks. Lacey took the opportunity to nab a few of the chocolates sitting on a silver tray as the chatter erupted.

Several hours and ten thousand dresses later, Adeline led the way back to the limo. She'd narrowed down some options but had yet to declare she'd found the one. Thank goodness the rest of their appointments were the next day. Lacey wasn't sure she could stomach another bridal store.

"Now's where we take over," Celeste announced. She distributed T-shirts to the women, who had no reservations about pulling their shirts off over their heads, even there in the back of the limo. "They're scratch and lick. Everyone has a different flavor."

Lacey glanced at the shirt she'd been given. A grid of what looked like circular stickers covered the front of the shirt. "Lick me?" she asked, her eyebrows shooting sky-high.

"They're for doing virtual tequila shots. Everyone has either a salt- or tequila-flavored shirt. Adeline has the lime-flavored one so she'll be at the tail end of everyone's shot. Make sense?"

No more sense than anything else they'd done so far today. "Yeah, great." Lacey tossed her shirt over her shoulder. No way was she subjecting herself to a myriad of unknown tongues, not even in the name of ensuring the wedding went off without a hitch.

"You've got to put your shirt on." Celeste nudged her chin toward Lacey. "Tell her, Adeline. It's no fun if we don't all do it."

Twelve pairs of eyes lasered in on Lacey's chest. "Fine. But the first guy who comes at me is going to get more than a taste of salt."

Adeline crossed her arms over her chest. "Come on, Lacey. You have to play. Have another glass of champagne."

The last thing she wanted was another glass of champagne. But to get Adeline off her back she pulled the T-shirt on over her head. "Happy?"

"Yes. Where to next, ladies?" Adeline relaxed back into the plush seat.

"We've got a big surprise, you'll just have to wait and see." Celeste pulled out her phone and began snapping pictures. "What's your Insta, Lacey?"

"Oh, no tagging me, thanks. Political figure and all. Wouldn't be a good idea." She unscrewed the cap from a bottle of water. Looked like someone was going to need to stay sober for the evening ahead. Might as well be her.

Celeste shrugged as she typed into her phone.

Fifteen minutes later the limo stopped. Lacey peered through the tinted window at an ornate set of doors. Sushi Tango. Great, now she had double the reason for making sure no one got out of hand. The combination of raw fish and too much to drink wouldn't end well.

"Bring on the sake." Celeste led the way into the restaurant and Lacey had no choice but to follow. For a moment she wished she'd stayed behind. Filling in armadillo holes, as horrible as that might be, would be ten times more bearable than subjecting herself to the rest of Adeline's party weekend. What was Bodie doing? Were he and Shotgun curled up on the couch taking it easy?

Thinking of the poor pup made her heart clench. Thinking of Bodie made other parts of her anatomy clench. Getting close to Bodie would mean nothing but trouble. First off, his family. She'd sworn an oath to work for the citizens of Ido. That meant she couldn't be caught colluding with folks who put themselves above the law. Second, her emotional-avoidance issues. Opening up her heart and letting someone in would result only in getting hurt. She'd learned that lesson over and over.

As she followed the line of women snaking through the restaurant, she clamped down on that thought. She'd do what she needed to do to save the town and wipe the smudge from her family name. That's all she'd signed up for. And that was more than anyone expected.

twenty-one

⌒♡⌒

Bodie paced the small office he shared with the rest of the Sewell County Sheriff's Department. His boss hadn't been the source of info he'd hoped for when it came to moving forward on the investigation involving his family. Sheriff Suarez wanted to remove Bodie from the case altogether, citing he had a conflict of interest.

"Even with me taking the lead, you still don't have the manpower to do a thorough job on this." Bodie stopped in front of the sheriff's desk, his hands set on his hips. Heat raced through his veins. They couldn't take this away from him. He couldn't trust anyone else to do a good-enough job.

"You're not exactly a neutral party here. It's time to step aside, Deputy Phillips. If I need to bring in additional resources, I will." Sheriff Suarez signed the paper in front of him then set down his pen.

Bodie nodded, taking in a breath through his nose. Wouldn't do him any good to lose his cool now. Not when the future of his involvement with this case depended on it. "You think I'd put my family first?"

Sheriff Suarez set his lips in a line and shrugged. "Happens to the best of us."

"You know I wouldn't work that way." Bodie leaned over the desk, placing his palms flat. Maybe he had in the past. If there was a way to get his family out of this without them getting into serious trouble, he'd do his best. But that line he shouldn't cross seemed to have a little wiggle room in it.

"You trying to intimidate me, son?" Sheriff Suarez had been in office longer than anyone before him. He was a fixture in town. Almost as ingrained as the Phillips family.

"No, sir. Just trying to convince you that you can trust me to do my job, to uphold my oath, and to not put personal relationships before the law." A muscle in his jaw began to tick.

"No one's accusing you of that. Hell, I know you're a trusted member of my team. But when push comes to shove . . ." Bushy eyebrows furrowed, making him look twice as stern.

"There's not going to be any pushing." Bodie tapped the toe of his boot on the linoleum floor.

"You've got your hands full enough with making sure our new mayor stays out of trouble. Keep your focus on that and I'll take care of the rest."

Bodie groaned, careful to keep his mounting frustration from blowing his top. "If you won't let me be in charge, at least let me help with the investigation."

"My hands are tied." The sheriff stood and made his way to the hook on his wall. He grabbed his hat and turned toward the door. "Now, I've got a meeting with some supporters, so if you'll excuse me."

"Yes, sir." Bodie followed him through the door and out into the parking lot. The sheriff might be able to keep him from officially working the case, but he couldn't stop him from having a conversation with family. All of a sudden Mayor Little's offer seemed somewhat appealing. For the first time in his career, the first time in his life, Bodie considered crossing that line instead of just nudging it farther away. If he got elected sheriff of Sewell County, he'd be able to dethrone Sheriff Suarez and take care of his family. Did the ends justify the means? In this case, he wasn't sure.

If only Luke were around. He knew Bodie's heart better than anyone. He'd always been a safe sounding board in times of doubt. But his friend was off on some top secret mission and not even available by e-mail for the next couple of weeks. At least Shotgun was going to be okay. That seemed to be the only bright spot he had going for him at the moment.

Twenty minutes later Bodie pulled his truck to a stop in front of his dad's office. Pops sat outside, whittling something with his ancient pocketknife.

Bodie settled into the rocking chair next to him. "Getting some fresh air?"

Pops didn't answer right away. He was a man of few words and even fewer emotions. "Smells like rain."

Nodding, Bodie took a better look at the piece of wood in his grandfather's hands. "What are you working on?"

Pops paused, holding the figurine up for Bodie to take a closer look. The head of a beaver had started to take shape from the hunk of wood. Long buckteeth hung out of a smiling mouth. Nice. That left no doubt in his mind that Pops and Dad were up to their armpits in the illegal import business.

"Is Dad around?" Bodie asked.

Pops jerked his head to the side. "Yeah. He's hiding out. Doesn't want anyone to see the shiner he's sporting."

Just thinking about confronting his family made Bodie's palms sweat. He rubbed them against his jeans, trying to shake off the nervousness. "I need a word with the two of you."

"Oh yeah?" Pops growled. "About what?"

Bodie turned a pointed look to the beaver. "I believe I figured out why you and Dad wanted those figurines back."

Pops nodded, a slight movement. "We should talk."

"That's what I figured."

"I'll get your father. Meet us in his office in five." Pops handed the partially carved animal to Bodie as he stood. "It's a shame you never learned how to whittle."

Before Bodie had a chance to respond, Pops turned and ambled up the walkway leading to the house. Bodie turned the carving over and over in his hands, not looking forward to the talk ahead.

By the time Pops returned, with Dad in tow, Bodie's stomach had knotted over and over, turning his gut into a tangled mess of nerves. He'd faced down notorious biker gangs, held his own against drug ring members, and even managed to arrest Lacey's dad without batting an eye. But facing down his own flesh and blood made him want to lose his lunch all over his mom's formal succulent garden.

"Shall we?" Pops gestured toward the door.

Bodie got up and followed him into the office. "How are you feeling, Dad?" Asking about his dad's recovery was a safe place to start. Then he'd move the conversation over to their cigar smuggling. Nice and easy.

"So you're here to bust our balls over the cigars, is that right?" Dad cut the end off what Bodie now recognized as the same brand of cigars he'd found in the warehouse.

"Not exactly." Bodie glanced toward his grandfather, who'd begun to clean underneath his fingernails with his pocketknife. A surefire act of intimidation. Bodie wouldn't let it get to him though.

"Then, what is it?" Dad lit up the end of his cigar, huffing and puffing to get it to catch.

"Why didn't you tell me what you were up to?" Bodie

took a seat in the chair across from his dad's desk. Pops continued to stand, leaning against the wall and working on his manicure like he didn't have a care in the world.

"We didn't know if we could trust you. Seems like you've forgotten about putting family first since you took on the deputy title." Dad set his cigar on the edge of a giant Texas-shaped ashtray. The right side of his face sported a mottled mix of blue and purple. Bodie winced just looking at it.

"You think your 'accident' was related?"

"It was a message," Pops said. "We sent one back of our own."

Bodie's head jerked to look at his grandfather. "What are you talking about? Who are you working with on this?"

"You ready to take sides?" Dad asked. "No sense getting you involved unless you're going to back us up."

"Take sides against who? Y'all are lucky you haven't been brought in for questioning yet. Suarez yanked me off the case so you don't have to worry about me." The little white lie rolled off his tongue as easy as if he'd been chatting about the weather. True, he'd been taken off the case, but he still intended to get to the bottom of things, no matter how deep he had to dig.

"Well, that's a relief." Pops pushed off the wall and took the seat next to Bodie. "You had us trembling in our boots."

"It's not a joke, Pops. Suarez suspects something. He's going to be trying to figure out what's going on. You'd be better off coming clean and letting me see if we can figure a way out of this rather than waiting for him to come down on you."

"We'll take care of Suarez. He's a sucker for that brand of whiskey, what's it called again?"

Bodie glanced from his dad to his grandfather. "You've got Sheriff Suarez in on this, too?"

"Nah. He has no idea what's really going on. We just

keep him happy so he looks the other way. But once you're elected sheriff we'll have an ally on the inside."

Bodie funneled his hands through his hair. "What the hell are you up to? I'm not signing on for anything without knowing exactly what the two of you have done."

Pops spread his hands then placed his palms on his knees. "All right, all right. I suppose if you're going to go all in with us you have a right to know."

As much as he wanted to figure out what his dad and pops were up to, Bodie wished for a half a second that he could remain oblivious. Once he had the information there would be no going back. He'd have to decide what to do about it. He swallowed the doubt that had formed a giant lump in his throat and nodded. "Tell me."

twenty-two

Lacey groaned into her ice water. She thought maybe the party would have mellowed out a bit at the restaurant but instead, things had kicked into high gear. They'd been seated in a private room in the back and the trays of Cherry Blossom Chillers hadn't stopped coming. Music blared over the speaker system, pounding into her head, making her wish she had a pharmacy of painkillers at her disposal instead of her ineffective ibuprofen.

"More sushi?" Celeste dropped into the seat next to her. "The spicy tuna rolls are really good."

Lacey couldn't stomach raw fish right now. She wanted to get to the hotel, check in, and take a long, hot soak in the tub. "No thanks. So, what's the plan after dinner? I know Adeline's got a full day of shopping planned for tomorrow. Are we turning in early?"

Celeste smiled, the kind of patronizing smile she might give to a child who'd asked a crazy, stupid question. "We've got entertainment on the way. Then we're heading to Ice Blue, it's one of the best dance clubs in Dallas."

"Right." Lacey twirled her straw around in her glass. Time for another refill of H_2O. "So I've got a monster headache coming on. Do you think you could drop me at the hotel on the way?"

"Don't be silly." Celeste bumped her shoulder into Lacey's. "You're not going to want to miss what we have planned."

Oh, don't bet your push-up bra on it. Lacey stopped herself from actually uttering those words out loud. Maybe she could sneak out and grab a cab. Or download one of those ride apps she'd never had the chance to use. She was about to excuse herself to find a quiet place to make a call when the door to the dining room opened.

Three men walked in, dressed in dark blue uniforms. Sunglasses shaded their eyes. Lacey's first thought was that they were being busted for drugs. She'd seen the joint Celeste had tucked into her purse. When the tallest guy flashed a badge and held out handcuffs, she cradled her head in her hands. They were going down. All of them. She never should have agreed to come to Dallas with Adeline.

Celeste nudged her in the side. "Here comes the fun."

Lacey looked up. Two of the men sandwiched Adeline between them. The guy with the handcuffs spoke. "I hear you've been some naughty, naughty girls."

Strippers. That might be even worse than the bride-to-be getting busted. Lacey's head went from throbbing to pounding as Adeline squealed, her smile giving her away that she was all in on this particular turn of events.

The men fanned out. One settled Adeline into a chair and started doing things to her that Lacey had only heard about. She couldn't stick around for this. No amount of ibuprofen would be a match for the headache she'd get from witnessing a room full of bridesmaids shrieking over a muscled man whipping off his pants.

She stood, intent on making her way outside to call

that cab she'd thought about. The tall guy blocked her path.

"Going somewhere?" He arched a brow.

Lacey glanced up at his face. It was a nice face. Looked like he'd shaved recently, probably to cut down on leaving scruff marks behind when he nuzzled his chin between some unsuspecting woman's breasts like his buddy was doing to Celeste. Blue eyes appraised her, his mouth curling into a smile.

She nodded, attempting to keep her cool. "I'm going to head outside and get some fresh air."

He reached for her wrist. "But the party's just getting started."

Lacey pulled away. "Not my kind of party. But y'all have fun."

The giant dropped to his knees in front of her. "You mean it's not your kind of party yet."

"What are you doing?" Lacey tried to take a step back but he caught her around the waist.

"You can't go before I get a taste of your T-shirt." His mouth closed in on her navel.

She couldn't move. His lips moved closer and closer as his arms wrapped tighter and tighter around her hips. Stomach knotting, palms sweating, Lacey watched the tip of his tongue slip out, heading straight for the scratch-and-taste circle in the center of her breastbone. She put her hands on his shoulders, pushing him away. Her knee flew up, connecting with his nose. His head snapped back. Blood flowed down his chin.

His fingers went up to his lip. "You busted my nose."

Red dots spattered across the front of her *Lick Me* T-shirt. Lacey's eyes widened as her hands began to shake. Oh no. Oh no, no, no, no, no.

Celeste took one look at the blood then ran out the door on her stilettos. The two other strippers stopped what they were doing, leaving the theme song from *Cops* booming through the speakers. If it hadn't been so horrifying Lacey might have burst into laughter. As it was, she fought like mad to beat down the beginnings of a panic attack.

"Ice. Here, put some ice on it." Celeste returned with a napkin full of ice with two more uniformed officers in tow.

"Is there a problem here?" one of the men asked.

Great, more strippers to join the fray. "Not unless you want to try to lick me, too," Lacey said, stepping in front of them.

"Excuse me?" The officer who'd entered first looked her up and down. "Are you responsible for the assault on this man?"

"I suppose so. And there's plenty more where that came from if you don't get out of my way." She wasn't sure where her instant confidence had come from, but there was no way another man was going to try to lick her tonight, not even if her raunchy shirt practically demanded it.

"Are you threatening an officer, miss?" The other uniformed man stepped beside his buddy.

"If that's what it takes to get out of here." Lacey clamped her hands to her hips.

"I think you need to come with us." Officer Number One took her arm.

"Don't you think you're taking this too far?" Lacey jerked her arm away. "Just take off your pants and be done with it. I've got a headache the size of Texas and I'm heading to the hotel."

"You're not going anywhere." Officer One nabbed her arm again.

Lacey groaned, then rolled her eyes and stomped on his toe with the heel of the stupid strappy sandals she'd worn. At least they'd been good for something.

"That's it." Office Number Two spun her around, took both of her wrists in his, and clamped a set of cuffs on her.

"Very funny." Lacey struggled against the handcuffs. Solid. Not like the kind her boyfriend in college had given her as a gag Valentine's gift one year.

"Let's go, miss."

"I'm not going anywhere with you. Let me go."

"You assaulted an officer."

"I stepped on someone's toe." She cast a quick glance to where Officer One hopped on one foot, his shoe with a hole in the toe held in his hand.

Officer Two put an arm on her shoulder and spun her toward the door. "You have the right to remain silent . . ."

He continued to read her her rights. Or at least she thought they were her rights. She tuned out right about the time she realized this wasn't part of the entertainment. She was being arrested. For assaulting an officer of the law.

"So you're not here to take off your clothes?" She winced as she realized the mistake she'd made. "Adeline? Celeste?"

"You ruined my bachelorette," Adeline shrieked. She must have finally realized what was going on. It didn't take her but a few seconds to storm across the room and step in front of Lacey. "You'll never make this work. I should have known better than to try to work with you."

"Me?" Lacey tried to cross her arms over her chest, forgetting they were secured behind her back. "All I've done is try to help you."

"I'm done. Find someone else to do your story on." She took one more look at Lacey, letting her dark brown eyes slide up and down Lacey's pathetic attempt to fit in. "Just go."

Lacey's heart did a slip and slide all the way down to her toes. "Adeline, wait. We can work this out."

Adeline and Celeste turned their backs on her, probably afraid she'd contaminate them with her sheer awkwardness and stupidity. Great, just great. Four hours from home and it looked like she was on her own. Surely they'd follow behind in the limo. Someone would come bail her out. She couldn't spend the night in jail. She was the mayor.

Suddenly, the sheer severity of her actions crashed down on her. She'd failed herself. She'd failed her family. But most important, she'd failed her hometown.

twenty-three

Bodie stared at his dad from across the desk and waited for him to start talking.

"We didn't intend to get into the cigar-smuggling business." Dad gestured to where his cigar sat on the edge of the ashtray. "You know how much I enjoy them."

"Go on," Bodie said, his nerves coiled tighter than a spring.

"Last time I was down in Mexico I was sitting on the beach, minding my own business. We were at that resort your mom likes so much, what's it called?"

Bodie let out an exaggerated sigh. "Doesn't matter what it's called. What happened?"

"Guy saw me enjoying a stogie. Started up a conversation. Next thing I know we're making cash hand over fist by just bringing in some shipments for him occasionally."

Pops grunted. "Easiest money we ever made."

"Too easy. You had to know you'd get caught." Bodie rolled his eyes.

"We wouldn't have if your dad hadn't gotten so damn greedy." Pops narrowed his eyes as he flipped his knife closed.

Dad put his hands out, palms facing Bodie. "I'll admit, we got in a little over our heads."

Bodie's phone rang. Tempted to ignore it, he glanced at the screen. Dallas area code. Probably someone trying to sell him something. He dismissed the call and set his phone on the desk.

"Go on, Dad."

Before Dad could say a word, the phone rang again. Same number. Dammit. He couldn't even sit and have a conversation without someone bothering him. Ready to give whoever was on the other end of the phone a piece of his mind, Bodie barked, "Hello?"

"Bodie? It's Lacey."

He pulled the phone away from his ear to check the number.

"Are you there?"

"Yeah, I'm here. What's wrong?" Something had to have happened. Why else would she be calling from a strange number? Come to think of it, why would she be calling at all?

She took in a ragged breath. Her voice came out shaky. "I've had a bit of a misunderstanding."

It didn't take a cop's intuition to know something was wrong. Very wrong. "Are you okay? Where are you?"

"Well, that's the thing"—she let out a shaky laugh—"I've been arrested."

"Arrested?" The chair screeched on the tile as he stood. She had his full attention. "What the hell happened?"

"Um, I've only got three minutes so I don't think I can cover it all. Is there any chance . . ." She paused, clearing her throat.

Bodie's entire body tensed while he waited for her to continue.

Her voice came out quiet and small. "Do you think you might be able to come get me?"

His pulse thudded through his temple as he tried to wrap his head around what she said.

"I'm so sorry. Never mind. I shouldn't have called. I just didn't know who else to try. I'll figure it out."

"Wait." The line went dead. Now what was he supposed to do? How did Lacey go from dress shopping with Adeline to sitting in a jail cell in Dallas somewhere?

"Can y'all excuse me for a minute?" He left his dad and pops sitting at the desk. As he made his way to the door, he tried to call back. After too many rings to count, the call flipped into an auto-answer. Bodie navigated through the voice mail system until he found someone to talk to. After verifying his credentials, the clerk on the other end of the phone line was able to confirm that Lacey was being held in a station on the west side of Dallas. Bodie called to let them know he was on his way. What else could he do? She didn't have anyone else. It's not like Luke would swoop in and save the day. And Mr. Cherish was restricted to house arrest.

Dammit, arrested. The one thing Lacey was most ashamed of—her dad's arrest—had happened to her. She must be going through hell. Which meant the sooner he got to her, the sooner he could figure out what had happened and how to get her out of the mess she must have found her way into.

He ducked back into the office. "Can we finish this later? I've got to go."

"Cherish girl got your boxers in a wad?" Pops asked.

Bodie didn't have time to argue with him. Not with Lacey waiting. "This conversation isn't over."

Over four hours later Bodie sat on a plastic chair in the soulless lobby of the Dallas police station, waiting for Lacey to be released. He'd gone over the details of the night with the arresting officer. She wasn't going to face charges as long as Bodie promised to take responsibility for her until she left the Dallas jurisdiction. He stifled a yawn as he cut his gaze from the door to the clock. The second hand ticked. It was after one in the morning. The smell of burned popcorn hung in the air from someone's late-night snack. If she didn't come out soon he might fall asleep right there on the unforgiving, bright orange chair.

A door squeaked open. Lacey emerged, arms clamped around her middle like she'd just survived a traumatic experience that would haunt her for days.

"You okay?" He jumped to his feet and rushed to her side.

She nodded.

"Okay, let's get out of here." He put an arm around her shoulders and steered her toward the parking lot.

She followed his lead, her head tucked against his shoulder. The night air was a welcome change from the stale interior of the station. As they walked toward the truck Bodie pressed the fob to unlock the doors. He wasn't going to force Lacey to talk; he'd wait until she was ready.

He held her door and helped her climb in. She seemed so fragile. What had happened to the woman who'd told him to *"back the hell off"* a few weeks ago? She had to be in there somewhere. Maybe a good night's sleep would help. By the time he'd walked around the truck and climbed in, she'd buckled her seat belt and stared straight ahead. Her shoulders slumped, her chin didn't hold that same confident angle he'd grown accustomed to.

"I'm not sure I'll be able to make the drive back home tonight. How do you feel about finding a room here in town and we can head back first thing in the morning?"

She nodded.

Okay. He pulled out of the parking lot and pointed toward home. On the outskirts of town there was a decent hotel he'd stayed in before. If Lacey didn't offer up any opinions, he'd take charge. She might bust his balls tomorrow but in the state she was in right now, she didn't appear to have the energy left to give him a hard time.

They drove in silence until he stopped in front of the hotel. "So, is one room with two beds okay or do you want your own room?" He wasn't sure how to broach the subject. The idea of sleeping anywhere near Lacey almost made the enchiladas he'd scarfed down for lunch reappear. Not that he was opposed to sharing a room. But Lacey wasn't the kind of woman he could mess around with. Even if she was, knowing her brother would kick his ass for touching her would ensure Bodie kept his hands to himself.

"One room is fine. I don't have the cash to cover my own." She tilted her head but didn't meet his eyes. "Two beds, right?"

Bodie bit his lip and nodded. "Yep. Two beds. You want to come in with me or wait in the truck?"

"I'll wait here."

"I'll leave it on. Back in just a sec." He needed to say something but he had no idea what. Something that would put a smile back on her face and chase away the sadness in her eyes. One step at a time. First step—he needed to get them a room.

The clerk at the desk didn't give him any trouble. Check-in took about three minutes from start to finish and before he'd had a chance to come up with step two, he was headed back to the truck. He hadn't thought to pack a bag and Lacey didn't have anything with her so there was no need to worry about any kind of luggage.

He knocked at her window to get her attention. She startled then rolled it down.

"Room two-forty-two. You want to turn off the truck and hand me the keys?"

She did before grabbing her purse and climbing out of

the truck. Standing on the pavement next to him, she seemed to shrink.

"Come on. Let's get you tucked in. Nothing that a good night's sleep won't cure."

Lacey followed behind him, fresh out of attitude. The silence seemed louder than any griping she'd done before. He'd never admit it to her, but he kind of liked her loud attempts at trying to run the show better than this complacent quietness.

The room wasn't anything special. Two double beds with a small nightstand between them.

"Which one do you want?" he asked.

"Doesn't matter." She tossed her purse on the one closest to the window. "You don't snore, do you?"

He hung his jacket in the small closet area. "It's kind of late to be asking about that, don't you think?"

The start of a smile lifted the edges of her lips. He'd take it.

"You don't by chance have an extra shirt, do you?" Lacey took off her jacket and turned to face him. Rows of circles lined her shirt.

He squinted, reading the print at the top. "*Lick Me?*"

"No thanks. When the last guy tried that I ended up in jail." She slumped into the chair next to the TV. "I never should have come to Dallas."

Bodie had been waiting for a conversation starter like that to fall into his lap. "It's not your fault. The officer said you pack a mean stomp on the foot."

Lacey groaned as she cradled her head in her hands. "How did I not notice the difference between the stripper cops and the real cops?"

"Maybe because the real cops were just as buff as the strippers?" Bodie tried to joke. Somehow the thought of a stranger putting his mouth on her shirt fired up a few nerves. *Easy now.* Even though he'd always kept an eye out for Luke's younger sister, Lacey wasn't his to protect.

She snorted. "I wasn't in the mood to check out their pecs."

"How about now?" He flexed, first one position, then another, in trying to get another laugh out of her.

Shaking her head, she blew off his lame attempt at humor. "Can I ask you something serious?"

He put a hand on the back of her chair and spun her around to face him. The bed creaked as he sat down on the edge. He wanted to give her his full attention. "What's up?"

"Why did you come and get me?" Her palm landed on his knee. She kept her gaze trained on the spot where her fingers rested against his leg.

His heart kicked up a notch at the contact. "Because you called."

"But I hung up on you." Blue eyes met his, ratcheting his pulse up even higher.

He put his hand on hers. "I'm there for you, Sweets. Anytime. Okay?"

"Because of Luke." She nodded, sliding her hand out from under his.

"No." The firm tone in his voice surprised her. Hell, it surprised him. She met his gaze again. "Because of you."

"What do you mean, because of me? I've done nothing but try to boss you around since I took over as mayor. And all you've done is try to help me." Her eyes reflected a combination of confusion and hurt.

Wanting to reassure her, he took her hand again. She didn't pull away. He ran his gaze over her fingers. "I'll always be there for you, Lacey. We've got a history together and your family has always been there for me. Even when mine . . ." He stopped. The shit his dad and pops had going on was too near the surface to share.

She stood, pulling his head to her chest, wrapping her arms around his shoulders. "I know."

His hands went to her back, rubbing small circles over her spine. She smelled like someone had spilled a gallon of vodka all over her then sat her out in the sun. Her shirt stuck to his cheek. He was tempted to flick his tongue out and see if the circles really did taste like salt. But this was Lacey. So what if she'd grown up in the time she'd been away? It didn't matter that being this close to her made him painfully aware of just how much she'd changed from the gangly girl she'd been.

"For what it's worth"—she leaned back and searched out his gaze—"I'm sorry."

He pulled back, his cheek sticking to her shirt. "No need to apologize. I've got your back and you've got mine. We're like . . ."

"Family." The way she said it made him think she didn't like having to claim him as some sort of kin.

"That's not a bad thing, you know." His hands fell from her back as he stood.

She shrugged before she stepped away. "It can be."

twenty-four

Lacey took in a breath through her nose. The smell of home washed over her. Silly girl. It wasn't home. It was the scent of Bodie's shirt that made her feel warm and snug inside. She was playing with fire right now and she knew it. Nothing good would come out of her and Bodie hooking up. But a whole lot of bad sure might. As much as she wanted to hold him close, nestle his cheek against her chest, and let them both forget about everything waiting for them back home, she couldn't. He'd never think of her as more than Luke's little sister. No matter how much she might want him to.

"What's wrong? What did I say now?" He stood, his chest filling her vision as he rose to his full height.

"Nothing. It's just been a long day. Do you care if I use the bathroom first?" She tried to rewind to a time when she didn't crave Bodie's touch. When being this close to him didn't make her want to throw herself into his arms. It didn't work. For as long as she could remember she'd had a major crush on Bodie Phillips.

He studied her for a moment, making her skin feel like it was baking under a hot July sun. "Go ahead."

She stepped into the bathroom, eager to wash the frustration of the day away and douse the warmth being alone with Bodie had sparked. Without a change of clothes she wouldn't be able to do much, but at least she could scrub the makeup off her face and freshen up a little bit. Too bad she didn't have a shirt to change into. She'd give about anything to swap out the stupid *Lick Me* shirt for something more comfortable and less of a reminder of how she'd failed the family name.

When she finished in the bathroom, she opened the door a crack. "I'm coming out now."

Bodie's answer came from close by. Too close. "Thanks for the heads-up."

"Are you decent?" She couldn't afford to surprise him with his pants down. The sight of him fully clothed sent her hormones into a tailspin. No telling what might happen if she actually caught a glimpse of forbidden skin.

"Pretty much." He held his shirt in front of the door. "Sorry I don't have anything else to offer, but if you want to change, I just put this one on before I left tonight."

Nothing would make her happier than to trash her stupid T-shirt, but could she spend an entire night surrounded by the remnants of Bodie's body heat and still be able to hold herself in check? The scent of fabric softener drifted past her nose, a much better option than the mixture of hopelessness and despair her shirt had absorbed in the holding cell. She snaked her hand through the crack in the door and grabbed it. "Thank you."

"You bet."

A moment later she stepped out of the bathroom, Bodie's shirt hanging halfway down her thighs. Just having the opportunity to wipe off her face and swap her shirt had given her mood a little bit of a boost.

"Wow." He stood by his bed, his gaze drifting over her.

"What?" The sheer intensity of his stare made her cheeks warm. She briefly met his gaze then sucked in her breath as her eyes roamed over his bare torso. She'd been right—his pecs were carved from granite. No wonder every time she'd pressed against them it felt like solid rock under her hands.

"Nothing." He ducked his head but not before she caught a flush of pink on his cheeks. Maybe they both felt a little out of their element. Instead of making her feel better, that thought caused a bolt of awareness to crackle through her. Bodie probably just felt uncomfortable being saddled with her for an evening. He couldn't have the same kind of thoughts about her that she'd had about him.

She shed her shoes and jeans while Bodie took his turn in the bathroom. As she curled up in a ball and pulled the covers up to her chin, she tried not to think about the events of the evening. But she couldn't hold the memories at bay. Her stomach tightened as Adeline's last words looped through her head. *"You'll never make this work. I should have known better than to try to work with you."*

Her chance to save the town and redeem her family name had disappeared with Adeline's temper tantrum. Not that Lacey blamed her for being upset. Lacey had single-handedly ruined the bachelorette party. Why couldn't she have just let the guy suck on her shirt and called it good?

She clenched her hands into fists then released them, trying to alleviate some tension. She couldn't because she didn't want some stranger, granted a very good-looking stranger, putting his lips anywhere near her. It was her right to decide who had access to her body. And the only man whose lips she wanted roaming over her didn't want to have anything to do with her. At least not in that capacity.

The bathroom door opened. "I'm coming out."

"Okay."

"Damn, it's dark out here." His feet shuffled on the

carpet. The sound of Bodie getting settled under the covers brought a slight sense of comfort and a tidal wave of anxiety. "You okay?"

She waited a beat before answering. "Yeah."

"It's going to be fine. You believe me, don't you?"

Rolling to face the direction of his voice, she took in a deep breath. "I want to."

"It will. You'll find someone else to have the first wedding."

"But the story . . . I don't know if the reporter will be on board if we don't have Swynton royalty involved."

Bodie's chuckle sent a wave of warmth through her. "Swynton royalty? Is that a thing?"

"May as well be. I think Adeline's crowned herself queen."

"We don't need Adeline. You'll figure something out." He yawned. "You always do."

His faith in her ability to always find a solution had to be misplaced. She tried to close her eyes, give in to the sheer exhaustion she'd been battling since she climbed into the limo this morning. Her body craved sleep. But her brain operated on overdrive, trying to sort out options on how to handle the latest development in her quest to save the town.

Bodie's breath evened out. She lifted the neck of his shirt to her nose, hoping his scent would calm down her frayed nerves. All it did was make her hyperaware of how close he was. Close enough to reach out and touch. Close enough to hear the breath leave his lips on an exhale. Close enough to guarantee she wouldn't get a wink of sleep.

She lay there for what seemed like hours. The more she tried to fall asleep, the more wide awake she became. Until she finally gave up and threw the covers off in frustration. She'd cycled through the first five stages of grief since she'd been lying in the dark, a process she was unfortunately too familiar with, thanks to the therapy sessions her dad had forced on her when her mom passed. Now she was stuck in the all-is-lost phase.

"What the hell's going on over there?" The sound of Bodie's voice made her heart stop.

She tried to infuse her voice with sleepiness. "What?" she mumbled.

The mattress groaned as he shifted. "You've been tossing and turning more than a pig in a mud bath over there."

"Nice." Figured he'd compare her to a swine. If she'd harbored even a smidgen of hope that he might consider her a romantic interest, comparing her to a muddy pig had obliterated any chance.

"Neither one of us is going to get any sleep if you don't talk about it."

She stuck her lower lip out in a pout. He couldn't see it though so it wasn't worth the effort. "I blew it. I may as well resign as mayor and turn everything over to Swynton."

Bodie's mattress creaked then he sat down on the edge of her bed. "Look, you had a setback but all's not lost."

She scooted away, not wanting to roll toward him into the indentation he'd made. "It feels that way. I finally had everyone working toward a common goal. People were excited about being featured in the magazine. It would have given us such a boost."

His hand patted the mattress, coming closer and closer. It landed on her hip. "Where the hell are you? Give me your hand."

Heat prickled her hip. That wouldn't do at all. She slid her hand on top of his, breaking the connection with her lower body. The hip bone connected to the pelvis bone. The pelvis bone connected to . . . she couldn't go there.

"You're being way too hard on yourself."

She sat up, dropping his hand. "I got arrested. For assaulting an officer."

Bodie laughed. "It was an honest mistake."

"Have you ever been mistaken for a stripper?" As the question left her lips she immediately regretted it. With a body like his, Bodie definitely could have been a stripper. Based on what she'd seen of him, he put the actual strippers to shame.

He sighed. "I can't say that I have."

"I'm an idiot."

"Come here." He reached for her, drawing her into an awkward hug.

Her cheek pressed against his naked chest. His scent surrounded her, invading her personal space, heating her blood to an uncomfortable degree. With her face smashed against him, he wrapped his arms around her.

"Bodie, I . . ."

"Shh. I don't want to hear you being so hard on yourself. You can't even see how important you've been to the town, to the people who put their faith in you, to . . ."

"To what?"

"To me."

Her cheeks tingled. He had to be able to feel the heat radiating from her face onto his chest. She pulled her head back and tilted it up in the direction of his. Darkness shrouded the room but she could make out the outline of his chin by the sliver of light that came through a crack in the curtains.

"What do you mean?" she whispered, her heart stalling while she waited for a response.

His hand came up to cup the back of her head. "You're special, Lacey."

"Special as in I require major adult supervision, or—" His lips sought hers, cutting off her self-deprecating remark. Heat exploded inside her chest, rocketing through her veins, igniting every nerve ending she had and some she hadn't been aware of before.

His mouth on hers was so much better than the almost-kiss they'd shared at the warehouse. She hadn't been able to stop thinking about it for weeks. She wrapped her arms around his broad shoulders, clinging to him as his kiss took her soaring, like climbing to the top of that wooden roller coaster she used to love as a kid.

He pulled back first. "I'm so sorry. That was out of line, I—"

She got to her knees, meeting his mouth with hers again. Her tongue played along the seam of his lips, testing, tasting. His hands roamed her back, tangled in her hair. She'd imagined how it would feel to have Bodie's lips on hers so many times over the years. Tonight far exceeded her expectations. Her hands danced over the curve of his shoulders, hard biceps, the contours of his back. His skin was smooth under her touch. So much better than what her limited imagination had been able to conjure.

The darkness provided a layer of safety. Tomorrow she'd have to face him and the repercussions. But tonight, tonight everything she needed, everything she wanted, was right there in front of her.

She wrapped her arms tight around his shoulders and pulled him down next to her on the bed.

twenty-five

Thoughts that he should put on the brakes, slow things down, get his hands and his lips off Luke's little sister rattled at the edges of his brain. Then she pulled him down next to her and his brain became incapable of any rational thoughts.

His hands roamed over her curves, so eager to feel her, to memorize the contours of her body. Her mouth matched his, kiss for kiss, never letting up. She was vulnerable. She didn't know what she was doing. She would regret it in the morning.

It took everything he had to break contact. "Lacey, I'm sorry. I shouldn't have done that."

She didn't say anything for a long moment. "Because you didn't want to? I don't want you feeling sorry for me."

"No." Did she think he'd kissed her out of pity? The thought made him want to pull her tight against him and not let up. "I'm sorry because that came out of nowhere. I don't want to take advantage of you when you're feeling down, when you're vulnerable."

She let out a quiet laugh. "You silly, silly man. The only thing I'm sorry about is that you didn't do that a long time ago."

His breath caught. "What?"

Her fingers played with the hair at the nape of his neck, making a shiver roll through him. "Can we talk about this tomorrow? I don't want to talk anymore tonight."

"Sure." He took her hands in his and brought them to his lips. "You get a good night's sleep and we'll chat in the morning."

"Are you really that dense?"

"What?"

She wrapped her arms around his shoulders and brought her head close to his. Her lips grazed his cheek, trailing kisses down to his chin then up the other side. He resisted the impulse to clamp his hands to her waist, waiting to see what she would do next.

"I don't want to get a good night's sleep." Her breath blew across his ear.

"What do you want, then?"

She nibbled on his earlobe, sucking it into her mouth before running her tongue along the shell of his ear. Need, pure raw need, shot through him.

"I want to be with you tonight, Bodie."

"You sure you won't regret it tomorrow?" That was his worst fear—that she'd come to her senses in the morning and whatever they shared tonight would change everything between them. Having to face Luke followed. What would his friend say if he found out Bodie had ravaged his sister? A chill began to seep through his blood, cooling the consuming heat that Lacey's touch had sparked.

Her hands went to his waist and she lined her torso up with his. "Why in the world would you think that? Do you have any idea how long I've imagined this?"

Her pelvic bone pressed against his crotch. His hard-on nudged into her. He didn't need any more encouragement, her confession erased any lingering doubts. His hands went behind her back, lowering her to the bed. He stretched out beside her, finally free to give in to the sheer desire that had been consuming him for weeks.

She threw her leg over his hip as her mouth crashed into his. Need rolled through him. His fingertips danced along the hem of her shirt, skimming the top of her thigh. Her moan spurred him on, and he continued to explore the soft skin of her navel.

Her hands played over his pecs, running up and down his side. Where did little Lacey Cherish learn to kiss like this? A sharp pang of jealousy pierced his gut. But then she reached between them and edged past the waistband of his boxer briefs. He splayed a hand across her back, pulling her even closer while he dipped his head down to cover the sweet skin of her neck with hot, wet kisses.

"Bodie, do you have anything?" she mumbled against his mouth.

"Have anything?"

"A condom. Do you have a condom?" she asked.

"I don't know."

"Well, check." She slid her hands between them, pushing on his chest.

"Are you sure?" Things were moving so fast. He wanted to make sure she was absolutely certain.

"Yes, I'm sure."

Anticipation slid through his gut. He hadn't had the need for any kind of protection in too long. He felt around for his wallet on the nightstand and breathed a sigh of relief when his fingers closed around the edges of a packet.

While he'd been groping around the nightstand Lacey must have taken the opportunity to remove the shirt he'd given her. His hands felt for her, closing around her shoulders. He trailed a finger down her collarbone then between her breasts.

Her breath hitched as his mouth followed. When his

lips met the rounded curve of her breast she hiked her leg behind him, drawing him against her. Her fingers fumbled with his waistband then slid his briefs down his legs. He kicked them off, no longer worried about the aftermath. All that mattered was here and now.

Lacey's hand reached for him, tentatively, unsure, like she'd suddenly shrugged off the bold attitude she'd been trying on. He slid a hand between them, past the waistband of her bikini-bottom underwear. That must have given her the encouragement she needed. Her fingers closed around his length, making him hiss in a satisfying breath. If he wasn't careful he'd lose it before he ever got to feel the slick heat of her surround him—something he hadn't been able to stop thinking about since he saw her back in town so many months ago.

He slipped a finger over her then dipped it inside, her wetness turning him on even more. The damn panties needed to be gone. He slid them down her legs. She tucked her knees up closer to her chest so he could ease them all the way off. Skin to skin, heat to heat, their bodies collided.

Losing track of whose hands were where, he lost himself in her touch, in the sheer closeness of having her pressed against him. Before he could talk himself out of it, he rolled on the condom. She rose to straddle him, taking control. His hands reached for her, closing around her waist, guiding her down on top of him.

He eased into her, holding back while they adjusted to joining together. His pulse thundered, rushing through his ears. The need to bury himself deep inside her raged through him. Until finally, she took all of him, surrounding him with her heat, clenching around him.

Groaning, he bucked up, needing to fill her, to make her feel as completely lost to him as he was to her. She pressed her hands to his pecs, lifting her hips then lowering back onto him, over and over again. He rose up, sliding her onto his lap until her legs clasped behind him. His mouth closed around a nipple, sucking, nibbling.

"Bodie . . ." His name on her lips drove him on, faster and faster until he couldn't hear anything except the sound of their bodies coming together. Her moan started in the back of her throat, rising until it vibrated against his ear. She clenched her legs, squeezing his waist between her thighs. He wished he could see her face when she came; he wanted to memorize the look he'd put there. Pausing, he held her tight against him while the momentum of her release exploded through her. She clung to him, her fingers gripping him so hard he'd probably have finger-shaped bruises on his shoulders. He loved how she didn't hold back, how she let herself go, how she wrung out the last bit she could, riding her release until her hips stilled, her chest heaving against his while she caught her breath.

Then he laid her down gently on her back. Hovering over her, he lowered himself onto her, into her. It didn't take but a few deep thrusts for him to lose himself. He strained, not wanting to crush her under his weight, as the power behind his own release flowed through him, draining him.

Spent, he collapsed, pulling her over so she sprawled on top of him. His fingers trailed from the base of her spine all the way up her back then down again. Feelings he didn't want to experience crowded into his heart. He couldn't be falling for Lacey. It would cause too many problems. Things were already too tense between his family and the town.

But any resistance he felt was shattered by the way she climbed back on top of him. His dick stirred against the wet heat of her core. "Can we do that again?"

twenty-six

Daylight. It had to be morning. Lacey opened her eyes to the hard planes of a man's chest. A naked man's chest. Remnants of the early-morning hours pieced themselves together as she lay there paralyzed, afraid to move. Bodie's rib cage rose and fell as he took even breaths. Thankfully he was still asleep. She tried to get up but something had her pinned. His hand splayed over one of her butt cheeks. Her naked butt cheek.

Embarrassment prickled along her nerve endings. She'd been so brazen last night. Taken from him so freely. As she chased sleep away, she did a quick body check of all of her parts. A delicious soreness ached between her legs. Her thighs chafed from where his whiskers had rubbed against them. Had that been during round two or three? She almost laughed out loud at the ridiculousness of the moment. Talk about an awkward morning after.

She ducked out from under his arm and took refuge in the bathroom. As she flipped on the light, she gasped as she caught a glimpse of herself in the mirror. Two, no make that three, hickeys dotted her neck. One more sat on top of her left breast. Her core quivered at the memory of Bodie sucking and pinching and licking and, oh hell, she had to stop thinking about it or she'd get turned on again.

Clean clothes or not, she had to shower before he saw her. She turned on the water and let the icy stream rush over her, cooling her skin, washing all traces of Bodie Phillips away. What if he regretted it? What if he was pretending to be asleep just so he wouldn't have to face her? What if . . .

Her heart jumped into her throat as the bathroom door creaked open. Then completely left her body as Bodie peered around the shower curtain. One hand tried to cover her breasts, the other shot to her crotch.

"Want some company?"

The smile on his face sent a wave of heat to her cheeks. She tried to speak but only a squeak came out.

"I can scrub your back," he offered as he slid the shower curtain back and stepped in.

Lacey kept her eyes above shoulder level. In the safety of a darkened hotel room she'd been brave, maybe even foolish, but definitely not inhibited. But now, in the harsh light of day, she couldn't help but wonder about all the lines they'd crossed and what the fallout might be.

"You okay, Sweets?" His voice caressed her raw nerve endings.

This was Bodie. Goofball, steady-handed, even-keeled Bodie, not some one-night stand. She turned her back to him and ducked her head under the running water. "How are you feeling this morning?"

He ran a washcloth over her back. A sliver of desire worked its way through her. "I feel good, really good. How about you?"

She peered over her shoulder, catching sight of the way the water coursed over his chest, running in little rivulets down his torso, over his stomach, to his . . . Her head snapped up. "Good. Do you feel a little, um, weird about anything?"

"Hey"—he put his hands on her shoulders and slowly spun her around to face him—"you okay? I'm serious."

Her gaze stayed down, trained on her feet. If she moved just a tiny bit she'd catch sight of all of him. She wasn't sure she was ready for that, even though she hadn't been shy about running her hands over every delectable inch of him in the dark.

"Lacey?" He put a finger under her chin, tipping her head up to meet his gaze. "Are you sorry for last night?"

The water beat down on her backside. She could lie, tell him it was a huge mistake. Then she wouldn't have to decide what to do about this new complication between them. But as his eyes searched hers, she realized she didn't want to. The feelings she'd had for Bodie had been a part of her since she realized there was a difference between boys and girls. He'd always had a piece of her heart—he'd just never known it.

She shook her head. It was a tiny movement, almost imperceptible. But the consequences were major. "Are you?" She shouldn't have asked. What if he said yes?

"No." His hands went to her upper arms and he gave her an encouraging squeeze. "The only thing I'm sorry about is that we didn't do this sooner."

The icy grip of dread loosened its hold on her heart. "Really?"

He nodded. "Yes."

"But what about Luke? What about me being mayor and your family trying to ruin the town? What about—"

His lips crushed to hers, stopping the words from falling out of her mouth. Stopping everything except for her undeniable desire to lose herself in Bodie's embrace and spend the rest of her life with her lips locked to his.

He pulled back, searching her eyes. "None of it matters. Nothing except you and me, okay?"

"Okay."

"Good. Now let's get cleaned up and get you home. I have to get things ready to pick up Shotgun tomorrow and we need to figure out how we're going to get another bride to take Adeline's place." He grabbed the washcloth and began to soap up her skin, running the cloth up one arm, down the other. As he did, she finally let herself take a good long look at him. All of him.

He stopped, letting his hands hang to his sides. "Like what you see?"

She laughed. "Aren't you a bit cocky?"

"The only cocky thing I've got going on is what's between my legs." He lifted a brow and she dragged her gaze down. Past his chest, over the dark hair trailing down his navel.

Her inhibitions shredded with the realization he might be just as into her as she was into him, she backed him against the tile wall. "Think we can get a late checkout?"

Three hours later she slid her sunglasses into place as she buckled into the front seat of Bodie's truck. He shut the door behind her and rounded the front end to climb in the driver's side. He handed her the coffee he'd snagged when he checked out of the hotel and nestled his cup into the console. After the awkwardness in the shower Lacey had decided to abandon her reservations and lean into whatever was blossoming between her and Bodie. That had been easy to do on the receiving end of his attention: his kisses, his encouraging words, the way he used his mouth to send her over the edge, not once, but twice. But now that they were on their way back home, doubt niggled at the edges of her brain.

He kept up the conversation, talking about nothing at all until they reached the edge of town. "You want to come home with me?"

"I think I'd better get home."

"Doesn't your dad still think you're in Dallas until to-morrow?"

She nodded. "Yeah, I haven't told him what happened. Not sure I ever will."

Bodie covered her hand with his. "You don't owe any-one an explanation."

The contact bolstered her confidence. "No, but I'm sure Adeline won't be shy about broadcasting the events of the evening. Everyone will hear about it sooner or later."

He squeezed her hand. "Let it be later, then. Spend the night with me and I'll run you home tomorrow."

Temptation to bury her head in the sand, if only for another twenty-four hours, made her seriously consider Bodie's offer. "I don't want to hide anymore."

Nodding, he let out a deep breath. "I get it."

The appealing thing about Bodie was, she knew he did. He'd always seemed to understand her, even when she didn't understand herself. She waited until he'd turned down the street where she grew up before she built up the courage to ask him the question she'd been dreading all morning. "What next?"

He eased the truck to a stop at the curb then looked over at her, that combination of boyish charm and wicked reck-lessness she loved reflected through his grin. "I'm hoping we can pick up where we left off earlier today. Maybe din-ner and whatever else might follow at my place tomorrow night?"

She bit her lip. "Does that mean you want to start see-ing each other?"

"Seeing? Hell, Lacey, I don't want to see you, I want to consume you."

Her heart expanded, filling her chest to the painful point that she rubbed a palm over her breastbone to make sure it wouldn't burst. "Okay then."

"Okay then?" He leaned across the console and worked

an arm around her shoulders, pulling her close. "I want to see this through."

She let out a breath. See it through. Suddenly the fact that she'd lost their first client and spent several hours in the slammer seemed worth the possibility that there could be some sort of future between them.

twenty-seven

Bodie looked at the vet tech like she'd sprouted another head. "That's impossible."

The woman gave him a nervous smile. "Actually, it's not."

He shook his head. "How could this have happened?"

"It's actually quite simple. Surely you're familiar with a little lesson you've probably heard before about the birds and the bees?"

Groaning, he lifted his shoulders and let them fall again. "But when? Since I've had her she hasn't been out of my sight."

The tech ran her finger down a piece of paper. "You sure about that?"

He had taken her with him to his mom and dad's place. Maybe one of the farm dogs had gotten to her. That had to be it. There was no other way. "For Pitties' Sake has got to take her back. I let them talk me into fostering her for a bit, but damn, I can't handle a pregnant pit bull."

"I'm sure they'll take her back. And in their defense, unless they were planning on spaying her soon, they probably didn't know. Most pups don't go through their first cycle until they're older."

He wasn't going to do this. He wasn't going to talk about a dog's menstrual cycle with a complete stranger. "Yeah, okay. I'll let them know when I return her."

The tech closed the folder and met his gaze. "She's a very sweet girl who's been through a lot. It might do her good to be with someone she loves and trusts while she goes through her pregnancy."

Bodie stepped back. "Whoa. I said I'd watch her for a few weeks, max. Never signed up to foster a pregnant dog."

"I'm sure you'll work it out." She slid a piece of paper in front of him. "If you'll just sign here I'll go get her for you."

He flicked his gaze over the long list of items. Intravenous hydration, twenty-four-hour supervision, electrolytes. It all added up to the tune of over three grand. And all because of his dad and his pops. They'd be hearing from him about this. If he hadn't spent the past twenty-four hours tracking down Lacey they would have already had another visit.

Bodie scrawled his signature over the credit card slip. There went his boat fund. The tech disappeared and came back a few minutes later with Shotgun. The dog sniffed cautiously at the floor, uncertain about her whereabouts.

"Hey, girl." Bodie squatted down to run a hand over her head.

At the sound of his voice she launched herself at him, covering his face in big, sloppy kisses.

"She trusts you," the tech observed.

Bodie stood and took the offered leash, choosing not to acknowledge that comment. "Anything else?"

"Nope. Should be good to go. But you'll want to check

in with her regular vet to monitor her pregnancy." She took a treat out of a canister on the counter and offered it to Shotgun. "Good luck with her. She's a sweetheart."

"Thanks," Bodie muttered. How had he gone from living the single life, a confirmed bachelor, to getting tangled up with Lacey and taking on a pregnant dog? He'd have to see if Zina could take her back sooner rather than later. He could barely keep his own life in order. There was no way he could become responsible for Shotgun and a couple of pups.

Before he did anything else though, he had to have a conversation with his dad and pops. With everything going on with Lacey and her plans to turn their corner of Texas into wedding central, he couldn't afford to get tangled up with the likes of Mayor Little and Swynton. His career aspirations would have to wait.

By the time he got Shotgun settled at home and checked in at work, he was hungry, tired, and cranky—the perfect time to resume the conversation with his family. He was already in a bad mood so Pops wouldn't have a chance to ruin it much more. He pulled into the drive next to his dad's fully loaded truck. At least he was here and not off scheming with Buck.

Bodie entered the office to the sound of Johnny Cash crooning over the built-in speaker system. "Dad?"

No answer. Bodie walked farther into the office.

"Out here," Dad called from the back. The office building shared a patio with the main house. Dad sat on the stamped concrete patio surrounding the huge crystal-clear pool.

"What are you doing outside?" Bodie pulled out a chair and sat down at the table. Temps were in the low fifties this time of year, not exactly poolside weather.

"I think my office is bugged."

"What makes you think that?"

Dad pointed to his face where the purple and blue had faded to a gruesome greenish color. "How else would they have known what was going on?"

Bodie ground his molars together. "Dad, you've got to come clean with me and tell me what's going on. Otherwise there's no way I'm going to be able to help you."

Dad shrugged. "I changed my mind about telling you. Your pops and I have it under control."

If "under control" meant continuing to dodge someone who obviously had it out for them, then they weren't doing such a great job. His phone rang, preventing him from saying as much. Lacey. His heart warmed at the sight of her number. But now wasn't the time. He swiped at his phone then set it back on the table.

"Doesn't look like you and Pops have a grip on things. Why don't you let me handle this?"

Dad shook his head. "You give any more thought to Buck's offer? Bodie Phillips, sheriff of Sewell County. Has a nice ring to it, don't you think?"

"It does," he agreed. His lifelong career goal, handed to him on a silver platter. Was he being too rash in declining the offer?

"Think of it. With you as sheriff it won't take long to run the Cherish girl out of town and then Buck can take over. He's got a vision that will put Swynton on the map."

"I bet he does. But—"

Dad's phone rang. He put up a finger, silencing Bodie. "Yeah?"

While he waited, Bodie checked his phone. For some reason it appeared to be midcall. "Hello?"

The sound of the line disconnecting hit his ear. Lacey. *Shit, shit, shit.* Instead of dismissing her call he must have answered. Which meant she'd probably just heard the conversation between him and his dad.

"I've gotta go." He dialed her number and got sent

straight to voice mail. With no time to spare, he shoved his phone in his pocket. The conversation with his dad would have to wait . . . again. He had to get to Lacey and find out what she'd heard. If she thought he was working against her she'd doubt everything that had happened between them. He couldn't afford to have that happen. No matter what his dad and pops had their greedy fingers into, it was high time he separated himself from their undermining efforts.

Now he just needed to find Lacey and tell her that before she came to conclusions on her own.

twenty-eight

Lacey gulped for air. Her lungs seemed to be collapsing in on themselves, making it impossible to catch a breath. She'd called Bodie only to confirm their dinner plans. If he'd been telling the truth when he dropped her off yesterday then she was ready to take the next step. She'd even made his favorite, brisket, that had been simmering all day along with cowboy baked beans and apple crumble for dessert.

But now . . . she rubbed her ears, trying to erase what she'd just overheard. Had Bodie been plotting against her all along? Had he been in cahoots with his dad, his pops, and even Mayor Little to try to run her out of office?

No, she didn't want to believe it. But all signs pointed otherwise.

She stomped through the kitchen. He must have known she was on the phone. She had to get out of there before he showed up on her doorstep making flimsy excuses.

"Dad, I'm heading out for a bit. Dinner's in the oven."

Let her dad enjoy Bodie's home-cooked meal. Zina would help her figure out what to do.

"Smells delicious, sweetheart." Her dad caught up to her in the foyer as she shoved her feet into her boots. "What's the occasion?"

"Just wanted to make something special tonight." She wouldn't tell him she'd opened herself up to Bodie, heart and soul, like a damn fool. "I'll be back later, okay? Everything will be ready in a couple of hours, just keep it on warm in the oven."

Dad kissed her on the temple. "You take such good care of me."

He wouldn't think so if he knew she'd fallen prey to Bodie's plans. Or that she'd spent Friday night in a jail cell in Dallas. She swallowed back the emotion clogging her throat.

"I'll be back." Then she grabbed her jacket and her keys and made her way to her truck as fast as she could.

Ten minutes later she'd pulled into Zina's empty drive. Lacey should have called first. Clearly Zina wasn't home. Probably putting in extra time at the shelter this afternoon. Lacey didn't want to go there. The last time she'd been at the shelter it had been with Bodie while they were dropping off Shotgun. She thought of the darling dog he'd taken into his home. Was that part of his ploy, too? While she sat in Zina's drive, the truck running, she ran through Bodie's actions of the last month. Was everything a lie?

She needed some time for herself. Time to clear her head. Turning her truck toward the one place she knew she'd be able to breathe, she let out a sigh. Spending a couple of hours on the back of a horse would make her feel better.

Her phone rang just as she pulled into the stable where she boarded her palomino. A number she didn't recognize flashed across her phone. Grateful it wasn't Bodie, she answered.

"Mayor Lacey Cherish?" a woman asked.

"Yes, this is she."

"Hi, it's Samantha Cross. We spoke about the story in *Texas Times* magazine?"

"Right." The story that wouldn't be happening now. Lacey's stomach whipped into a knotted frenzy. "What can I help you with?"

"I had a phone call from Ms. Monroe. She said she's no longer having her ceremony and reception at your new event venue and invited us to cover her wedding over at a venue in Swynton instead. I really enjoyed learning the history of the building last time I was there. But without a bride, I just don't see how we can put a story together."

"I understand." Lacey rested her forehead on the steering wheel. It physically pained her to let an opportunity like this slip through her fingers. There had to be some way to salvage the story. *Think, think, think.*

"Unless you fill that date with another wedding, I'm sorry, but we'll have to move our coverage to Ms. Monroe's wedding in Swynton."

Another bride. Who could Lacey throw into the frying pan? Someone who would be easy to manipulate, someone who would go with the flow just until the story came out in the magazine. That ruled out Zina. She'd never go along with this kind of plan. Jojo came to mind. But she was overwhelmed at the diner. And she wasn't even seeing anyone. Where would Lacey come up with a groom?

"Mayor Cherish?" Samantha asked. "Are you still there?"

A vision of Bodie sealing the deal with Buck Little played through her head. She ought to out him to the town, lump him together with the rest of his no-good family members. Could Jojo pretend to be engaged to Bodie?

"Mayor Cherish?"

"Yes, I'm here." A plan began to take shape. Lacey shook off the alarms ringing in her head. She didn't have a choice. Something had to work out. "I didn't want to say anything because I didn't want to steal the limelight from Adeline . . ."

"Do you have another couple willing to be featured?"

"I do."

"Fantastic. Can you give me their names so I can follow up? We'll need to make contact right away to make sure we don't miss out on any of the planning. We've got the story scheduled for the June issue, which means the wedding needs to happen by the middle of May in order to make our deadline."

Crap. She couldn't expect Jojo to cram a few months' worth of wedding planning into her already busy schedule. That left Lacey with no choice. As much as it chafed her to tie herself to Bodie in any capacity, he was her last hope. "The groom is actually Deputy Phillips. I believe you met him the day you visited the house?"

"Oh, that's fabulous. He didn't say anything about being engaged at the time. How perfectly romantic, what with him having such history with the town. Now, who's the lucky bride?"

Panic set in. Lacey took in a deep breath through her nose. *Here goes nothing. Here goes everything.* "The bride is me."

twenty-nine

♡

Bodie knocked at the door of the Cherish home, trying to brace himself for a confrontation with Lacey. As the door opened he straightened his stance and held the bouquet of carnations out in front of him.

Mr. Cherish eyed the flowers then glanced to Bodie's face. "You shouldn't have, son."

His cheeks radiating heat like they'd been set on fire, Bodie let the flowers drop to his side. "Is Lacey home, sir?"

"You just missed her. She tore out of here about ten minutes ago like the devil himself was on her tail. Is there a reason you're bringing my daughter flowers?" He cocked his head, his eyes narrowed.

"No, sir. I mean, yes, there's a reason, but it's nothing special." Not unless he wanted to admit to Lacey's dad that he'd spent the early hours of Saturday morning testing out the theories of physics on his daughter's limber body.

"What'd you do?" He held the door open, an invitation to come inside and spill his guts. Bodie had taken advantage of several invites like this from Mr. Cherish over the years. He respected the man's opinion and often sought out his advice over his own father's. But not today. He couldn't very well admit to screwing up where Lacey was concerned. Especially screwing up over screwing Lacey.

"Lacey overheard something she shouldn't have. I need to find her to make it right."

Mr. Cherish nodded. "Odds are she's either over at Zina's or out at the stables."

"Thank you, sir." Bodie stood there, the flowers still clutched in his hands. "Would you mind making sure she gets these? In case I don't catch up to her today?"

"Sure. Good luck, Son. You know as well as I do when she gets upset about something it can take quite a while for her to calm down."

"Yes, sir." Bodie handed over the flowers. They'd seemed like a good idea when he ran into the mini-mart but now they looked wilted, like a lame attempt at an apology, as Mr. Cherish held them in his hand. He took a final look at the blooms then steeled himself to track down Lacey.

A drive by Zina's house and a quick pass by the shelter didn't turn up Lacey's truck. Unless she was going to great lengths to hide and didn't want to be found, she hadn't gone to either place. That just left the stables out on Highway 75. She'd been boarding her horse there ever since he could remember. He and Luke used to have to run her back and forth for lessons after school and on the weekends. Bodie had always enjoyed watching her ride. She was a natural in the saddle.

He pulled up next to her truck in the dirt parking lot. If she'd taken her horse out it might be an hour or more before she returned. He walked through the barn in search of the horse's stall. Empty. That left him two choices. Either wait around for her to come back or head over to the Phillips House to check on the armadillo-removal attempt. Having good news to share when she returned might make their confrontation go a little smoother.

As he walked the length of the barn to head back to his truck, he ran into one of his old high school pals. He and his family owned the ranch. Like most of the folks around town, the land had been in their family for generations.

"Hey, Bodie. What brings you out here today?" Callan stopped mucking out an empty stall and stood.

"Just trying to track down Lacey. I've got some official town business I need to fill her in on. You see her around?"

"Yeah." Callan wiped his brow with his sleeve. "Came through here about twenty minutes ago, fit to be tied about something."

"Oh yeah? She say what?"

"Nah. Whatever she was working through, she didn't want to talk about it. You want to borrow old Mercury and chase her down? She probably just went on a loop around the property."

"That's okay. I'll catch up to her later."

"Sounds good." Callan resumed his job on the stall.

Bodie was halfway through the barn when Callan called out behind him. "Oh, I forgot to offer my congratulations."

"Yeah, thanks." Congratulations on what? He didn't want to take the time to ask about it. Could be he'd heard Bodie had taken in a dog. Or maybe it was a belated congrats on the public safety award he'd won back in December. Either way, it didn't matter. All that mattered was finding Lacey.

He didn't want to think about what might be going through her head. After the night they'd shared on Friday, she had to be madder than a wet hen, thinking he'd played her like a fiddle. He picked up his phone and tried her number again. Straight to voice mail. Served him right. He should have shut down his dad's ridiculous offer the first time he'd brought it up. Now look where it got him. On the outs with Lacey, right when he'd finally found an in.

He tried not to think about it as he drove over to the

Phillips House. The pest-removal truck sat in the drive. Either the armadillos had multiplied and dug even more holes or the person trying to trap them had been creating more piles in an attempt to figure out where the damn animals were hiding.

He walked the perimeter of the house before he caught sight of the wildlife expert. The man held a live trap in each hand. Bodie closed the distance between them, hoping for good news. He had to have something positive to tell Lacey. Something to balance out the bad.

"How's it going?" Bodie tipped his hat at the man.

"Been at it all weekend. You've got some wily critters, that's for sure." He held up the trap in his right hand. A small armadillo peered at Bodie through the wire cage. "Just got two more. The traps have been snapping all night."

"What are you going to do with them now that you've caught them?" As much as Bodie wanted the damn critters long gone, he didn't want them turned into boots or belts or something else.

"We release 'em way out in the country." He shrugged. "It's the most humane thing to do. Got about six already. I'll reset the traps again tonight but I think we may have caught them all."

Bodie nodded. "Great, thanks. Y'all planning on filling in the holes all over the yard, too?"

"Sorry, Deputy. Mayor Cherish didn't pay for the all-in-one service. Said she'd take care of that herself."

Figured. Lacey would cut as many corners as she could to save a few bucks. "All right, then. I'll figure that out."

"Saw a shovel in the garage." The man nodded toward the building that used to operate as the carriage house.

"Thanks." Bodie waited until he reached his truck and loaded the traps into the back. With nothing but time on his hands and a giant hole he needed to dig himself out of, he might as well start by filling some in. He found the shovel in the garage and got to work. An hour passed, then two. By the time the sun began to disappear behind a bank of heavy gray clouds, he'd filled in all the holes he could find. That ought to put a smile on Lacey's face. One less thing for her to have to worry about.

Thinking of Lacey made him wonder where she was. Had she blown off some of the anger he'd created? Hopefully giving her the afternoon to cool down would work in his favor. As he put the shovel back in the garage he pulled out his phone, ready to track her down again and try to make amends.

"Hey, Bodie." She answered on the second ring, her voice calm, clear, and sounding the slightest bit happy.

"Hi. Where have you been this afternoon? I stopped by the house."

"My dad gave me the flowers you dropped off. That was so sweet of you. Thanks for thinking of me."

Why wasn't she swearing up a storm? Did he get it wrong? His gut told him to proceed with caution. Something wasn't right. The singsong tone in her voice was a dead giveaway. "You're welcome."

"I went out for a ride. It's been so long since the poor horse got a chance to stretch his legs. I'm sorry I missed you. You should have told me you'd be stopping by. I made a brisket and some apple crumble for dessert. Do we still have dinner plans?"

He checked his watch. It was almost six and the only thing waiting on him at home was a knocked-up dog and a freezer full of frozen tamales. "I'm over at the Phillips House right now. I need to swing by home and feed Shotgun but other than that I'm not doing anything tonight."

"I could make up a couple of plates for us and run them over. What do you think?"

She sounded genuine. His gut warmed at the thought of a home-cooked meal and practically sparked as he envisioned the kind of things they might be able to get to after they ate and he came clean about the offer from Mayor Little. "Yeah, that sounds great."

"I'll see you in a little while, then." Her smile traveled right through the phone. There was no way she was pissed at him. He'd seen her angry before and if Lacey had one area where she struggled it was in wearing her heart on her sleeve. She'd always been like an open book. A weight lifted from his shoulders and he smiled.

"Looking forward to it, Sweets."

"Oh, me, too." She disconnected.

Hell, what had he been so worried about? He looked around the yard. He'd just wasted a couple of hours filling in holes for no reason. Granted, Lacey wouldn't have to worry about it now but he'd wasted hours' worth of energy worried she'd never want to see hide nor hair of him again.

The thing with his dad and pops must be making him paranoid. He'd do best to come clean with Lacey tonight before she caught wind of it otherwise. Having her find out from someone else would definitely put a kink in their budding relationship. A relationship . . . is that what he wanted?

Luke wouldn't like it. But he was thousands of miles away. By the time he made it home it would be old news. Mr. Cherish might have a bone or two to pick. It's not every day he was arrested by the man who'd become his daughter's boyfriend. Bodie shook his head. *Boyfriend* sounded too juvenile. Lover. No, that didn't work, either. Made it sound like they were having some sort of illicit fling. Significant other?

Was he ready for a significant other? She couldn't just be an "other." He spent the drive home trying to come up with a way to classify whatever was growing between him and Lacey but making no progress. By the time he'd taken a shower and put on a fresh pair of jeans and a pressed button-down flannel he'd about given up. Why did he have to name it?

He'd let it grow naturally. Someday in the future, the distant future, they'd figure it out together. So when the doorbell rang, he rose from the couch, a little extra pep in his step.

Shotgun got there first, her rear end wiggling so fast she knocked herself over. Bodie pulled the door open, a smile on his lips, ready for a kiss from whatever she wanted to call herself.

"Hey there, Lacey." His smile faded slightly at the sight of Lacey standing on his doorstep, a familiar woman in tow.

"You remember Samantha, don't you, sugar pie?" Her eyes widened then narrowed.

"Sure I do." He held out his hand to the reporter. Why would Lacey be coming over with the magazine reporter? Especially on a Sunday night?

Lacey brushed past him, her arms full of foil-wrapped containers. "Samantha was in town this weekend but has to head back tomorrow. Since Adeline backed out I didn't have any choice but to tell her our news."

"Our news . . ." Bodie trailed behind the two women to the kitchen, Shotgun at his heels.

"Lacey told me how the two of you didn't want to steal Adeline's thunder. I think that's so sweet. Readers are going to love it."

Bodie nodded, a smile pasted on his face. What was she talking about? He tried to catch Lacey's eye. She looked comfortable in his kitchen as she opened up cabinets, pulled out plates, and set up on the counter the dinner she'd brought.

"So are you ready to talk about the big event?" Samantha asked. She opened up a notebook and clicked her pen. "Tell me, Deputy Phillips, what does it feel like to be engaged to the mayor?"

thirty

Lacey waited for Bodie to respond. Knowing him as well as she did, he'd go one of two ways. He'd either play it off, leaving her to fill in the details or he'd go along in an attempt to save face. Either way she had the lying deputy exactly where she needed him. At least for now.

"It feels, um, well, Lacey, you've kind of caught me by surprise here. You sure you want to do this?" His face had paled under the seemingly constant layer of scruff.

"What with Adeline canceling, it didn't really give me a chance to find another bride and groom willing to share their big day with the media. I know we talked about having a fall wedding, but really, it should be us that gets married there first, don't you think, love bug?" She stepped next to him, put her arm behind his back and rested her head against his chest.

His heart thudded, a much faster beat than it had the other night when she'd lain in his arms. When she thought he meant what he'd said. When she thought they were for real.

"Sure. Can I just grab a quick word with you? You

don't mind giving us a minute or two, do you?" he asked Samantha.

"Not at all." She set down her pen and waved them away. "Take all the time you need. I'll just be out here drooling over whatever Lacey has hiding here in this pan."

"It's brisket. Cooked all day. Feel free to help yourself, we'll just be a minute or two." She smiled, then tugged on Bodie's arm, dragging him down the hall to where she presumed his bedroom was. How could she pretend he was her fiancé when she'd never even seen where he slept?

"What the hell's going on?" He closed the door behind them then turned on her. "Fiancé?"

"That's right. Congratulations to us. It happened so fast it just left my head spinning." She practically spit the words at him. Being in his room, alone with the man who'd left her heart full of buckshot almost made her regret what she'd told Samantha. Almost.

"Where do you get off telling people we're engaged? Who else have you told about this?" He towered over her, the glint in his eye proving he was beyond finding this an amusing little prank.

"You didn't leave me much of a choice." Arms clamped around her middle, she held her ground. This was his fault, after all.

His arms spread wide. "What are you talking about?"

"You tell me, Sheriff Phillips." She emphasized the word *sheriff*.

He stopped gesturing and put his hands to his hips. "So you were on the phone earlier today."

"That's right." She tried to squelch the raw emotion that threatened to bubble up inside. "I heard everything. How you and your dad are working with Buck Little." Her eyes watered. She couldn't have that. Reaching up, she ran a finger under her lashes, wiping away any trace of emotion.

"Lacey, I can explain. My dad made me an offer but I went there to turn him down."

"Sure you did. Does Sheriff Suarez know you've got your eye on his job?"

"It's not like that." He reached for her.

She sidestepped him, whirling around to stand in front of his bed. A bed she'd hoped to spend some time in up until a few hours ago. "I don't care what it's like. All I know is that your dad and grandfather are trying to pull a fast one and you've taken their side. Just like you always do."

"I do not." His jaw set. A muscle ticked along the edge.

"You do, too. And I'm not going to let you get away with it. Not this time."

He scoffed, shook his head, and rolled his eyes. "Unbelievable. After everything that happened the other night? You think I'm working against you?"

Her heart seized. Could he be telling the truth? She wanted to believe him. Wanted to think that everything they'd done had been because of feelings they'd been hiding over the years. Not because of some plan he was trying to pull together to keep his family out of trouble.

"You have two choices, Bodie." She held up two fingers to emphasize her point.

"Really? Do tell. I can't wait." He took a step closer.

She backed up, her thighs bumping against the edge of his bed. Not willing to be intimidated, she drew in a breath and lowered her voice. "You can go out there and pretend to be my adoring fiancé—"

"Or?" He matched his tone to hers—low, almost a growl.

"Or you can tell her it's a sham and I'd be happy to return the favor by paying a visit to Sheriff Suarez and telling him all about the plans you've been making with Buck."

"I'm not making plans with Buck." He glared at her.

"So you're not trying to cover up the fact your family is involved in some illegal importing activities and you've been offered his job?"

His left eye twitched. She'd hit a nerve.

"I just haven't had a chance to fill him in on everything just yet. Once I get to the bottom of it I'm going to tell him everything."

The power shifted. She could almost feel victory in the air. "But you haven't yet."

Bodie put his hand to his temple. "Not yet. You know as well as I do that my dad's made a few, let's just call them 'less than legal' decisions over the past few years. I don't want to see anything bad happen to him."

"Yeah, I didn't want to see anything bad happen to my dad, either. Imagine what it's going to feel like when my own father isn't able to walk me down the aisle at our wedding."

"Seriously? How far are you going to take this? You don't expect me to actually marry you, do you?"

"Of course not," she hissed. "We'll fake the ceremony and no one will be the wiser. Don't you see, this is our chance to put the town on the map? You owe it to me, Bodie. It's your family's fault this whole thing happened in the first place."

He opened his mouth and she waited, expecting an argument. Instead, he threw his hands in the air. "You're right. Fine, I'll be your fiancé. But you've got to promise you won't spill a word about the import stuff or the offer from Buck until I have a chance to figure out what's happening on my own."

"Deal." She thrust her hand at him, ready to seal the agreement with a handshake.

His hand closed around hers, warm and firm and reminiscent of how it felt to be lost to his touch. Was that just the other night she'd spent hours in his arms? Seemed like a lifetime ago. And now, by calling him out and blackmailing him into being her fake fiancé, she'd pretty much guaranteed that would be the last time she'd have her way with Bodie, in or out of the bedroom.

thirty-one

Bodie gestured for Lacey to enter the kitchen first. "After you, sugarplum."

She shot him a thinly veiled glare—the kind that might have leveled him if he hadn't been in on her deceitful little game. "Thanks, snuggybug."

"Have you always had nicknames for each other?" Samantha sat on a stool at the kitchen counter, pen in hand.

"Not always," Bodie said. "She didn't like me for the longest time."

"Oooh, an enemies-to-lovers tale? Do tell." Samantha scooted closer to the counter, where her blank notepad waited to be filled with stories detailing his and Lacey's love affair. Lies, all of them. But he'd always been a big fan of the advice to go big or go home. Since he was already at home, he didn't have a choice but to come up with the biggest, most ridiculous background story he could. If Lacey wanted to play with fire, he would make sure she got a little singed around the edges.

"Yeah, she always had the hots for me but . . ."

"Unrequited love?" Samantha's pen flew over the paper.

"Not exactly." Lacey leaned her elbows onto the counter. "I didn't want to catch anything, if you know what I mean. He's been clean for a few years now, isn't that right, honey bear?"

Samantha's eyes widened.

"I don't think you should put anything about that in the story." Lacey brought a finger to her lips. "Let's keep that just between us."

Score one to Lacey. If that's how she wanted to handle things, he'd be willing to take a stab or two at creating a history for her that was just as colorful as the one she seemed to want to make up for him.

"Yeah, that was nothing though compared to what poor Lacey went through as a teen." He picked up a plate and forked a nice piece of juicy brisket. "Did she tell you about her IBS issues? I'm surprised she made brisket tonight." He held a hand up to his mouth like he was about to share a big secret. "Gives her horrible runs, red meat always has."

"Oh." Samantha glanced at her plate of half-eaten brisket.

"Crazy what true love will make you do, isn't it?" Lacey asked. "I know how much he loves it so even though I can't enjoy it like I used to, I still want him to be able to experience it."

"That's such a great story," Samantha said.

Yes, it was. Bodie would have to up the ante if he wanted to cast Lacey in a bad light. Before he had a chance to come up with something equal parts ridiculous and embarrassing, Samantha tapped her pen to her lip.

"I notice you're not wearing a ring. Did he give you one? I'm sure our readers will want to know how he popped the question."

Lacey glanced down at her ring finger. "Of course he

gave me a ring. I was just out working with the horses today so I didn't want to risk losing it. I'll make sure to wear it next time you come to town."

Next time? Bodie's heart stuttered to a stop. What exactly had he committed to? Temporarily distracted from his goal of throwing Lacey under the bus, he cleared his throat. "When exactly is the next time?"

Lacey twined her fingers with his and rested their joined hands on the counter. "We're going to be featured in the magazine. Samantha is going to want to follow our journey from proposal to happily ever after."

"That's right. So tell me, how did you propose?"

Bodie glanced to Lacey. "You sure do tell it better, honey pie."

Her eyelashes fluttered. "Well, if you insist . . ."

He insisted, all right. What fictional tale would Lacey feed to the reporter? He sat down on a barstool and picked up his fork. It would be a shame to let all of that home-cooked brisket go to waste.

"He's always been so romantic," Lacey started. "In fact, he used to write me love poems while we were growing up but was too shy to give them to me."

Bodie almost choked on a piece of brisket. Love poems? The only poem he'd ever memorized was his dad's version of grace: Good bread, good meat, good Lord, let's eat.

"How sweet. Do you remember any of them off the top of your head?" Samantha glanced to Bodie.

He shoved a bite of beans in his mouth and shook his head.

"He's too embarrassed to say." Lacey leaned over and squeezed his shoulder. "How did that one go? Grass is green, sunflowers are yellow, I wish so bad that I was your fellow?"

He sucked in a breath, sending the bite of beans down the wrong pipe. Coughing, he tried to catch his breath.

"Are you okay, angel love?" Lacey's mock concern

made him want to abandon the project right then and there. If he had to put up with crap like this until May he'd rather risk facing the town. She handed him his water and he took a nice, slow sip.

"Sorry, I wasn't expecting you to share something so personal." The way he glared at her should have shut her down. Should have turned her knees the consistency of his grandma's rhubarb jelly.

But instead she tapped him on the shoulder and leaned toward Samantha. "What did I say? He's so sensitive."

"And the proposal?"

"It was incredibly romantic." Lacey smiled as she dipped her head. "All day he kept leaving me little poems. I won't repeat any of the others since they're so personal." She glanced at Bodie, one side of her mouth quirking into a smirk. "But we had dinner plans that night so I figured it was just a lead-up to our date. He picked me up that afternoon and we drove to Houston. Nice restaurant, gorgeous view of the city. Then the waiter brought a special dessert to the table next to ours."

Bodie wondered where she was going with the storyline. But he waited, ready to intervene if necessary.

"The gal squealed because there was a diamond ring sitting on top of her flan. Just resting there. Poor Bodie kept craning his neck, and I wondered why in the world he was so interested in their dessert. I mean, the man does love his flan, but it was ridiculous. And then he gets up from the table and walks over there and I almost died. He stuck his finger in the flan and grabbed the ring."

"No." Samantha gasped.

He could see where she was going with this so he decided to ad-lib a bit. "It was my ring. The waiter took it to the wrong table. Like hell some other guy was going to get credit for my proposal."

"Not to mention that two-carat yellow diamond." Lacey laughed as she skimmed her hand over his arm. "That poor woman was so sad. The other couple left the restaurant with her in tears."

"After you stomped on her foot," Bodie added. Lacey squeezed his arm. "She really thought the schmuck she was with was proposing. She told everyone they'd been dating for seven years. So she tried to take the ring back from me."

"But you held on tight, right?" Samantha asked.

"No." Bodie shrugged. "She caught me off guard. Grabbed it right out of my hand as I went down on one knee. It fell on the floor and Lacey got down on her hands and knees to find it. You should have seen her crawling around in that miniskirt she had on. I think one of the busboys got some video of it."

"I'm assuming you captured the moment as well."

"Of course," he said.

At the same time Lacey blurted, "Sadly, no."

"So which is it?" Samantha asked.

Lacey glanced to Bodie, her hand to her temple, a question in her eyes.

What was the big deal? "I'm pretty sure we got at least one good one."

"I'd love to include it in the article. I'm thinking this could be bigger. Maybe we'll do a small piece in the issue ahead of the big one. Can you get that to me by the end of the month?" Samantha reached into her bag.

While she rummaged in her purse, Lacey elbowed him in the gut. So maybe he'd taken it a tad far in his effort to one-up her. He'd find someone at the station to fudge a pic of them together. No big deal.

"I'd love to. I can probably even send one or two of our early dates if you'd like." He glanced at Lacey. Her eyes just about bugged out of her head. This was fun.

"The two of you are so right together. I'm sure our readers would love that."

"So right." He wanted to belly laugh at that remark. If

he and Lacey were so right together then how come everything had gone down so wrong?

"Tell me what it's like working so closely together?" Samantha changed the subject. "Have you ever had any conflict of interest seeing as how Lacey's the mayor and you're the sheriff?"

"Sheriff's deputy," Lacey corrected. "Although rumor has it my main squeeze has some pretty big career aspirations." The glint in her eye could have sparked a fire.

"It's good to have dreams," Bodie said.

"Have you clashed over city issues? Where's the conflict?"

"We have plenty of sparks, if you get my drift." Bodie lifted a brow, trying to make light of the gray area they were wading through.

"Yes, we've had conflicts," Lacey answered. "His family closed down their business recently, causing half the town to lose their jobs. As mayor, that put a giant wrench in my plans to keep our economy going."

"Bodie, how's that possible? How involved are you in the family business?"

"My dad and grandfather handle everything. They don't run their decisions past me. It's unfortunate but you'd have to ask them for their reasons."

"You said you wanted to talk about how the wedding plans are going," Lacey said, changing the subject.

Grateful for a bit of a reprieve, Bodie kept quiet while she and Samantha talked about all of the upcoming decisions they'd have to make. What kind of flowers did they want? Were they going with a theme? How about a groom's cake? Would there be a bachelor and bachelorette party? Hell no to that. He'd seen the kind of damage Lacey could do when let loose with the girls for an evening.

He finished his brisket and went back for another helping. Lacey might be a hot mess when it came to some things, but the woman sure could cook.

"So Bodie, you'll get that photo to me? And one with the ring?" Samantha asked as she slid her notebook into her bag.

"Sure. I'll get right on that." And by "get right on that" he meant he'd try to figure out a way to manipulate something that would pass.

"It would be great if you could include the name of the restaurant. Couples are always looking for places to pop the question."

"It was the Cattleman," he offered.

"Oooh, I've heard that place is nice." Samantha turned to Lacey. "You're a lucky woman."

"Don't I know it." Lacey blew him a kiss then stuck out her tongue as Samantha reached back to put on her jacket.

Why was she giving him the stink eye? He'd gone along with her crazy talk. For now. Someone would have to set the record straight though before this got out of hand.

"Thanks again for sharing your story. I'll be in touch with some potential dates for the camera crew to come down."

Lacey held the door open, the casual grin on her face not giving any outward sign of what was going on inside that crazy head of hers.

"That sounds great. I'll talk to you soon." She shut the door gently, letting it barely click closed before she spun around and glared at him.

thirty-two

Lacey advanced, her pointer finger leading the way, jabbing the air with sharp thrusts. "What was that?"

"What was what?" Bodie sidestepped her attack.

Was the man really so dense that he didn't realize he'd just made the situation at least twice, if not three times, as bad? "Why didn't you let me handle that? I told you to be quiet and play along."

"That was before you made me out to be some nerdy poet. *'Sunflowers are yellow'*? Are you kidding me?"

"That's better than telling her we got engaged at Cattleman's. And that you have photographic proof. Where are you going to come up with those pictures you promised her?" She could feel a migraine coming on. The kind that would require complete darkness and silence, not an argument over their fake engagement.

"I'll figure it out. That's nothing compared to the two-carat yellow diamond engagement ring you said you got." He ran a hand through his hair, making it stick out in all directions. Reminded her of how he looked when she woke up next to him yesterday. How could that have been only a day ago? So much had changed since then. Almost gave her whiplash trying to wrap her head around it.

"Can we pick this up again tomorrow? I need to get home."

"Sure, why not? You seem to be the one in charge here. No matter that I didn't have a say before you outed me as your groom. Did you even think to ask me first?"

Lacey tried to tune him out. Her headache was coming on like a freight train and she needed to take one of her pills and lie down before she ended up missing the chance and having to spend the next two days in bed. "I'm sorry, okay?"

He paused in his rant and put his hands on the counter. "So what next, Mayor Cherish? What's the big plan?"

She took one look at him and made a mad dash for the bathroom. Her knees barely hit the floor when the little bit she'd had for dinner came back up. Damn migraine. Damn Bodie. Damn everything.

"Lacey, are you okay?" He paused in the doorway to the bathroom, genuine concern evident in his eyes.

"Headache," she managed to mutter. "Pill's in my purse."

"I got it." He disappeared down the hall, leaving her to curse herself for not heeding the early signs. She knew from experience when she felt one of her migraines coming on she needed to drop everything, take a pill, and go to bed. But with Samantha giving them the third degree it had been her chance to set the publicity plan in motion—something she needed to do if she had any hope of saving the town.

Bodie came back, a glass of water and one of her pills in hand. "Here you go." His voice lacked the sharpness of earlier.

She nodded, taking the pill and swallowing. How was she going to get home? She couldn't see straight enough to walk down the hall, much less drive herself ten miles in the dark.

Bodie must have read her mind. "You can take my bed tonight. I'll sleep on the couch."

"It's okay. Just let me lie down for a few minutes." She rested her head against the cabinet, too tired to even think about getting up.

"Come on, Sweets." Bodie leaned down and scooped her up into his arms.

She groaned at the movement. It had been a long time since one of her headaches had come on so fast and fierce.

"I've got you." He angled her through the bathroom door then took soft steps down the hall.

"Don't be silly. Just put me on the couch and I'll get myself home when I feel better." She tried to push against his chest. Her head seemed to weigh forty pounds and all she wanted to do was close her eyes and wish her headache away.

"Shh." He stepped through the doorway to his bedroom and gently set her on the bed. "What can I do for you?" he whispered.

"Just leave me alone for a while." She wanted to roll out of his arms but didn't dare move.

He pulled back slowly then climbed on the bed beside her. "Come here." With long, gentle strokes his fingers smoothed the hair back from her temple.

The tension in her head eased a bit. Bodie continued to stroke her hair, his chest pressed against her back. Maybe it was the calming scent of what had to be freshly washed sheets. Or it could have been the warmth she felt with his front pushed against her back. Whatever it was, it eased her headache from debilitating to slightly less so.

She waited until her pill took effect then closed her eyes. Taking a short rest before she tried to head home would be the smart thing to do.

* * *

She woke to the *thump-thump-thump* of a heartbeat against her ear. It was impossible to see in the inky darkness. She remembered Bodie, arguing in front of the reporter from the *Texas Times* and then a monster headache coming on.

Propping herself up on an elbow, she squinted at the clock on the nightstand. Four thirty in the morning? Her dad had probably been worried sick about her. She tried to get up but something pinned her in place. One of Bodie's arms clamped around her middle. Just like the other night. For a moment she wanted to lie still, linger in his arms, and pretend they were just a guy and a gal, not the warring deputy sheriff and mayor, both trying to protect and save something they loved that happened to be in direct conflict with each other. Wriggling, she tried to free herself.

"Hey." His breath brushed against her cheek. Sleepiness edged his voice, making it sound gravelly, even borderline sexy. "You feel any better?"

"Yeah, I should go. Dad's probably wondering where I am."

Bodie's arm tightened. "I called him last night. Told him you had a migraine and were going to stay here."

"You did what?" She tried to flip around to face him. He loosened his grip a little and she rolled over.

His hand skimmed up and down her back. "Didn't want him to worry."

"I need to get home."

"Why?" His question gnawed at her resistance. "Alarm's set for six thirty. Just go back to sleep."

"I can't sleep with you." She spoke into the soft cotton of his T-shirt.

His chest rose and fell as he let out a soft laugh. "Too late for that. Besides, aren't we engaged now?"

Heat slapped her cheeks. Engaged. That's right. If she

wanted to hang on to the promo opportunity, she and Bodie would need to pretend to be engaged. With his arms enveloping her, the sound of his heart against hers, and the intoxicating scent surrounding her, she wished with all her might she'd picked someone else to be fake engaged to. But her options were limited. No one else had as much to gain or lose by keeping up the charade.

"You know I wouldn't have done that if I thought I'd had a choice." His shirt muffled her words. At least he had one on. For a brief moment she let herself remember what it felt like to be cradled against his bare chest the other day. The heat moved from her cheeks, down her neck, across her breastbone, then lower, uncomfortably lower.

"So here we are." He reached up, running a finger down her cheek. "How are we supposed to play this now, Mayor?"

"I don't know. Adeline's wedding was scheduled for mid-May. That means we only have to pretend to be engaged for a couple of months."

"Surely you'll be able to put up with me for that long."

As his hand ran over the contour of her hip she doubted her resolve. She couldn't let herself get involved with Bodie. Not now. Not when she knew for certain he'd been hiding things from her.

"You know, I'm going to run home." She rolled away from the indentation he'd caused in the mattress and let her feet hit the floor.

"You sure?" His fingers wrapped around her arm. "How's your head?"

"It's fine. Thanks for taking care of things last night." Her heart swelled as she remembered what it felt like to get swooped up in his arms. He might have been thrown off by the fake engagement but the concern and gentleness he'd shown had been real, she was sure of it.

"So I'll see you around?" he asked. "Have you given any thought to how we're going to break the news of our engagement to everyone?"

No, of course she hadn't. It had been an impulsive re-action to feeling all of her hopes and dreams for Ido slip-ping away. "I'll figure it out."

He let go of her arm. Her breath returned to normal.

"Let me know when you do. I want to make sure I play a convincing role." There it was, the tiny bit of bitterness she'd been expecting.

"It's not like you left me much of a choice." Even in the dark she could sense his glare, the weight of his disap-proval heavy enough to sit like a boulder on her shoulders.

He let out a frustrated breath. "I told you, I don't want to say anything about the import stuff until I figure out what's going on."

"I get it, really I do. But the deal with Swynton and your offer from Buck . . . it's too much. I don't know which side you're on anymore, Bodie."

The mattress shifted and she felt him stand next to her. "I'm on the right side. I would never do something shady to get ahead. You ought to know that about me by now."

She felt around for the lamp on the nightstand then flipped the switch, lighting up the room. Bodie stood, his arms crossed over his chest, the look in his eyes daring her to doubt him. She wanted to believe him, she really did. But a tiny sliver of doubt wedged its way in between her heart and her head. It would take more than his denial to show her he meant what he said.

"Can we talk about this later? I need to get home." What she meant to say was she needed to get away from him, from his broad shoulders and warm hands. She couldn't think straight in Bodie's bedroom. Heck, she couldn't think straight no matter where she was if he was anywhere near her.

"Yeah, go. Just make sure you let me know who I'm supposed to tell what and when." He ran a hand over the scruff on his chin, the scratch of fingers on whiskers mak-ing her want to crawl back into bed and let those strong arms wrap around her, shield her from all of the problems she had waiting for her.

"I'll put a spreadsheet together."

"A spreadsheet to track our fake engagement?" His brow furrowed.

She wanted to smooth out the lines creasing his forehead. If she was being honest with herself, she wanted to do a whole lot more than that. But denying herself was one of her superpowers—one she needed to employ more often if she wanted to keep her wits about her.

"Yes. Now that we're planning a wedding we'll need to figure out all the details. I'll also make note of who needs to know and what we tell them so we don't mess anything up. Why don't you get to work on those photos?"

"Yeah, okay." He followed her to the front door, pausing every time she stopped to scoop up a personal belonging. Seemed like her stuff had exploded all over Bodie's apartment. Her purse sat on the kitchen counter, her shoes had been kicked off and left on the living room floor.

"Oh, and you may as well keep the brisket." She turned on him as she reached the front door. "Seeing as how I can't fully enjoy it due to my massive IBS issues."

He snickered. "Hey, you were painting me out to be the world's worst poet. I had to strike back somehow."

"Touché." Her hand closed around the doorknob. "I'll be in touch, okay?"

"You got it."

As the door closed behind her she fought the temptation to fling it open again and bury herself in Bodie's arms. That's the only place she'd felt sheltered from the storm she'd created that now raged around her.

thirty-three

♡

Bodie sat back from the computer. He'd been doing research all morning on cigar importing, except for the breaks he took to look up engagement rings. Did Lacey know the going rate for a two-carat yellow diamond ranged from five grand to over two hundred thousand dollars? Probably. He'd gone from jewelry store websites to costume jewelry websites real quick. The ring he'd chosen should arrive by the end of the week, putting an end to the reporter wondering about the ring. Now he just had to hope she wasn't some certified gemologist who'd be able to spot a fake.

With the ring issue resolved, he still had to figure out a way to get some photos created. Why'd he have to go and give the name of Cattleman's? The ultraexclusive steak place didn't have any interior pictures on their website and he'd never actually been inside. Would Lacey be willing to take a day trip to Houston to snap a few images? If he couldn't figure out how to fake it, they just might have to.

The threat of someone discovering the fake engagement paled in comparison to the threat of finding out his dad and pops were into something much more sinister. As he scrolled down another web page, Shotgun sat up from where she'd been lying at his feet and whined.

"Need to go out, girl?" He patted her head, still not comfortable with the fact that she was going to be a mother. As an only child he'd never had to care for anyone or anything younger than him. Sure, they'd had kittens from the barn cats and an occasional calf or two but that fell under his grandfather's jurisdiction. Bodie might have helped a little bit but raising animals was typically left to the ranch hands.

He clipped Shotgun's leash onto her collar and led her out of the stuffy office. Shotgun sniffed along the mulched flower bed before heading toward the bushes on the side of the building. While he waited for her to do her business, his phone buzzed in his pocket.

Dad. The text wasn't really an invitation to lunch, it was more of a demand. Bodie hadn't talked to his dad or his pops since the blowout they'd had. His desire to keep his family safe battled with his need to get to the bottom of whatever asinine plan they had. It was time to come clean. If he wanted to be able to help them dig themselves out of the hole they'd fallen into, they'd have to trust him.

He was about to respond when a text from Lacey lit up the screen.

> We need to meet. Can you come to the funeral home at 3pm?

> The funeral home? About what?

> Spreadsheet's done. We need to sync schedules and I need to show you something.

Her and her damn spreadsheet. If he left soon he could chat with Dad and Pops and still have time to meet her by three. What could she possibly want to show him at the funeral home though? Knowing Lacey, it could be anything. The thought of her all decked out in white sent a cold shiver through him. She'd make a beautiful bride. Someday. For someone else.

What would Luke say when he found out about the phony wedding? If all went well, he never would. Bodie would follow Lacey's lead and let her figure out the plan. He had his hands full enough with his own family issues.

Twenty minutes later his dad greeted him as he walked into the office. "You said you needed to see me?"

Dad stood and walked around his desk. "I think it's about time we put this deal to bed, don't you?"

"I told you, I'm not going to fix the election. Now, why don't you come clean with me and tell me exactly what's been going on?"

"That won't be necessary." Mayor Little swiveled around in a chair, a thick cigar clenched between his teeth. "We've got some business to discuss."

"What's this?" Bodie spread his hands. "I told you, I'm not selling out to Swynton. I don't care about the sheriff's job. Just tell me what your involvement is in the cigar-smuggling ring. If all goes well I can use the info you give me as a bargaining chip and we can figure out who's at the top of the line."

"Deputy Phillips"—Mayor Little stood—"you may want to rethink your options."

Bodie's head shook from side to side. "I've made my decision. The cigar ring is going down."

"Even if it means taking your entire family with it?" Buck's eyes gleamed.

"Dad? Want to tell me exactly what your role is in this? Who are you working with?"

His father didn't speak but the look in his eyes said more than if he'd launched into a long-winded explanation.

Bodie turned his attention to Buck. "You seem to be running the show. Why don't you tell me exactly what's going on?"

"Oh, I will. But first we need to make sure you're not going to do anything with the information we share. A little insurance, if you will." Buck slid his phone out of his pocket.

"What's he talking about, Dad?"

"I didn't mean for it to come to this." Dad hung his head. Bodie had never seen him look so haunted, so wrung out, so low.

If he thought his dad and pops had been messing around, Bodie's mind was completely blown by the image staring back at him from Mayor Little's phone screen. Lacey stared into the camera, her eyes smudged with makeup from crying, her cheeks stained pink, probably from shock and embarrassment.

"Where did you get your hands on that?" Bodie asked.

"I happen to have a penchant for mug shots. You think the people of Idont—"

"She's changing the name to Ido," Bodie corrected.

"Doesn't matter. When the folks see their beloved mayor splashed across the front page of the paper they won't care what name she wanted to call the town. I can see it now." Buck lifted a hand and made his point by punching the air with his palm. "Small-town Texas mayor arrested for assaulting an officer."

Bodie's hands clenched into fists at his sides. He couldn't overreact. That would just fuel whatever fire Buck had started building. "What do you want?"

"I think you know, Son." Buck slid his phone back inside his linen blazer.

"Fine, the beavers are yours. Cigars, too. I'll go get them tonight and meet you wherever you want." He couldn't let Lacey take the fall for something his family had started, not even if he went down with them.

Buck waved the notion away like a pesky fly. "That's the least of it."

"Then what?" Bodie spread his arms wide, at a loss. Obviously Buck was in charge of whatever his dad and pops were involved in. What more could he want than the damn cigars?

Buck tapped his cigar against the ashtray on Bodie's dad's desk. "Find anything interesting while you were digging around in the yard the other night?"

Bodie's forehead creased and he rubbed at a knot in his shoulder as he tried to make sense of Buck's question. "I was filling in holes from the armadillos."

"You sure those critters are what made those holes?" Buck kicked his feet up on the edge of the desk, making it crystal clear who was running the show.

"You buried something in the yard, didn't you?" Bodie stepped forward and slammed his hand down on the desk. "You sick sonofabitch. There's something out there you can't get your hands on now, isn't there?"

Buck tapped a finger to his forehead as he cast a long look at Bodie's dad. "I knew you got the smarts in the family."

"What's out there?" Bodie crossed his arms over his chest, his patience for Buck's style of fun and games quickly dissipating.

"I want to make you an offer. You get me what I want and I don't leak your girlfriend's picture to the AP. Sound good?" Buck offered a hand.

Bodie ignored it. "I'm not willing to consider any kind of offer until you tell me everything."

"Your boy's got a backbone." Buck spit the words out toward Bodie's dad. "Turns out your pops didn't necessarily trust the local bank with his savings."

"What?" Bodie glanced to his dad. "What's he talking about?"

Finally, his dad shifted in his seat and a little bit of color returned to his face. "Pops was his own bank. He preferred to keep his cash right under his nose."

"You mean . . ."

"Yes. Your grandfather stashed pockets of cash all over the yard of the house. Figured with it being so close to the warehouse and under the town's protection that it would be a safe place to store it."

"And he can't go dig it up himself?" Bodie asked.

Dad shook his head. "He doesn't necessarily know we're going after it."

"Whoa." Bodie put his palms out. "There's no way I'm crossing Pops."

"Would it make a difference if I told you it's not his?" Dad asked. "He owes some very dangerous people quite a bit of cash."

"Then why won't he dig it up himself?" Bodie asked. Even though his pops might bend the law from time to time, his word was as good as gold. "Pops always honors his commitments."

"Not this time." Dad lowered his head. "Our customers lost patience with the disruption in service. Buck sent him up to Oklahoma to stall. But we're not going to have enough, not unless we make up the rest with the stash from the yard."

"You've got to be kidding me." Bodie wiped the back of his hand across his brow.

"Wish I was. Then we'd all be happy," Buck said. "I've agreed to help your grandfather out this time. But I still need to answer to my higher-ups. You get me fifty grand from the yard and I'll let your grandfather live. Oh, and keep little Lacey Cherish from gracing the front page of the paper."

Bodie slid his gaze from Buck to his dad. "Pops doesn't know about this?"

"He hasn't checked his stash in years," Dad said as he handed Bodie a creased piece of paper.

"What's this?" Bodie took it, recognizing his grandfather's chicken-scratch writing.

"A map. Just take some from each hole until you get what Buck needs. Pops will never know and we'll get him off the hook. Lacey, too."

"And then you'll leave everyone alone?" Bodie directed the question to Buck.

"You've got my word." Buck held two fingers up like he was making some sort of pledge.

Bodie regretted the words before he even uttered them, wishing he could take them back as they spilled from his mouth. "Fine, I'm in."

"Great. I realize this will take quite a bit of effort so I've decided to be generous. You've got a month. If I don't have that cash in hand by then you can kiss your pops and your mayor's future good-bye."

Bodie waited until Buck swaggered out the door until he turned on his father. "What the hell were you thinking? Do you have any idea what kind of position you've put me in?"

"Would have been a hell of a lot easier if you'd gotten us the damn beavers when we asked for them in the first place." Dad cradled his head in his hands.

Bodie's palm smacked the edge of the desk. "Would have been a hell of a lot easier if you'd been straight with me from the get-go."

Dad looked up, his eyes streaked with pink lines like he hadn't slept in days. The side of his face still held a greenish-purplish tinge. "I guess we both learned something from this experience."

Not wanting to justify that remark with any kind of a response, Bodie took a final, long look at his dad then folded up the treasure map and slid it into his back pocket.

His grandfather and father had sealed their own fate. But Lacey . . . she was only trying to do the right thing. He couldn't let her take the fall for something his family had done. He needed to come through for her on this, and sooner rather than later. Hopefully she'd never find out about it.

thirty-four

Lacey flipped through pictures of funeral wreaths. Some were shaped like horseshoes, some like hearts. Flowers in every color of the rainbow decorated the wire frames. That wasn't exactly what she had in mind when she'd set up the appointment to chat about flowers. Since Adeline canceled and took all of her vendors with her, Lacey would have to get creative when it came to finding people to help her with wedding plans if she wanted to keep the business local. They didn't have a local florist so she'd reached out to the only place in town that used flowers on a regular basis . . . the funeral home.

Bodie pushed through the door, his boots not making a sound on the plush carpet. He took the seat next to her in the front room. "Hey. Sorry I'm a few minutes late."

"That's okay. I was just looking through some of our options." She turned the photo album toward him so he could see. "I think I'm leaning toward the heart-shaped wreath with the *Holding You in Our Hearts* banner."

Bodie's eyes widened. "Really?"

"No, not really. But Suzy hasn't ever done a wedding, just a corsage or boutonniere for a dance or two so she didn't have any pictures to look at." Without thinking she set her hand on top of his in an effort to ease his concern.

"And you're sure you don't want to find a florist in Swynton or bring in someone else?"

She let her hand drop from his and leaned back in her chair. "If we're going to be wedding central we need to be able to offer all of the services a bride will need. Besides, Adeline booked everyone else for the same date. She's still mad at me about ruining her party. Suzy can handle it, I'm sure."

Speaking of Suzy, the front doors opened and the woman rushed in amid a whirlwind of flowers, papers, and bright red hair. Lacey and Bodie both made a move to help. Bodie grabbed a large wire easel dragging behind her while Lacey bent to pick up the papers strewn across the floor.

"I'm so sorry I'm late." Suzy bustled over to the coffee table and dumped the contents of her arms on the sparkling glass top. "I had a woodchuck to finish up."

Bodie tilted his head toward Lacey, a question in his eyes.

"Suzy works full-time for the taxidermist out on Highway 87." Lacey set the papers she'd gathered on the table before taking her seat again.

"How interesting," Bodie said. He moved the easel holding a wreath of fake orange roses closer to where the women sat.

"I usually only do flowers when someone dies," Suzy twittered. "My husband says I just can't get enough of being around stiffs."

Lacey's gaze flew to Bodie, who bit back a laugh. "Thanks so much for meeting with us."

"What's the occasion?" Suzy asked. "Are we talking cremation, closed casket or open? Jacinda does a great job on lips if you need someone to do the makeup. So lifelike, you'd hardly know they were dead."

"Um, we have another kind of event in mind," Lacey said. "We're not ready to go public quite yet"—she reached for Bodie's hand—"but Bodie and I are engaged."

Suzy stood stock-still, her mouth agape. For a split second Lacey wondered if her news had given the poor woman a heart attack.

"We were hoping you'd be able to do flowers for the wedding." Bodie squeezed Lacey's hand, infusing her with a jolt of confidence.

"Suzy?" Lacey prodded.

"Well, hell's bells. A wedding. The two of you?" Suzy moved her pointer finger from Lacey to Bodie and back again.

"Yes." Lacey cleared her throat and summoned a smile. Breaking the news wasn't quite as hard as she thought it would be. At least this time. "We're planning a wedding for the middle of May at the Phillips House. I'm sure you've heard it's being restored and reopening as an event center?"

Suzy laced her hands over her belly and giggled. "I sure did. What a crackpot idea."

Lacey's pulse twinged against her temple. "Since the import business closed its doors, we're hoping the event center will create jobs for all of the workers who have been displaced."

"Oh." A slight burp escaped through Suzy's orange-painted lips. "Excuse me."

"Will you help us?" Bodie leaned in. "With the flowers? Lacey's trying to build up the town, put us on the map, and give everyone something to work toward together."

"I see." Suzy flipped through the stack of papers on the table. "I haven't done a wedding before. Closest thing I've ever done was a double funeral for a couple of married teacup poodles. I have pictures here somewhere."

Bodie scooted forward in his chair. "Did you just say married pood—"

"We'd love to see them," Lacey interrupted.

While Suzy searched for the photos, Bodie cleared his throat. "We're trying to keep this quiet for now so we'd appreciate your discretion."

"Oh, don't you worry about that." Suzy waved a hand in the air as she set a color-printed sheet on top of the stack. A small bouquet sat on top of a tiny casket. Miniature white roses were strewn around the edges, caught up with clusters of ribbons and netting. "They were so small they put them in one together."

"That's just lovely." Lacey gave Bodie's hand a squeeze. "Isn't it lovely, sugar bum?"

"Sure is. I've never seen anything like it."

Lacey could tell by the wide eyes he was telling the truth. She'd never seen or heard of anything like it, either. But with time running short and no other option, she swallowed any doubts and thrust her hand at Suzy. "You're hired."

"But you haven't seen all of my pictures. I've got a great one here somewhere of a float I did for the funeral home for the county fair a few years back." Papers fell to the floor as she shuffled through.

"It's okay, I've seen enough to know you're the one for us." Lacey pumped Suzy's hand up and down. "We're thinking something pretty simple. Do you have any suggestions?"

Suzy glanced from Lacey to Bodie and back again. "Well, if the wedding is in May you know tulips will be in season. I could do a bouquet of tulips with some accents of freesia."

"I love it." Lacey glanced at Bodie. "Anything to add?"

He shook his head. "No, this is your big day, Sweets. I want it to be everything you've ever dreamed of."

Lacey furrowed her brow. He was being awfully accommodating. She knew him well enough to know that could mean only one of two things: either he truly didn't give a rat's ass about what kind of flowers they had at their fake wedding, or he was going along because he wanted something.

With her pen flying over her notepad, Suzy counted aloud. "Two dozen, no, probably need three for the bridal bouquet. How many bridesmaids?"

"Oh." How had she missed that question on the quick wedding-planning checklist she'd downloaded from the Internet? Who would she ask to stand next to her? The only person who came to mind was Zina, and she'd probably pitch a fit when she heard the news. "Probably just one."

"Who?" Bodie asked.

"I was thinking of asking Zina." Lacey picked at a ragged cuticle. "Are you planning on having anyone stand up next to you?"

"I hadn't really thought about it."

"Well, now's the time. You'll need a best man, won't you?"

"Just a best man or will you have groomsmen, too?" Suzy nibbled on the end of her pen. "And ushers? I suppose I didn't ask about all of the details. Where's the ceremony going to be?"

"Inside the house," Bodie said.

At the same time Lacey blurted, "Outside on the lawn."

"Oh, an outdoor wedding?" Suzy looked back and forth between them. "May can be a fairly unpredictable month for weather."

"I don't think everyone will fit inside for the ceremony." Lacey fluttered her lashes at Bodie. "Don't you think we should have the reception inside and keep the ceremony outdoors?"

"How many people will you be inviting?" Suzy's pen poised over the paper.

"Yes, just how many guests do you think we'll have?" Bodie leaned toward her. "How many people need to witness this production?"

Lacey cleared her throat. "It's going to be on the small side. But we will have coverage from the *Texas Times*. That's a magazine and they're doing a big spread about the wedding and the preparations."

"Oh, I do love being featured in magazines. I'll make sure I put some extra Suzy magic into your flowers." She leaned over and patted Bodie's knee. "You know I was a centerfold once."

Bodie glanced to Lacey with a *where in the hell did you dig this woman up?* look on his face.

"Really?" Lacey asked. "That must have been quite a moment."

"It was. My dad was so proud when I showed him. He took that issue to work and passed it around the lunchroom for a week. I still get a chuckle when I think about that."

Bodie coughed, covering his mouth up with his fist.

"I think I have a copy of it with me." Suzy rummaged through her pile. "Oh, here it is."

Lacey closed her eyes. This was too much. She'd put all of her hope into the people of Ido and they just couldn't hack it. Maybe they weren't ready for the event center. She'd forced it on them when all they wanted was to go about their business, stuff woodchucks, and pose for whatever magazine centerfolds that moved them.

"Suzy, I—"

"This is really something," Bodie said.

A pang of something akin to jealousy—if she'd been the jealous type—sliced through her chest. Lacey opened her eyes to find Bodie holding a copy of *Taxidermist Today*.

"Check it out." He flipped the magazine so she could

see the centerfold—a picture of Suzy surrounded by stuffed woodland creatures.

"Wow." A gurgle rose in her throat. Hopefully Suzy would keep her animal friends away from the wedding setup.

"So did you decide on ushers? Are we sticking with a maid of honor and no best man?" Suzy drummed her fingertips on the barrel of the pen.

"Can we get back to you on that?" Lacey asked. She and Bodie had to hash out the details if they wanted to present a united front to the other vendors.

"Absolutely. Just let me know when you've made up your mind. I usually have Tuesday and Thursday mornings off. Sometimes a Friday, too." She gathered her papers. "Y'all can go ahead and keep the wreath if you want."

Bodie put his hand to his forehead and leaned onto his elbow like he was trying not to laugh.

"That's very generous of you, but are you sure you don't need it for a . . ." For a what? A client? How would one refer to a dead person in this particular situation?

"Nope, this one was a loaner. It's been around enough that people are starting to recognize it. I need to make up a new one."

"What do you mean 'it's been around'?" Bodie asked.

She stood, closing her notebook and hiking her purse strap onto her shoulder. "I mean I loan it out for wakes and funerals. Half the town has seen this one though. Time for something fresh and new."

"Thank you." Lacey stood. The sooner she could get Suzy out of here, the less likely it would be that Bodie would insult the only florist available. "We'll be in touch."

"Congratulations on your engagement. I sure can't wait to tell my sister. She'll get a kick out of—"

"Remember, it's a secret." Lacey put her pointer finger to her lip. "Shh, okay?"

Suzy smiled, nodded, and winked before she disappeared through the front doors.

"How long until she spills the beans?" Bodie asked.

At that moment both of their cell phones rang. "Not long."

thirty-five

Bodie took a long draw on his beer. He'd called in sick to work today to hide out in the relative privacy of his own living room. After Suzy left the funeral home yesterday, his phone had continued to ring until he'd finally silenced it by turning the damn thing off. How was he to know that agreeing to the wedding charade with Lacey would mean instant notoriety?

A knock sounded at his door. Suspect of everyone and everything, he tiptoed to the door to peer through the peephole. Lacey stood on the stoop, the giant orange wreath in hand.

"I'm not home."

"Hurry up, someone's pulling up to the curb and I don't recognize them." Lacey tried the knob.

Bodie peeked again. Sure enough, a white van had stopped at the curb. The driver got out and opened the side door. "It's probably someone delivering a package to a neighbor. I need an evening off of wedding planning."

"He's coming this way," she hissed at the door.

"Fine." He fumbled with the lock, opening the door to Lacey and the giant orange wreath as the man reached the stoop.

"Bodie Phillips?" the driver asked.

"Who wants to know?" He tipped his beer up and downed another sip.

The guy launched into song. "Congratulations to you! Congratulations to you! Congratulations, Bodie and Lacey! Congratulations to you!"

"That's it?" Bodie cocked a hip. What kind of stunt was that?

"And a cookie couplet for the happy couple." The guy produced a cookie in the shape of a heart. Red frosting across the center read *Congrats on your engagement! Mayor Little.*

Dammit. Buck was mocking him.

"Why would Mayor Little send us a singing telegram?" Lacey asked.

"I'm sorry, it's not a telegram, it's a sing-a-gram," the man corrected. He didn't move from the stoop.

Bodie grabbed the cookie and shut the door.

"Didn't you tip him?" Lacey asked.

"For what?" Bodie shook his head. "I've owned dogs who could sing better than that." To prove his point, Shotgun sat down, her tail wagging like a broom, and let out a half howl. "See?"

"Why aren't you answering my calls?" Lacey barreled into the room, toting the ugly orange wreath with her.

"Do you have to bring that here?" He eyed the monstrosity. It was like a giant jack-o'-lantern but seven months too early.

"Why didn't you answer my question?" She set the easel in the corner of his living room, blocking his view of the classic football game he'd been watching.

"What was the question again?" He smirked. At least

he still enjoyed giving her shit, even though he couldn't leave his house without being assaulted by well-wishers.

Lacey snagged the beer bottle out of his grip. Didn't matter, it was almost empty anyway. "What's going on with you? You said you were all in on this and you're practically ghosting me."

He padded to the kitchen on bare feet to grab another beer from the fridge. Based on how the conversation was going, he might need two. He pulled out another and popped the top.

"Bodie?" She'd followed him into the kitchen and stood next to the counter, her hip cocked, arms crossed over her chest.

He handed her the beer he'd just opened and popped the top off the other. "I didn't realize what a splash news of our engagement would make." He made air quotes around the word *engagement*.

"I told my dad." Lacey took a deep swallow from the bottle.

Bodie's heart stalled. "You told him the truth?"

She shook her head. "No. You know what a big mouth he has when he drinks, even if he is housebound. I figured it would be best to string him along like everyone else until the wedding. If word got out that this wasn't for real we'd probably lose the publicity, don't you think?"

No, he didn't think. He hadn't thought this through at all. Playing along with Lacey's idea to secure publicity seemed like a no-brainer at the time. But now that he was living through the repercussions, he'd begun to regret being so flippant about it in the first place.

"Everyone seems really excited for us." Her lips curved up in a smile.

"That's fantastic." He wanted to kick himself in the nuts for the way the bitterness in his tone caused her mouth to turn down until that smile had morphed into an unsure frown.

"I talked to Helmut today. He said he'll do the catering." She set her bottle down on the edge of the table.

"Banzai Shakes for everyone," he joked.

"You know, he hasn't been slinging burgers his whole life. He used to be a real chef up in Seattle once upon a time."

Bodie knew he was being an asshole. And he really didn't intend to be. It was just, all this hubbub with Lacey on top of the threats from Buck, it had been rolling around like a tumbleweed in west Texas, gathering momentum, picking up dirt and dust and getting bigger and bigger. "I'm sure the food will be terrific. Thanks for handling everything." He tipped his beer in her direction then headed back to the living room.

"Bodie . . ." She trailed behind him, reminding him of yesteryear, of times he'd walk away from her just like that and she'd follow behind. Even then she hadn't given up on him.

"What do you want?" He whirled around, almost knocking her off her feet.

Her hands wrapped around his biceps to steady herself. Taking in a long, slow breath, he raised his gaze to meet hers.

She worried her lower lip with her teeth, her fingers tightening around his arms. "I know you didn't want to pretend. I'm sorry for asking you to lie about it." Her words came out soft, almost a whisper.

Dammit. How could he tell her how right she was? He didn't want to pretend. But it didn't piss him off, it scared the shit out of him. He didn't want to pretend anymore because the feelings he'd been faking had become all too real. What was he going to do when the fake minister pronounced them husband and wife and he had to lean down and kiss her?

"Don't you dare apologize. I went into this with my eyes wide open. I just wasn't expecting so many people to be so interested in us."

The radio switched from a commercial to a slow song, one of his favorite classic country tunes. Lacey took the beer bottle from his hand and set it down on the coffee table. "May as well start practicing our first dance. Will you dance with me?"

His throat seemed to close, making it difficult to take in a full breath. "I'm not a very good dancer."

"It's okay, neither am I." She nestled herself against his chest, putting one hand on his shoulder. "Just take my hand and I'll follow your lead."

Against his better judgment, he slid his hand into hers and pulled her into his arms. She stepped forward, burrowing even closer into him. The scent of butterscotch surrounded him, even though he hadn't seen her eat a butterscotch candy in years. She had to be able to feel his heart—it seemed like it was going to beat its way right out of his chest. If Lacey noticed his strange behavior, she didn't say anything about it. After an awkward start, he caught on to the rhythm of the song and guided her around his small living room in a halfway decent dance.

"You're not so bad," she said as he twirled her away from him. "Lots of practice?"

He shook his head. "Nah. Just a natural, I guess."

"What's that like?" She batted long, dark eyelashes at him, her eyes twinkling.

"What?"

"To be a natural at something? Seems I have to fight tooth and nail to figure things out. Just once I wish something would come natural to me."

He drew her tight against his chest, wrapping both arms around her. "Hell, Lacey, I'd say you've got a lot of natural talent."

"Yeah, I'm a walking natural disaster." She ducked her head, a self-deprecating smile on her lips.

"Stop." His tone came out sharper than he intended,

making her look up. "You've got more natural talent in your pinky finger than I do in my entire body."

Her gaze raked over him. His blood heated, sending warmth coursing through his veins. "Is that so? Why do people always bring up the pinky finger?"

"Fine. How about I say you've got more natural talent in your big toe?"

"My big toe?" Her forehead creased. "I didn't think you were a foot man."

He wasn't. Or at least he never had been before. But with Lacey he was an everything man—from her toes to the tips of her hair, and everything in between.

"Feet are underrated," he joked. Especially Lacey's feet. He loved how she kept her toenails painted, usually a bright shade of pink. He'd never been particularly drawn to feet before, but he could imagine himself doing all kinds of things to Lacey's toes.

"Don't tell me you've developed a foot fetish." She rested her cheek against his chest as one song led into another.

"No." He didn't have a foot fetish. He had a Lacey Cherish fetish and that was ten million times worse. What was he going to do when it was all over? When she didn't have a reason to come knocking on his door on a Tuesday night? When she moved on to dance with some stranger in another living room? His gut clenched at the idea of Lacey wrapped up in someone else's arms.

He was being ridiculous, he knew that. And why couldn't they have a shot at a real future? There was nothing holding them back. They were both adults, both consenting, contributing members of society.

He'd almost convinced himself it would be no big deal to dip his head down and claim her mouth with his. They'd acted on desire before and in his own humble opinion, neither were the worse because of it.

"Hey, Lacey?"

"Mmm?" She lifted her head from his chest. The imprint of his button pressed into her cheek, reminding him of the time he and Luke had dared her she couldn't stay up and watch the entire *Star Wars* saga with them. She'd fallen asleep with her cheek on the zipper of her sleeping bag. Luke teased her about it for days.

"Nothing." Reality check. Luke. Luke was the reason he couldn't jump into a fling with Lacey. That and he didn't want to put her in any danger. Once his dad and pops were out from under the threat they'd been fighting, once he had a chance to run this by Luke, once he knew for sure he wouldn't lose his heart in the process—then he'd give in and see where this might go.

Until then, he needed to keep his head in the game and his heart completely out of it.

thirty-six

———❤———

"You want how much?" Lacey squinted at Helmut from across the counter.

He flipped another burger patty with one hand while he juggled the fries in the deep fryer with another. "Two thousand bucks. It's a family recipe."

"That's ridiculous. Our entire wedding budget is only five thousand dollars. I can't afford to spend forty percent of that on the cake."

"It's good cake." Helmut plated a Banzai Burger Special while she performed math acrobatics in her head.

"I don't care how good the cake is, I don't have an extra two grand. Now, will you make the cake or do I need to work with someone else?"

Helmut wiped his hands on his apron before settling his meaty paws on his hips. "Who else will you find to make you a cake?"

Lacey matched his stance. She'd had just about enough of the local vendors trying to rake her over the coals and price-gouge her. Didn't they know she was doing this for their own good? "I'll check with my good friend, Betty Crocker."

He smirked as he waved her off. "Good luck."

"I'll make you a cake." Jojo stopped at the counter to clip an order ticket on the spinning rack. "What's the occasion?"

Lacey inhaled a deep breath through her nose. The smell of fried onions assaulted her. "It's a wedding."

"Oh, I love weddings." Jojo clapped her hands together. "Anyone I know?"

Enthusiasm. Lacey could work with enthusiasm. "It's actually, well, it's me."

"What?" Jojo grabbed Lacey's hands in hers and squeezed. Then she flipped Lacey's left hand over. "Where's the ring? Who's the groom? When's the date?"

"You ask too many questions." Helmut set two burger plates in the serving window and chimed the bell. "Order up."

"I'll fill you in later," Lacey promised. "But really, you can make a cake?"

"I did one for my cousin's best friend's grandma's birthday a few years ago. Ain't nothin' but a little baking. And you know how much I love baking."

"Yeah, we all know." Helmut waved them off. "Food's getting cold."

"Later," Lacey said. Then she grabbed the two Burger Banzai platters and delivered them to the couple she didn't recognize sitting at table four.

Jojo hunted her down after the lunch rush. "So about this cake. How many people does it need to feed?"

Lacey had just sat down in a back booth to work her way through her club salad. It was a lot more lettuce and a lot less of "club" anything but she'd always been grateful for the free meals Helmut offered, especially when she was a starving college student home on break. Of course, now she was a starving mayor who had the future of an entire town resting on her shoulders. It might take more than a club salad to fuel her efforts.

"What's the scoop? Tell me everything. Where did y'all meet? What's he look like?" Jojo slid into the booth opposite her with an expectant grin on her face.

Lacey toyed with her straw. "Well, you actually know him."

"I do? Who is he?"

"Bodie Phillips." Lacey sighed as she kept her gaze trained on the contents of her glass. Bubbles floated to the top then burst, kind of like how the bubbles in the pit of her stomach felt as she waited for a reaction from Jojo.

"You're getting married to Deputy Phillips?" Jojo leaned back, slumping against the back of the booth. "He's a hottie, that's for sure. But really? I haven't seen the two of you so much as smile at each other without one of you getting mad enough to chew up nails and spit out a barbed wire fence. What's going on?"

Jojo's reaction didn't surprise Lacey. She'd been waiting for someone to call her out and point out the obvious— that she and Bodie went together like whipped cream and cow patties. Now she had two choices: give Jojo her most convincing story or admit everything was a farce and hope her friend wouldn't sell her out. As she contemplated which way to go, the bell over the door jangled.

Lacey glanced to the front of the restaurant. "I'll get this one."

"Go ahead. Then come back here and tell me all about your sordid secret love affair with the good deputy." She pulled the latest issue of her women's magazine out of her purse.

Before she had a chance to stand, Bodie stopped at their booth, leaned down, and planted a kiss on Lacey's cheek. "Hi there."

She pulled back in surprise as he sat down next to her.

Jojo's eyes just about bugged out of her head at the sight of Ido's most eligible law enforcement officer.

"Jojo." He nodded at her.

"Deputy." She nodded right back.

"How's my girl today?" Bodie slid an arm over Lacey's shoulders and dangit if her bra didn't immediately feel just a little too tight.

"Lacey just told me the good news," Jojo stammered.

"Is that right, bubblewubble?" He nudged his nose into Lacey's ear, whispering, "The engagement, right?"

She nodded. As if there were something else newsworthy to share. "Jojo and I were about to start talking about the cake. She offered to make us one after Helmut tried to charge me two grand."

"For a cake?" Bodie asked. "Better be frosted in solid gold for that amount of money."

Jojo cleared her throat. "About the frosting."

"Yes?" Bodie and Lacey turned to her at the same time, speaking in unison.

"I can make you a cake that'll melt in your mouth but I can't frost worth a damn." She screwed her mouth into a frown. "We'll have to find someone else to pitch in on that part."

Bodie cocked his head. "So you'll make the cake?"

"Oh, absolutely." Jojo nodded, her earrings bobbing up and down along with her head.

"But we need to find someone else to put the frosting on? Isn't adding frosting part of making a cake a cake?" A line appeared, bisecting his forehead.

"I didn't say I could frost a cake, only that I could bake one. If y'all want to find someone else—"

"No." Lacey reached across the table to latch on to Jojo's wrist. "I appreciate your willingness to pitch in. I'll find someone to do the rest."

"Okay then." Jojo lowered herself back onto the red vinyl bench. "Now, how many people do we need to serve?"

"I don't know." Lacey let go of Jojo and shook her head. "I still don't have a final list. Bodie, can you get me your guest list ASAP?"

"I'll do it now. My mom, my dad, and my pops." He held up three fingers.

"That's it?" Lacey frowned.

"Hell yeah, that's it. I don't want the whole town witnessing the show."

Jojo's eyes narrowed. What was Bodie doing? He was about to give up the whole secret.

"Look, I know you're nervous about things, sweetums, but we're all friends here." She scooted closer to him on the booth as she leaned across the table toward Jojo and lowered her voice. "He's so sensitive. You wouldn't know it by looking at him, but he's like a big cream puff inside."

"Mmm." Jojo clasped her hands together.

She wasn't buying it. Bodie needed to get with the program or the entire engagement would be blasted as a fake. She snaked a hand up around his neck and pulled his head down. At first he resisted. She leaned up and murmured against his ear, "You're blowing our cover."

He turned his torso to face her, a glint of challenge in his eyes. "I'm sorry, cinnamon bun, you're right, I do get shy about us. But that's going to change, I promise." Then he wrapped his arms around her shoulders, angled his head, and pulled her into his chest. His lips sought hers, playing along the seam of her mouth until she opened for him. His tongue dipped inside. He tasted like coffee and something sweet . . . doughnuts, maybe. Her hands instinctively tangled in the hair at the base of his neck. She forgot she was sitting in a back booth at the Burger Bonanza. Forgot Jojo sat across from them, taking everything in. Forgot her own damn name as the sensations she'd been dreaming about since the last time he'd kissed her rocketed through her system.

He took the kiss deeper, angling her head back, cradling her skull in his large, capable hand. She pressed her fingers into his shoulders, drawing him closer as she tried to think of one good reason not to climb onto his lap.

"Ahem." Something clunked against the table. "Ahem." Jojo cleared her throat again.

Lacey broke away from Bodie's lips. Dazed, she glanced around, forgetting for a moment exactly where she was, exactly who she was.

Jojo pulled her shirt away from her body with one hand as she fanned herself with the other. "I take it back. Y'all seem evenly matched." Then she got up from the table. "Break's over. I'll roll the silverware if you bus tables."

Lacey nodded, waiting for Jojo to move beyond earshot. Then she glanced up at Bodie and wiped a smudge of pink lip gloss from the corner of his mouth. "Thanks, that was very convincing."

"Yeah." His finger traced the spot where hers had been. "That's what we're after . . . convincing, right?"

She nudged him with her shoulder. "I've got to get back to work. Did you stop by for something?" Something beyond laying a deep, earth-shattering kiss on her? One she'd be feeling for days?

"Yeah, uh, I talked to one of my pals from high school who owns his own carpentry business. He said he'd build us a thing to stand under when we take our fake vows." His fingers drummed on the table. "What's it called? Not a gazebo, but . . ."

"An arbor?" She waited for an answer, keyed up at the idea of one of her childhood dreams coming true. She'd always wanted to stand under an arbor with the sun setting behind her and her groom.

"Yeah, that. I saw that picture in your file and figured if we were having it outside it might make a nice backdrop."

Before she thought better of it, she reached a hand out and cupped his cheek. "Thanks, Bodie. I think that'll be beautiful."

His face flushed, just a teeny tiny tinge of pink. Enough to let her know he'd put thought into this.

"Well, I've got to go. There's a report on that pit bull ring that came in this morning. I think they're setting up another fight, close this time."

Her lungs seized. "Where?"

"Don't know yet. Maybe over in Springer. I'd love to find those jerks and take the whole thing down." His jaw clenched as he talked about it.

"You be careful. If there's money involved, those horrible people are going to do what they can to protect their investment."

"Don't worry, I won't leave you standing at the altar, Sweets." He tipped his hat as he scooted out of the booth and held out a hand to help her.

"Just watch yourself." She stood in front of him, not sure how to close the conversation. They were going more and more public with their fake engagement. People might expect them to be a little more affectionate toward each other. Thinking of what Jojo said, that she and Bodie didn't seem like they were in love, made her pull him against her for a hug.

"What's that for?" he asked, mumbling into her hair as his arms surrounded her.

"We've got to make people think we're really in love." She squeezed him tighter then let him go.

He nodded. "I see. In that case, I'll pick you up at seven tonight."

"For what?" What in the world could Bodie be planning? The cocky tilt of his lips gave nothing away.

"Date night. Isn't that what couples do?" He began to move toward the door, walking backward so she could still see the smug expression on his face.

"All right, then. Seven o'clock," she agreed.

"And wear something sexy." Then he ducked through the front door and was gone.

thirty-seven

Bodie fiddled with his tie, wondering if he'd made a mistake. Maybe he should have just handed Lacey the fake ring he'd picked up. But she wanted a public splash so he might as well make it a memorable moment for whoever happened to be there tonight.

He cut the engine and walked up the sidewalk to the Cherish home, a knot of nerves tightening in his gut. Everything had happened so fast—the engagement, the wedding plans. He hadn't had a chance to follow up with Lacey's dad to make sure he was on board with the whole idea. Surely Lacey had broken down and told him about the ruse. She must have. Otherwise he would have heard something from her dad or worse—something from Luke—by now.

He'd barely raised his hand to knock when Mr. Cherish opened the door. The man used to keep a clean-shaven chin but several months of house arrest seemed to sap the desire to keep up appearances right out of him. He stood in the doorway in ratty sweatpants, a stained T-shirt, and a pair of well-worn slippers.

"I wondered when you'd have the balls to show up around here." Mr. Cherish opened the door wide, motioning for Bodie to come in.

"Mr. Cherish, let me explain." He'd confronted hardened criminals with more confidence than he felt facing Lacey's dad.

"I wish someone would tell me what the hell is going on." He crossed his arms over his chest and pulled himself up to his full five feet ten inches, several inches shy of Bodie's six foot three.

"There you are. Ready?" Lacey spun into the room in a red dress that fluttered around her legs, drawing his attention to her slim waist, the low cut of the neckline, and bare arms. "Let me just grab my coat."

"Where do you think the two of you are off to?" Mr. Cherish stepped between Lacey and the closet, preventing her from passing.

"Date night, Dad. Bodie's taking me out . . . somewhere. Where are we going?" She glanced up at him, expectant.

"Dinner. That new place out past Swynton." Somehow, under the weight of both of their stares, he'd forgotten the name of the place where he'd spent the afternoon, making sure everything was ready for their big night.

"Suddenly you're a big spender?" Mr. Cherish asked. "Anything else you want to tell me, Son?" He practically spit out the word *son*, definitely intending it as an insult as opposed to an endearment.

"Lacey? You've talked to your father about this, haven't you?" Bodie asked, his gaze bouncing back and forth between them.

She sighed. "Yes and no."

"Meaning?" Bodie inched closer, waiting for her to reassure him that her dad wasn't about to go grab his twelve-gauge and take matters into his own hands.

"I told him our good news." She linked her arm through his. "About the engagement."

"And?" Bodie prompted.

"Fine. I didn't want to say anything because I'm terrified this is going to come back to bite us in the ass."

"Go on," her dad said, gesturing for them to sit down on a barstool at the kitchen counter.

"Bodie and I are faking the wedding so we can get some media coverage." The words tumbled out of her mouth as she slumped onto a stool.

Her dad's forehead creased. He opened his mouth like he wanted to ask a question then snapped it closed again.

"I know, it's ridiculous." Lacey waved her arms around her head. "But you once told me you wished you'd done more, tried harder, to make this into the kind of place you wanted to raise your kids. I took that to heart, Dad. If I have a way I can save the town, I have to try."

"Lacey, honey." Her dad took the stool next to her. "I didn't mean sacrificing your happiness, your own future."

Bodie rolled his eyes. "You're not suggesting that marrying me would be the worst kind of fate available to her, are you?"

Lacey stifled a laugh. "What are my other choices?"

Her dad reached for her hands. "Your willingness to put the town first, to put everyone's needs in front of your own is admirable."

She nodded, her gaze trained on their hands. Feeling like a total third wheel, Bodie put a hand on her shoulder. "I agree with your dad on this one."

"But it's not necessary. I know you've got your heart set on turning the tide for Idont."

"It's Ido now, Dad. I found out today the motion passed and the vote made it official." She lifted her head, the glint of a tear flashing in the corner of her eye. "When I decided to run for mayor I made a promise to myself. That I'd do whatever it took to make Ido a better place. Now's my chance. The town needs something to look forward to, something to put their faith in. The wedding venue could be it. They just need to see it in action."

"I hope you're right about this." Mr. Cherish gave her hands a squeeze then hopped off the stool. "Bodie, for what it's worth, thanks for doing your part."

He nodded. "You're welcome, sir."

A firm hand landed on his shoulder and Bodie looked into the unforgiving eyes of Lacey's dad. "Just make sure the fake engagement stays fake. No funny business."

"Yes, sir."

"You've got to keep this a secret, Dad. You can't tell anyone," Lacey said.

"Who would I tell?" Her dad gestured around the house. "The only person I see on a daily basis is you."

"Luke." Lacey lowered her head. "You can't tell Luke a thing. Not until it's over and the magazine article has been published. Promise?"

"What would he do, hop on a transport and fly home to break his best friend's nose?" her dad joked.

Bodie nodded to himself. That sounded exactly like something Luke might do if he thought Bodie was taking advantage of his baby sister. Better to set the record straight before word got around. "Maybe we should tell him—"

"No." Lacey whirled on him. "Absolutely not."

"Okay." Bodie shrugged. "It's your show. Now, come on, Act One is about to start and I need my leading lady."

With a question in her eyes, she took the hand he offered. "Do I even want to know?"

He grinned as he shook his head. "There ought to be some surprises, don't you think?"

Less than thirty minutes later they'd been seated at the table he'd picked out at the exclusive new restaurant on the other side of Swynton. It wasn't Cattleman's, but it would do. Based on the few pictures he'd finally managed to find of the interior of the swanky restaurant in downtown Houston, he figured he could make it look similar enough that no one would be able to tell the difference.

"Wow, you're certainly going all out," Lacey said as she placed the cloth napkin in her lap.

"Nothing but the best for my fiancée." He raised his water glass in her direction before taking a sip.

The corners of her mouth tipped up. The sadness from earlier was gone, replaced by a casual comfortableness. But there was nothing low-key about the dress she had on. He'd been trying not to notice how it clung to her curves, leaving little to the imagination. Having had his hands and his mouth all over every inch of her already, his imagination didn't have to do much work anyway to picture the creamy skin the dress barely covered.

Lacey picked up the menu. "Have you been here before?"

"Just once." He reached for the wine list. Maybe a bottle of something decadent and red would set the mood. He scanned the list. Or possibly a sparkling would be more in line with the tone he wanted to set for the evening. "Do you have a preference on wine tonight?"

She lifted a shoulder. "Surprise me. That's your goal, right?"

Sparkling, he decided. Something effervescent to add a little bubbly to the evening. "Is that a challenge?"

"Sure. Take it how you will." She looked around the restaurant, probably trying to see if there was anyone she recognized, or worse, someone who might recognize her.

"Challenge accepted." They should be somewhat hidden from prying eyes. He'd made sure of it when he stopped by earlier to pick the table and make arrangements with the waitstaff.

By the time they placed their order and the wine had been delivered to their table, Lacey appeared to relax even more. The candlelight played off her skin, making her red lips look even redder and her skin appear even smoother than he already knew it to be. He had to keep reminding himself that this was all part of her plan, not some form of foreplay. He'd be taking her back to her place after and dropping her off with her dad. There would be no repeat of the night they shared. Or the morning after.

Lacey kept up her side of the conversation during dinner, chatting about the decisions they still had to make for the wedding. He had no idea there were so many details to consider. What color bow tie did he want? He didn't care. Did he have a preference on which song they'd have their first dance to? Whatever she wanted. It's not like this would count.

He was happy to leave all of the planning up to her. All he wanted to do was show up and get it over with. Then maybe he could go back to thinking of Lacey as nothing more than a coworker. He'd already passed the point of not being able to think of her as a little sister. That ended the first time they kissed. There was no going back to the way things used to be. Not since he'd felt how magical it was to be inside her.

The waiter came to clear their plates. Bodie sat up straighter, his heart picking up the tempo. This was the part of the evening he was most concerned about. When the waiter asked if they'd like to see the dessert tray, he furrowed his brow. He'd made arrangements earlier for the special dessert—flan with a side of a yellow cubic zirconia engagement ring. Even though the whole engagement was fake, he wanted her to be surprised enough to get a few realistic photos.

Lacey looked to him for guidance. "What do you say? We could split a piece of that giant chocolate cake I saw on display when we came in."

"What?" Bodie had been craning his neck, trying to find the maître d' he'd spoken with earlier.

"Chocolate cake." Lacey reached across the table and put her hand on his. "You okay? You seem a little distracted."

He shook his head, trying to dislodge the feeling that something had gone wrong. "Yeah, chocolate cake sounds great."

The waiter nodded then disappeared with their plates.

"Can you excuse me for a minute?" Bodie asked.

"Sure." Lacey let her hand fall away. "This has been a really nice night. Thanks."

"Mmm-hmm." He pushed back from the table, intent on finding out what had happened to his engagement flan and, more important, where his fake engagement ring had gone.

thirty-eight

Lacey stared down at the flan the waiter set in front of her. "Oh, we ordered cake."

"It's flan, ma'am." He slid it to the middle of the table and produced two spoons.

"I see that it's flan. But we ordered chocolate cake." She tilted her head, wondering how an order of chocolate cake could turn to flan in the space of a few minutes.

"I'll check on that." He nodded his head as he turned to go.

"Wait." Lacey took the plate holding the flan with one hand. "Why don't you take this with you?"

"I'd prefer to leave it on the table if you don't mind." He gave her a forced smile.

"I do mind. We ordered chocolate cake." She put both hands on the plate and thrust it toward him.

"As you wish." He took the plate and turned toward the kitchen, disappearing through the door as Bodie approached from the other direction.

"Sorry about that." Bodie slid back into the seat across from her. "Had to sort something out."

"Is everything okay?" she asked.

"Yeah, it's fine. More wine?" He didn't wait for her to reply before he topped off her glass.

"You sure you're okay?" She took a small sip.

"Oh, absolutely." But the way he ran a finger around the inside of his collar told her otherwise. Something had him rattled, she could tell by the way he tapped his fingertips on the white tablecloth. Bodie had never been a tapper. But if he wanted to pretend all was cool, she wouldn't push the issue.

A giant slice of chocolate cake materialized in front of her. The waiter slid it onto the table along with two forks. "Your chocolate cake."

"But . . ." Bodie looked around like he expected the waiter to pull another slice out of thin air. "Where's the flan?"

"We ordered chocolate cake," Lacey said. "I sent the flan back."

"You what?" He stood from the table, towering over the waiter, who seemed to shrink under Bodie's heated glare.

"The lady refused the flan, sir. I returned it to the kitchen."

Bodie took a fork and dug it into the middle of the cake. Chocolate crumbs flew everywhere.

"What are you doing? Have you lost your mind?" Lacey pushed back from the table as Bodie massacred the cake. Chocolate frosting splattered over their wineglasses and covered his fingers.

Finally, he turned his gaze on her. "The flan. Our engagement story? I was going to get pictures tonight."

She put her hand to her forehead. That's what this was all about? He was trying to surprise her with a fake proposal? "I'm sorry, I don't even like flan."

"What?" He stopped rummaging through the cake. "Then why the hell did you tell the reporter I proposed to you with a ring on top of some flan?"

Her cheeks flamed. "I don't know. I was trying to come up with a good story."

"I've got to get that ring." He wrapped a chocolate-covered hand around the waiter's arm, leaving brown streaks all over the long, white sleeve. "What did you do with that flan?"

"It's in-n-n-n-n the k-k-itchen," the poor waiter stuttered.

Bodie reached for Lacey's hand. "Let's go."

She followed him through a set of swinging doors into the commercial kitchen. Someone holding a giant knife stopped chopping carrots and stepped in front of Bodie. "Sir, you can't come in here."

"I'm looking for my ring. You were supposed to deliver it to our table so I could propose." Bodie gestured to where Lacey stood half-hidden behind him. Confronting men with large knives wasn't her style.

"Where did the flan go?" The chef waved his knife in the air. "The one that was sent back."

"Took it to table seven." One of the servers raced by, his arms full of dishes.

"Which way is table seven?" Bodie asked.

"Follow me," the server said.

Bodie whipped around, still holding on to Lacey's hand, and pulled her out of the kitchen. As they entered the main dining room everyone erupted into a round of applause. A couple stood in the middle of the room, the woman holding her left hand out and admiring a huge yellow diamond sitting squarely on her ring finger.

"Dammit." Bodie let go of Lacey's hand and picked his way through the tables to the center of the room. Lacey waited where he left her, not wanting to put herself in the center of attention. Her goal of keeping a low profile had been blown to bits . . . again.

Bodie exchanged words with the man and woman. The woman clamped her hands to her hips while the man shoved his hands in his pockets and looked to his feet. A few moments later the woman slipped the ring off her finger and tossed it across the room. Lacey's heart skipped a few beats as the ring bounced across the floor and came to land under a table a few feet away.

She knelt down, trying to catch a glimpse. There it was. She crawled toward it, past a man's legs, finally grabbing the ring in her hands. As she stood, Bodie reached for her hand to help her up. He took the ring from her hand and knelt in front of her.

"Lacey Cherish, I know this isn't the way you pictured things, but I need to ask you a question."

Her stomach knotted, her throat closed. She couldn't make a sound if she wanted to so she nodded. Even knowing this was fake, that it didn't mean a thing, that he was doing this only for the pictures, her heart still surged in her chest.

"Will you marry me?" His eyes shone. He was putting everything he had into this performance. Without even thinking, she knelt down in front of him.

"Yes," she whispered. The word came out like a cross between a croak and a whisper.

He slid the ring onto her finger and her heart nearly burst. Feeling like she was floating on a fluffy cloud and looking down on the entire scene, she wrapped her arms around him and pulled his head down. He resisted for a flash of an instant then his mouth was on hers. Applause erupted all around them, drawing Lacey back from her dreamy cloud, back to where she knelt on the floor of a restaurant, back to where reality slammed into her like a two-by-four to the gut.

Bodie stood, helping her to her feet. "Think they got some good pictures?" he muttered under his breath.

Pictures. That's right. This was a stunt, staged solely for

the purpose of getting the pictures he promised to the reporter. Of course. Confusion and hurt meshed together, shielding her heart, cutting off any ridiculous hope she might have had that a teeny, tiny part of Bodie's performance tonight had been something beyond that . . . a performance.

"Yeah." She swallowed the ache of disappointment rising in her throat. What did she expect? That after a night of mind-blowing sex he'd want to throw caution to the wind and make their fake engagement into something real? She didn't have anyone else to blame but herself. This had all been her idea, part of her master plan. All he'd done was gone along with it, even when he didn't want to.

"Good." He brushed his thumb over her knuckles. "What do you think about the ring?"

She hadn't gotten a good look at it yet. As he led them back to their table, she held her left hand out in front of her. A giant yellow stone sparkled and glittered. Square-cut and set in a platinum bezel surrounded by small white diamonds, it exceeded anything she might have hoped for. "It's beautiful."

His hand brushed her hair back from her face. "So are you."

"Look over here, now." Their waiter held Bodie's phone up, ready to capture the photo they needed.

Lacey pasted on a smile, the kind she figured a woman who found herself newly engaged might project. Fortunately for her, it didn't require much effort. Despite his reluctance to admit his dad and pops were in over their heads, he'd really come through for her. And here she was, engaged to the man of her dreams. Fake engaged, she reminded herself.

She swallowed back the irony, trying to keep it from gobbling her up. "Did we get what we needed?"

"Yeah, I think so." Bodie let go of her hand to finish wiping the chocolate frosting onto a napkin.

"How about one with a kiss?" the waiter prompted.

"Um, sure." Bodie set the napkin down and held out his arms. "How about it, Sweets?"

For the camera. For the publicity. For the town. She reminded herself of all the reasons she should want his kiss. And tried to ignore the reality that she wanted his kiss because he was Bodie. And she'd been falling for him for years.

thirty-nine

Bodie grabbed Shotgun's leash as he came to a stop outside the Phillips House. Lacey had been working nonstop for the past three weeks. So had everyone else, making it impossible for him to sneak over and dig around the yard for his granddad's stash. The outside sported a fresh coat of light gray paint. The windows sparkled and shined. The weathered wood had been replaced and a new white railing surrounded the large wraparound porch.

Between following up on leads for the cigar ring and trying to hunt down the pit bull fights, he hadn't been out to check on things for a week or so. Any sign of the holes from the supposed armadillo infestation was gone, although Bodie wondered if his dad or Buck had been more to blame for trying to find his granddad's stash of cash. Either way, the whole yard had been replaced by a fresh layer of sod. That was going to make it incredibly difficult to do what he needed to do. But he was running out of time. If he didn't get out here in the next day or so, not only would his family be going down, but so would Lacey and her dreams of salvaging Ido.

Lacey stood on the edge of the lawn, a hose in her hand, watering the new grass. Her hair piled on top of her head in a messy updo and the shades sitting on her nose hid those gorgeous eyes. He hadn't seen her for over a week and the sight of her filled him with an unfamiliar feeling, one he didn't feel comfortable exploring. Not now, maybe not ever.

"Hey, Deputy." Jonah stepped onto the porch as Bodie and Shotgun exited the truck.

"Jonah, what are you doing here?" The last time Bodie had seen Jonah Wylder he'd been wrapped in chains and protesting the close of the warehouse. It was nice to see him doing something helpful for a change. Lacey had that effect on people. She was really turning the town around, getting everyone to work toward a common goal.

"Needed a little tuck pointing around the chimney." Jonah shrugged. "Guess I should have followed in my old man's footsteps a while ago. Turns out I'm a damn good mason."

"Good for you." Bodie shifted Shotgun's leash to the other hand so he could shake Jonah's.

"Sorry about all that ruckus about the warehouse." He tucked his hand into his pocket and cast his gaze to the ground.

"Not a problem. I'm glad to see you've found a new profession." And he was, too. It didn't do anyone any good to have a wild card like Jonah on the loose with no direction and a chip on his shoulder.

"Mayor Cherish is going to have me frost your wedding cake, too."

"What's that?" Bodie shook his head. He must have heard Jonah wrong.

"That's one way my dad said I could practice my mortar skills. Turns out frosting a cake is just like laying bricks. Consistency of the spread is key." He waved his hand in front of him like he was spreading a layer of mortar over an imaginary brick wall.

"Is that so?" Bodie glanced toward Lacey. She must have noticed his arrival since she'd turned off the hose and appeared to be headed his way.

"Yes, sir. You're going to have the best wedding cake this place has ever seen."

Bodie didn't doubt it, seeing as how it would be the first wedding cake the event center had ever seen. "Sounds good. I'll catch you later." He had more important things to do than chat with Jonah. He hadn't seen Lacey for over a week and his body seemed to actually be going through withdrawal.

"Hey, Deputy." She stopped in front of him, a grin on her face that reflected how he felt deep down inside.

"Hey, yourself." He couldn't help but smile. Seeing her erased the past seven days. Why had he stayed away for so long? He lifted her shades to sit on top of her head, needing to see her eyes. The look she gave him made heat flare in his gut.

Shotgun walked in a circle around them, wrapping them up in her leash, then tried to nose her way between their legs.

"Feeling a little neglected?" she asked Shotgun.

The dog whined, tail wagging. Bodie cleared his throat as he tried to untangle the leash from their legs.

"You ready for our interview today?" Free from the leash, she stepped back. "I've got a binder of stuff we can go over real quick before the reporter shows up."

"Don't you think we should hug or something? How would you greet your fiancé if you hadn't seen him for a week?" He leaned close, muttering against her ear. The scent of hay and horses did little to soothe his nerves. He'd been on edge for the past two days thinking about the meeting with the reporter this afternoon.

She wrapped her arms around his shoulders. "I suppose you're right. Is anyone watching?"

Holding her in his arms, he didn't care who was watching. He dropped his chin, grazing her lips with his. A lightness bloomed in his chest, radiating through his limbs. This is what he'd missed—holding Lacey tight against him, tasting her on his lips, breathing in her scent.

"Whoa, we don't want to give them too much of a show." She pulled back first. "I can't wait for you to see the inside. Come on."

He followed her up the steps and into the house. The floors had been refinished and now gleamed under his boots. Daylight filtered through the windows and the stained glass transom, casting tiny rainbows across the wood floors. The smell of lemon and ammonia surrounded him. The entire first floor had been restored to what looked like its original glory.

"This looks amazing. How did you get this all done?" Everywhere he looked progress had been made. He ran a finger along the mantel of the fireplace in the front sitting room. There wasn't a speck of dust anywhere.

"I had, I mean have, so much help. Jojo's been by several times. Even Helmut stopped in with lunch a couple of times for the crew. And Zina's been my right-hand woman."

"It's incredible." He slowly spun around, taking it all in. "You're incredible."

Her face pinked. "Honestly, all I've done is keep track of the to-do lists."

"I doubt that." Suddenly he had a new appreciation for Lacey. Was there anything the woman couldn't do?

"How's Shotgun?" She bent to scratch the pup behind the ears. "When is she due?"

He groaned. "Another couple of weeks or so."

"And then what?" Lacey glanced up at him, expectant.

Shrugging, he squatted next to her and ran his hand down Shotgun's back. "I don't know."

"I talked to Zina. She said she'd love for you to keep her."

"Puppies? I can barely take care of . . . oh, never mind."

"You weren't going to say you can barely take care of yourself, were you?" she asked.

"Of course not. It's just, it wouldn't be fair to her to have her sit around the house all day waiting for me. I'm gone so much."

"What if she came to work with me?"

"What do you mean?"

"She could be an ambassador for For Pitties' Sake. Maybe when people come to the house for an event she could greet them. If she makes a good impression then maybe we can find homes for some of the other dogs."

"You know, you might be onto something." He knelt down next to the pup. "You want to go to work with Lacey every day?"

Shotgun nudged her nose under his hand.

"I could keep her during the day and you could take her home at night," Lacey suggested. "Just like—"

"Shared custody," Bodie said.

"I suppose so."

Weird. He'd gone from being single to engaged and sharing custody with Lacey in less than two months. He waited for the panic to seize him, for his gut to clench or his throat to close. It didn't happen. Maybe it was because the gig was almost up. In just a few weeks he'd be faking *I do* with his best friend's little sister. That thought put him on the edge of a panic attack. But not—he realized—because he'd be fake-marrying Lacey. Because after that he wouldn't have a reason to see her on a regular basis. He'd have to pull that thought out later and mull it over. Now he needed to turn on the charm for the chat with the reporter.

"Want to finish showing me around?" He stood, Shotgun's leash back in his hand.

"Sure. Follow me." Lacey led him up the stairs to the bedrooms. They'd turned one into a bride's dressing room, made another into a small conference room, and kept two of the rooms as bedrooms.

"So you're going to rent rooms out overnight?" Bodie asked.

"I'm not sure yet. There's been talk of running some kind of bed-and-breakfast when there isn't a wedding scheduled. This lets us keep our options open."

Bodie noted the little touches of Lacey that appeared everywhere. Fancy soaps by the sinks, flowers on all of the tables, and the light scent of fresh-baked cookies that seemed to linger everywhere they went.

"How did you do it?" he asked as he climbed the stairs to the third floor, coming up behind her.

"I told you, everyone pitched in." She turned to face him as she neared the top. "You'd be surprised at how everyone's coming together. I think I finally got to them."

He stopped on the narrow staircase, two steps below her. His eyes lined up with her chest.

"Bodie?"

"Yeah?" Reluctantly, he pulled his gaze away from the V-neck shirt she had on. His hands itched to feel her soft skin under his fingers.

"You okay?"

What a loaded question. No, he wasn't okay. He had just a few days left to get the cash to Buck before everything he'd been working so hard to save came crashing down around him. Not to mention the upcoming wedding. He'd gone a week without seeing her and he felt like his heart had been ripped out and stepped on. What was going to happen when he had to stand in front of the entire town and pledge to love her *till death do us part*, knowing he'd never get to kiss her again?

"Yeah. Just have a lot going on." He wiped a hand over his chin. A few more weeks. He could handle that.

"How's the investigation going? Find out anything

new?" Concern creased her forehead. The kindness in her eyes slayed him.

"Um, getting close."

"But no cigar, eh?" She giggled. "Sorry, that wasn't funny but I couldn't resist."

He shook his head, grateful for the poor attempt at humor for lightening the situation. "So what's up here?"

She climbed the rest of the steps with him behind her. It took everything he had to not plant his palm on the curve of her gorgeous ass as he followed her.

"Potential living quarters. We might need a grounds-keeper or event manager to move in if things get really busy." The hope in her eyes made him wish he could come clean with her, warn her about the threat of Buck exposing her arrest. No. He'd have to eliminate that threat on his own. Tonight. He'd sneak back after dark and see if he could find his granddad's stash. Anything to keep Lacey's world from falling apart.

"You've done an amazing job." He reached for her hand and gave it a squeeze.

"Thank you." She turned to him, her mouth spread into a smile.

"Lacey? You up here?" a voice floated up the stairs from below.

Bodie seized the opportunity to get that kiss he'd been craving. He took her in his arms, dipping her backward, lining his lips and his hips up with hers.

Her arms clasped around his shoulders, holding on tight. Mouth to mouth, heart to heart, he teased her lips apart, sighing as he relaxed into the kiss.

"There you are." Zina huffed as Bodie set Lacey upright. "I see you two have been working real hard."

Lacey wiped at her lip, her gaze bouncing from Zina to him. "I was just showing Bodie what we've done to the third floor."

"Sure you were." Zina shook her head. "I can't believe the two of you are going through with this."

"Wait, you told her?" Bodie asked.

"Yeah. You don't have to pretend to love me around Zina. She knows." Lacey glanced at the floor.

"I know and I think it's one of the stupidest ideas you've ever had. You should know better"—she glared at Bodie, making him feel like he'd just been doused in ice water—"both of you."

"It's okay, she's not going to tell anyone," Lacey said.

Bodie looked to the ceiling. "So who else? Your dad, now Zina? Who else knows we're not for real?" *"Not for real."* The words dropped into his gut like a load of bricks, hollowing out everything on the way.

"That's it," Lacey said.

"Ahem." Zina cleared her throat. A look passed between the women.

"What aren't you telling me?" Bodie furrowed his brow. "Aren't we past the point of keeping secrets?" His heart squeezed tight. He was a fine one to bring that up. He'd been the one keeping the secrets all along.

"Well, there is the small problem of Adeline." Lacey's shoulders rose and fell. "She got so mad at me for ruining her wedding that she's opening up her own wedding venue in Swynton."

"So?"

"And she's taken every one of the vendors she lined up with her so we need to find a new band to play the reception."

"No big deal. I know a guy."

"And she's trying to convince Samantha to come cover her wedding instead." Lacey bit down on her lower lip.

Zina cocked a hip. "I think you should let her."

"But then we don't get the media coverage." Lacey stepped in front of Bodie and straightened his shirt. "So we have to be extra charming during today's interview, okay?"

Extra charming. Sure, he could do that. "When will Samantha decide which wedding she's going to feature?"

"She said she'll let me know by the end of the week. I know I've been asking a lot of you, but can we really turn it on today? Pretend we're really in love?" Her eyes shone.

"Yeah. I think I can manage that." He almost leaned in to kiss her again.

But then Zina whomped them both over the head with a pillow she'd picked up from the couch. "Y'all are asking for it, if you ask me."

"Good thing no one's asking you, then." Bodie winked at her, ready to play the part of the loving, head-over-heels fiancé. As he followed Lacey back down the stairs, he couldn't help but think, it wouldn't take much faking this time.

forty

Lacey carefully traipsed down the stairs in her strappy heels. She'd brought clothes to the house so she could get cleaned up here and not have to run home before the interview. If all went according to plan, she'd be walking down these same steps in just a few weeks on her way to marry Bodie in the garden out back.

He waited for her at the bottom of the ornate staircase, holding out a hand to help her down the last few steps. She took it, not letting go as she joined him and Samantha in the front room.

"It's so good to see you again," Samantha said. "How are the plans coming? I can't wait to hear all about them."

"Should we sit down?" Lacey gestured to the formal sitting room she'd finished with period furniture. An antique sofa sat in front of the ornate fireplace. Two sets of chairs had been placed on either side, creating the perfect place for conversation. Everything had been donated by folks in town. If this idea didn't take off she'd have a lot of items to return to their rightful owners.

Bodie waited for her to sit then nestled close to her on the love seat, his arm possessively resting over her shoulders. She took in a breath, letting his closeness calm her nerves. They could do this. Confident in their ability to reflect the picture-perfectness of a couple madly in love, she smiled at Samantha.

"Tea?" Lacey leaned forward, grabbing the handle of the pitcher.

"Sure." Samantha settled her notebook on her lap. "So how are the plans coming?"

"Great." Lacey handed her a glass of sweet tea before leaning back against the cushion, settling into Bodie's side. "Did you want some tea, babe?"

"I'm good." He smiled before brushing her temple with his lips.

So far, so good. Lacey glanced to Samantha, whose smile proved they were pulling this off.

"What's left to do?" Samantha asked.

"Oh, not much. I just got alterations done on my dress. Flowers have been selected, cake and reception menu were finalized a couple of weeks ago." Lacey held up a finger for each item as she went down the list. "Photographer's been paid. We're in good shape."

"What are you serving at the reception?" Samantha's pen poised over the paper, ready to capture all of the details.

"Barbecue, of course." Lacey grinned. "Ido has the best smoked brisket in the state of Texas."

"But can you eat that?" Samantha asked, worry lines creasing her forehead.

"Well, sure, why not?" Lacey asked.

"She's got pills"—Bodie squeezed her hand—"for the IBS."

"Right. Won't be a problem." How stupid could she be to forget Bodie had plagued her with lifelong bowel issues? She grinned up at him. "I wouldn't want to deprive my hubby-to-be of his favorite."

"She's so selfless." Bodie ran a finger along her cheek, sending a wave of chills down her spine.

She shifted her butt on the love seat, ignoring the goose bumps popping up on her skin.

"And the cake?" Samantha looked up from her notebook. "What did you decide on there?"

Lacey leaned forward. "White cake with raspberry filling. It's absolutely decadent."

Samantha cocked her head. What now? "I thought you were allergic to raspberries?" she asked Bodie.

Lacey looked back at him. Allergic to raspberries? Since when?

"Just slightly." Bodie turned his most charming smile on Samantha. "We'll have one layer that's plain vanilla. Lacey made sure."

Her heart thumped so loud she was sure Samantha could hear it from across the room.

"You two really are meant for each other," Samantha said. "It's nice to see two people who love each other so much they're willing to sacrifice for the other. Not like . . ."

"Like what?" Lacey asked. Maybe Adeline and Roman weren't as accommodating as they intended.

"Oh, nothing." Samantha waved the comment away. "Do you have the items we talked about? I'd love for Jay to be able to get some pictures of everything before the big day. I'm sure it'll be so busy, we'd rather get it taken care of ahead of time."

"Yes." Lacey stood, pulling Bodie to his feet next to her. "Our florist should be here any minute with the mockup of the bridal bouquet and the boutonniere. Do you want to sneak a peek at my dress before she gets here?"

"I'd love to." Samantha got to her feet. "Lead the way."

Lacey almost headed right for the stairs, but Bodie didn't let go of her hand. She whirled around. "You can't come with us, sugar pie. No peeking at the dress ahead of time."

He wrapped his arms around her and kissed her on the cheek. "I don't want to ruin the surprise. I'll wait down here for you, but I'll be missing you the whole time we're apart."

She rolled her eyes, making sure he was the only one who could see her. "Think you're laying it on a bit thick?" she whispered.

"Never." He grinned against her ear. She could feel his lips lifting into a smile. Then he palmed her ass and gave it a squeeze. "Hurry back, honeybuns."

Lacey nipped at his earlobe in retaliation. He chuckled, the rumble in his chest vibrated against hers, making her wish they weren't standing in the middle of the sitting room trying to convince a reporter that the feelings they had for each other were real when she'd been struggling so hard over the past few weeks to convince herself they weren't.

"Right this way." She pulled away from Bodie, letting her fingers linger in his for a long moment before leading Samantha and Jay up the stairs.

"You've done an amazing job with this place," Samantha said as she trailed behind Lacey.

"Thanks. It's been a labor of love for the whole town. They need something to believe in, something to put their hope in now that the import business is gone." She led Samantha into the larger bedroom, the one she would have chosen for herself if she'd been staying the night. Dark wood complemented the pale ivory walls. Stained glass windows lined the curve of the turret. Lacey had always wanted to be a princess when she was younger. What little girl didn't?

"This room is gorgeous." Samantha turned in a wide circle. "Is this where you and Bodie will be spending your wedding night?"

"What?" Lacey reached for the handle of the closet door, glad to have something to grab on to.

"You've got to admit, it's so romantic." Samantha jotted notes as Jay snapped photos of the room.

"It is." For a moment she let herself imagine what it would feel like to snuggle under the covers of the antique four-poster bed with Bodie next to her. Would he take her fast or slow on their wedding night? How would it feel to have his clean-shaven cheeks nestle between her thighs? The full length of him filling her, like he had before? Like she dreamed about him doing again?

Samantha cleared her throat. "Lacey?"

"Hmm?" Pulled from thoughts that she had no business thinking, Lacey focused her attention on the closet. The dress. "You wanted to see the dress?"

Samantha stepped closer. "Is there a story here? How did you know it was the one?"

Lacey opened the door, her breath catching in her throat like it did every time she set eyes on her mama's wedding dress. "It belonged to my mama. She died when I was little."

"I'm so sorry." Samantha's hand rested on Lacey's shoulder, offering comfort. "It's got to be hard for you to wear it."

Lacey lifted the hanger from the rod and turned around, holding the dress in front of her. "It is. Or I should say, it will be." She turned to face her reflection in the full-length mirror. "But it's also a way of having her with me on my wedding day." Lacey would have rather worn a white dress from the clearance rack of any one of the bridal shops Adeline planned on visiting that weekend they'd spent in Dallas. But time and budget constraints had forced her to reconsider her options. Wearing her mother's dress was the economical choice, even though it would wreak havoc on her already raw emotions.

"You're going to be a stunning bride," Samantha said as Jay lifted the camera to snap a few photos. "We won't publish those until after the wedding. Want to make sure your groom doesn't see the dress before the big day. You know it's bad luck."

Lacey nodded as she put the dress back in the closet. She needed all the luck she could get to make sure the big day went off without a hitch.

The sound of someone coming through the front door interrupted her thoughts. Heavy footsteps sounded on the stairs. "Lacey? The florist is here," Bodie called.

"Ready to see the bouquet?" Lacey turned to Samantha with a smile, hoping with all of her heart that putting her faith in Suzy wasn't about to bite her in the ass.

forty-one

Bodie wanted to warn Lacey before she walked in on the spectacle Suzy had created in the sitting room. But unless he wanted to tempt fate and catch a glimpse of the wedding dress, he couldn't very well get to her before she came downstairs. Which meant he was on his own with the taxidermist florist.

"What do you think?" Suzy stepped back to survey her handiwork.

Displays of silk flowers in every shape, size, and color rimmed the room. Bodie shrugged. "Is this what you and Lacey talked about?"

"I did take some creative liberties." She adjusted the ribbon stretching between two horseshoe-shaped floral arrangements. "I wanted to surprise her."

"Oh, she'll be surprised, all right." Bodie could absolutely positively guarantee that. He took a deep breath and headed back up the steps, hoping he could give Lacey a heads-up on the landing.

"I think it's so romantic you're wearing your mother's wedding dress." Samantha's feet came into view through the ornate wooden railing, followed by Lacey's heels.

"Thanks." Lacey's voice wavered, laced with emotion.

"Mind if we poke around the other rooms real quick before we head back downstairs?" Samantha moved down the hallway.

"Go ahead. I'm going to make sure the florist is set up." Lacey made her way to the steps where Bodie waited.

Her mother's dress? She hadn't told him she was going to wear her mother's wedding dress. Why the hell would she go and do a thing like that? The gravity of what they were doing pressed down on him. They might joke and smile and pretend that it was going to be a piece of cake— raspberries or not—to fake-tie the knot. But he had to come clean with her. Tell her that real feelings were getting involved.

"Bodie?" Lacey met him on the landing. "What's going on?"

He reached for her hand. "You're wearing your mother's dress?"

"Yeah." She looked away, not willing or not able to meet his gaze. "It was free, and—"

"You don't have to do this." He put a finger under her chin, tipping her head up, forcing her to look at him. Her eyes glistened, shining with the threat of tears. "Oh hell, Sweets. We can stop. Just say the word and we'll figure out another way."

She wiped under her eyes, brushing off his concerns. "I have to see this through."

"It's not worth it." He rubbed his palm over her arm. "Your mom's dress? You need to save that for your real wedding. Don't waste it on me."

"Is that what I'm doing?" Her jaw set. "Wasting things on you?"

"No, I just mean—"

"I know what you mean. But I've got to finish what I started. Everyone's depending on me. They need me to do this. My dad, the town."

"What about you? What do you need?" He hadn't planned on having this conversation. Not now, maybe not ever. Especially with a reporter and photographer roaming the floor above and a twisted kind of florist on the floor below.

"It doesn't matter what I need." Her eyes sparked. "Now, will you get downstairs and play the part of my loving fiancé so we can get this sham over with?" She brushed past him, heading toward the first floor.

He funneled his hands through his hair, wondering how he'd let it get to this. Why hadn't he refused to go along with this crazy idea when she first brought it up?

Because he'd do anything she asked him. The realization coursed through him like a truth he'd always known and hadn't been able to admit yet. With Lacey, he was all in. Always had been. He had to help her see this through. After the wedding, once things settled down, maybe then he could broach the topic of exploring the feelings he'd been having. He almost laughed out loud at the ridiculousness of the situation. Once he'd fake-married the woman he loved, maybe he could ask her out on a date.

"Bodie." Lacey's voice came from the lower level.

Suzy. Dammit. He hadn't warned her about Suzy. Scrambling down the stairs, he steeled himself for her reaction. She stood facing the display Suzy had so carefully put together.

Hands on her hips, the toe of her sandal tapping on the refinished floorboards, Lacey turned to face him. "What are we going to do about this?"

He joined her, wrapping an arm around her waist to prevent her from launching herself at the colorful floral display.

"I wanted to incorporate everything we all love about Idont." Suzy glanced over at them, a shy smile on her face. "I mean, Ido."

"You've certainly done that." Lacey's voice came out an octave higher than usual. She moved into the room, fingering the petals on a cross-shaped standing display. "Is that a chipmunk?"

Bodie glanced to the piece Lacey stared at. Some sort of furry creature tucked into the center of a heart-shaped wreath.

"Flying squirrel." Suzy put her hands on her hips, beaming with pride. "Worked on that one myself."

"We talked about tulips, Suzy." Lacey rounded, her cheeks stained pink. "It's a wedding."

"A Texas-style wedding." Suzy leaned over to grab a bouquet of flowers from the table. "Here's your bridal bouquet."

Lacey didn't reach for it. As Bodie waited to see what she would do next, he ran his gaze over the bright bouquet of flowers. Tulips of every color made up the large bouquet. Burlap and jute wrapped around the stems. That didn't look so bad. Flowers were flowers, as far as he was concerned.

"Is that a spider in my flowers?" Lacey lowered her voice to a whisper. A pissed-off whisper.

"It's just a tarantula. I put a scorpion over here. Wanted to reflect the area, you know." Suzy offered the bouquet.

Lacey backed up, moving away from the flowers until she bumped into Bodie. "I can't deal with this right now."

Footsteps sounded on the stairs. "I can't believe what you've done with the place. You're a miracle worker, that's for sure." Samantha's feet appeared on the steps, followed by the photographer.

Bodie wanted to pause time. He glanced back and forth from the horror on Lacey's face to Suzy's proud smile to the curious look on Samantha's face as she came down the stairs.

"Is this your florist?" Samantha asked.

Bodie glanced back to Lacey, whose shock had disappeared.

"Yes, she is. You'll never find another one like her." She smiled, took a step toward Suzy, and put an arm around her shoulders, propelling her forward.

He had to hand it to her, Lacey was a pro at masking her feelings. She'd be able to convince anyone of anything she wanted. It was a real skill. As Lacey chatted about how important it was to incorporate symbolism from the town and the region into their wedding, he considered what that might mean. She could have been a professional actress with the way she could turn her feelings on and off. Like a water spout, she could turn on the tears and then, just as fast, she could switch to looking like the happiest woman in the world.

Or the most in love.

Panic clawed at his chest. What if that's what she'd been doing with him? Two minutes ago he would have sworn on his own life that she had feelings for him. Feelings that went far beyond faking a wedding. Feelings that offered the possibility of a future.

But what if it was all fake? What if she'd been playing him just like she was playing the florist? Playing the reporter? Playing everyone in town?

"I've got to go." He needed air. He needed space. He needed to put some distance between himself and Lacey.

"Everything okay?" Lacey reached out for him, concern evident in the crease between her brows.

"Got a lead on a case I'm working on." He leaned forward, brushing his lips against her forehead. "I'll call you later, okay?"

"You sure?" She pressed a palm to his chest.

"Yeah. I'll talk to you in a bit." He squeezed her hand,

removing it from where it seared his skin, even through his shirt. "I'm sorry to cut out on you. Lacey's better at answering any questions you have anyway."

"Duty calls, we get it." Samantha waved. "I'll see you on the big day."

The big day. He nodded. "See you then."

forty-two

Bodie cut the engine a few blocks away and eased the four-door sedan to the curb. He'd borrowed a car from the impound lot for tonight's escapade. No need to alert anyone that he was out and about this evening. It wasn't likely that anyone would come across the vehicle unless they were headed to the Phillips House, but better to be safe than sorry.

He crept along the drive, keeping to the edge where the tall trees and bushes would hide his approach. The small shovel in his backpack clanged against something. He paused to readjust the contents of his bag. That's all he needed, was to get caught sneaking around the event venue. Of course he'd prepared an alibi just in case but he preferred not to use it. If luck was on his side he'd be in and out of the yard in the space of fifteen minutes. Ten, if he got really lucky.

He scaled the iron fence that separated the backyard from the front and dashed across the grass to press himself against the building. Nothing but the sounds of an early-spring evening greeted him. Crickets chirped. A bullfrog from the nearby pond croaked out a tune. The breeze danced across the yard, eliciting a song from the wind chimes Lacey had hung on the corner of the porch.

His heart slowed. He could do this. He had to. Lacey had been willing to put everything aside to do what she thought was best for the town. Now it was his turn. He couldn't move on until he'd neutralized the threat Buck Little represented.

Pulling the map out of his bag with one hand, he fumbled for his mini flashlight with the other. The small beam of light played over the hand-drawn map. If the drawing was to scale, two possible stashes sat immediately to his right. He set down the map and grappled for the small shovel. Two steps straight ahead and three to the right. Lifting the piece of freshly laid sod, he pressed the blade of the shovel into the dirt underneath. Assuming he could trust the notes on the map, he had to dig down only about eighteen inches before he'd strike gold. Or, in this case, a wad of his grandad's hoard.

Five minutes later he had yet to hit anything even though he'd dug a wide radius around the site of the supposed treasure. Dammit. He should have known better than to believe anything Buck Little or his dad told him. Sweat beaded along his hairline. He would have whipped the long-sleeve black shirt over his head if he wasn't worried so much about being discovered. Instead, he wiped a sleeve over his brow and studied the map again. Pops was meticulous. If he made note of a location, it had to be where he marked it. Accuracy was his style.

Bodie turned the map over. If he looked at the drawing from that angle, he was digging two feet away from where he should. He walked off the steps and dropped to his knees. If he didn't find anything this time, he'd have to give up. Dad could sell his truck or some acreage to get himself out of the tight space he'd wedged himself into.

The shovel scraped against something hard. It had to be what he was looking for. Bodie carefully dug around the metal box until he could make out the edges. He pulled it out of the ground and opened it.

The smell of dirt and earth and cold cash floated to his nose. Yes. He counted two thousand dollars in fives and ones before moving on to the next hidey-hole. As he tucked the bills into the canvas bag he'd brought along, he fought against his conscience. He didn't have a choice if he wanted to protect Lacey. It's not like he was stealing, just borrowing his granddad's cash to pay off the old man's debt.

By the time he collected the whole fifty grand, sweat soaked through his thin T-shirt. He spread the dirt over the hole he'd dug, careful to replace the sod and pat it down. Eager to get the job done and ready for a nice, warm shower, he packed up his bag and made his way back to the car.

Forty-five minutes later, hair still damp from his recent shower, he sat across the kitchen table from Buck. Bodie didn't want to have the money in his possession any longer than necessary and he needed to take action before he changed his mind, so he'd picked up his dad and dropped by Buck's to unload the cash and hopefully his guilt along with it.

"I gotta say, I didn't think you would do it," Buck said.

"Didn't seem like I had much of a choice." Bodie slid the backpack off his shoulder, letting it fall to the table. Mayor Little didn't look nearly as intimidating in a pair of plaid pajama bottoms and a plain white T-shirt.

"You're a smart kid," Buck said. "You're going to make a great sheriff."

"No. I don't want the two of you fixing any election."

Dad put a hand on his shoulder. "But, Son—"

Bodie shrugged it off. "This ends here. I'm done trying to save your ass. You and Pops are on your own now. I can't be a part of anything you've got going on." He'd thought about it as he dug up his grandfather's stash. Buying off Buck would fix only his immediate problem. If he wanted to make Ido a safe place for Lacey he had no choice but to do the right thing. Besides, after his fake wedding to Lacey, he'd need to get out of town. No sense agreeing to take on a job that would only keep him here, close to her.

"Fair enough." Buck reached for the bag. "Shall we see what we've got here?"

"It's all there," Bodie said. "Fifty thousand bucks to clear my dad and granddad's names. That's what we agreed to, right?"

Buck eyed him through narrowed lids. "Anything you want to tell me, Son?"

"No, sir. Just want your word that my family's satisfied their obligation to that little cigar ring you've got going."

Bodie waited for a response. Instead, Buck reached for a piece of paper and a pen. He scratched something across the paper then slid it in front of Bodie.

Are you wearing a wire?

Bodie stared at the black ink, his vision speckled with black dots. Of course Buck would think that. He'd screwed enough people around that he'd naturally be suspicious. Taking in a deep breath, Bodie tried not to wince as the tape he'd used to fashion a makeshift mic stretched across his stomach.

"Of course I'm not wearing a wire. You think I'd risk messing with you? I just want out." Bodie spread his arms wide, hoping the boost to Buck's ego would prevent him from initiating a full pat down. "The cash for the out, right?"

Buck nodded, his hand closing around the bag. "Let's make sure it's all here first, shall we?"

"Be my guest." Bodie stood, pacing the large kitchen, his boots clomping on the ceramic tile. He'd hoped that by catching Buck at home he'd throw him off guard.

Especially in the middle of the night. As he rounded the table, he cast his gaze over the wall of the office across the hall. Framed photographs hung from floor to ceiling. Bodie wandered over, his attention caught by a photo of Lacey's dad shaking hands with Buck. Must have been during his tenure as mayor.

Seeing how many people Buck had probably manipulated and blackmailed over the years lit a fire in Bodie's gut. He couldn't wait to see the man go down in a bonfire of his own creation, even if it took a piece of him with it.

"Is it all there?" Bodie returned to the kitchen, hands on his hips, ready to put this nastiness behind him.

"All there." Buck slid the piles of cash he'd counted back into the bag. "Pleasure doing business with you, Son."

"Don't call me son," Bodie said as he took the hand Buck offered. "You have the right to remain silent—"

"What's this?" Buck's eyes went wide.

Bodie flipped one hand around Buck's back and reached for the other wrist. "Anything you say can be used against you in court."

"What's going on?" Dad stood, looking older than his fifty-some years. "Bodie?"

"I'm sorry, Dad. I can't be a part of this anymore."

"What are you talking about? Family comes first." His dad slammed his fist against the heavy wood table.

The front door opened. As Sheriff Suarez and the two other deputies moved through the living room, Bodie's dad cracked open the door leading to the garage then disappeared into the darkness.

Dammit. This was going to be even worse than he thought. Bodie handed Buck over to the sheriff and followed his dad through the door to the garage.

"Dad? Don't make this harder than it needs to be." The smell of oil hit him as he rounded the front of Buck's oversized truck.

The door to the backyard hung open on its frame.

Bodie passed through and found himself standing on the deck of a giant in-ground pool. His dad was doing his best to put some distance between them but a bad knee and years of limiting his exercise to sitting behind a desk ensured he was no match for Bodie.

"Stop. Let's end this." Bodie jogged around the pool.

His dad glanced back over his shoulder. "I'm not going to let you take me down."

Bodie wouldn't have to. "Watch out!" He yelled the warning in time but it was too late. Dad didn't see the hose someone had stretched out to fill the pool. His boot caught on it, sending him tumbling to the ground. He fell on his arm, collapsing onto his chest and rolling right into the deep end of Buck Little's pool.

Bodie didn't hesitate. He dove in, headfirst, scrambling to reach the spot where his dad sputtered and splashed. By the time he had an arm around his dad's shoulders Sheriff Suarez had grabbed the life ring hanging from the fence and flung it toward them.

"Dad, grab on to the ring." Bodie pushed the ring into his dad's chest. The stubborn man wouldn't take it.

"Just let me drown," his dad wailed.

"You don't really mean that." Bodie dragged him to the side of the pool, where the deputies hauled him out of the water.

Bodie climbed out and took the towel Sheriff Suarez handed him. "We can take it from here, Deputy Phillips."

Nodding, Bodie turned toward his dad. "I'm sorry."

"I hope you're happy, Son." Dad huddled on the edge of a lounge chair. "You know Buck was just the front man, don't you?"

"Doesn't matter. I did what I needed to do to clear my conscience."

Dad shook his head. "You turned your back on your family. I thought I'd trained you better than that."

"No, Dad. You trained me worse. But despite that, I

still managed to do the right thing. I wish you luck." He waited while one of his fellow deputies snapped a set of handcuffs on his dad's wrists. Then he turned and walked toward the gate, his heart free from the burden of feeling responsible for his family, but heavy at the thought of what this decision had cost him. As he walked down the driveway of Mayor Little's home—make that the ex-mayor's home—he breathed in a sigh of relief. Lacey was safe. The threat Buck had issued was null and void. The only person he wanted to see was Lacey. But she was off-limits. He couldn't unload everything that had just happened on her, not when she'd never been aware of the threats Buck had issued in the first place. So he turned his truck toward home, where at least one warm body waited for him— albeit a four-legged one.

forty-three

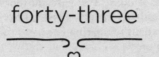

Lacey skipped up the steps to Bodie's place, hardly able to contain her excitement. She hadn't seen him or heard from him since he walked out on the interview a few days ago. Work must be keeping him extremely busy. She didn't want to bother him, but with the big day barreling toward them, she had to share her news.

She knocked on the door, too excited to stand still. "Bodie? I know you're in there, your truck's outside."

The door opened a crack. "What do you need?"

"Bodie?" She tried to peer into the darkness. He must have all the shades pulled.

"Yeah?" His voice came out rough, like he hadn't used it for a while.

"You okay?"

"I'm fine. What's up? I didn't miss anything, did I? Wedding's not for another week, right?" He shielded his eyes from the sun as she pushed the door open a bit more.

"What's going on?" The stale smell of air that had been

undisturbed for too long wafted past her. She wedged her way between the door and the frame. "I'm coming in."

"Oh, that's not necessary. I need to clean up first. Place isn't fit to be seen—"

She elbowed her way past him into the foyer. He had on a pair of shorts, no shirt. She sucked in a breath at the sight of his bare chest. Her gaze moved from the scruff covering his chin to the pizza boxes littering the kitchen counter. The thrill of sharing her news faded. "What the heck is going on?"

"It's fine, really. Just taking some time to work through some stuff."

"What kind of stuff? Why didn't you come talk to me? To Dad?" She turned on him. "What's happening with you?"

"Nothing. Just doing my part to keep the good folks of Idont safe."

"Ido," she whispered.

"That's right." The edges of his mouth tipped up in a flimsy smile. "Have I told you how proud I am of you?"

She let out a laugh. "You're proud of me? The man who wears a gun every day, risking his life for strangers?"

"Not anymore." He turned away from her, heading toward the couch. "Gun and badge have been turned in. At least until I get cleared."

"Cleared? From what?" She'd been crazy busy trying to finalize the details for the upcoming wedding and the grand opening of the Phillips House. Had she missed something? Had she been so focused on herself and her goal of securing the article in the magazine that she completely missed something major going down?

"I didn't want you to worry." He slumped onto the sectional. "It's going to be fine. Suarez will go through the evidence and realize I didn't have anything to do with it. But until then . . . I guess I get to catch up on all those TV shows I never have time to watch."

"You took down your dad?" A ball of dread plopped into her gut while she waited for him to respond.

He nodded. "It was for the best."

"Oh, Bodie." She climbed onto the couch, pulling his head against her chest. "I'm so sorry. That must have been so hard."

His hands roamed over her back. She relished the way she fit against him.

"Arresting your dad was harder."

She pulled away, meeting his gaze. "Are you okay?"

"I'll be fine. Dad's pissed, Pops is livid, and my mom has pretty much stopped speaking to me. But it was worth it."

"Why did you do it?" His family had skirted the law for years. What had they done that made him finally turn them in?

He shifted her off his lap, settling her next to him on the couch. "It's not important."

"Why didn't you call?" She and her dad were the closest thing he had to family, even before his dad and granddad got arrested. "I would have come over. You could have talked to my dad."

"By the way, your dad should be getting cleared sometime soon. Turns out Buck had something to do with him ending up behind the wheel of that golf cart that night."

"What?" Her father had a history of drinking too much. Even if it hadn't been all his fault, he still made the decision to get behind the wheel.

"I'm not saying he's totally free, but I think they're going to lift the house arrest. Maybe not in time for him to attend the wedding but shouldn't be long after that."

The wedding. The whole reason she'd come over was to tell him her good news. "Hey, this probably isn't a good time, but I just found out Samantha chose us to showcase in the magazine article. Swynton is out and Ido is in."

"That's great." He gave her a smile, a real one this time. "You did it, Lacey."

"We did it." She grinned at him.

"You're right. I should get cleaned up, we need to celebrate."

"Aw, you don't have to do that. I can tell you're not feeling up to it."

"And that's exactly why we need to. We've only got a few days left before you never have to see me again. People ought to see us out in public. We need to remind them how in love we are, remember?"

She swatted at his chest, a part of her wishing for nothing more than to stay in all night and hold him close instead. "One night won't matter."

He let out a sigh, like the weight of the world rested on his broad shoulders. "You're so close to making it happen. Don't give up now, okay? Give me ten minutes to shower."

"Okay." She waited while he took his time dragging himself off the couch. Then she gathered the empty cans, paper plates, and take-out containers from the coffee table and took them into the kitchen. Shotgun followed, her tummy hanging low to the ground. Lacey bent down to run a hand over the dog's back. "What's going on with Bodie, huh?"

Shotgun didn't answer although life would be much easier if she could talk. Maybe then Lacey would know what Bodie had been going through while he'd been keeping his distance. It had to be killing him to know he was the reason his dad and his pops were arrested. While she waited for him to get cleaned up, she filled the dishwasher and took the trash to the bin in the garage. As she walked back into the kitchen, her phone pinged.

Lacey groaned as she read the message from Adeline:

You're going to be sorry.

Why couldn't she leave well enough alone? Adeline had been a thorn in her side for far too long. It was time to put their petty rivalry behind them. Lacey typed out a reply.

Wishing you nothing but the best.

Adeline might have the tastiest cake, the most beautiful flowers, the biggest ring, the most people at her reception, but she'd never have what Lacey had—an entire town supporting her dreams.

Bodie came out of the bedroom, his muscular thighs encased in a pair of clean jeans and a concert T-shirt snug around his shoulders. Lacey grinned. She had one more thing that Adeline never would—one hell of a hot fiancé. Even if she wouldn't be able to keep him, he was hers for the next week and Lacey planned to enjoy him, even if what they had wasn't real.

forty-four

"So where are we going?" Lacey asked as she pulled her legs into the cab of the truck.

"What are you in the mood for?" Bodie leaned in the open door of the truck, getting his fill of just looking at her. Busting his dad and his grandfather had dragged him down. Seeing Lacey brightened his mood like he'd just gotten his own personal shot of concentrated sunshine.

She shrugged. "I'm easy. Whatever you want to do is fine with me." Then her cheeks pinked. "By *easy* I mean I'm flexible."

"Yeah, I've seen how flexible you can be." He chuckled as she flushed a shade closer to red.

"You know what I meant."

"Yeah, I know." He pushed the door closed behind her then walked around to the driver's side. He'd miss the adorable way she looked when she thought she'd embarrassed herself. For a moment he didn't want to spend the evening with Lacey. It would be one more night of showing him what he'd never have.

But then she leaned across the front seat and pushed open his door. "So you coming or are you going to stand there all night?"

He shook off his hesitation. One more night with Lacey was one more night with Lacey. He'd be a damn fool to pass that up. "You want to go into Swynton for dinner? I hear they've got a new place on the other side of town."

"No. Let's just go to the Burger Bonanza. There are a few things I want to show you on the way."

"You're the boss, Mayor Cherish." He fired up the truck and headed toward downtown.

"Did you see we planted some flowers around the square?" Lacey asked.

He shook his head. He'd been so busy trying to chase down the dog-fighting ring and worrying about how to handle his family that he hadn't paid much attention to what had been going on around town. "Sorry, I haven't noticed."

She nodded. "Lots of folks are pretty excited about putting Ido on the map. Helmut even ordered a new sign for the Burger Bonanza."

"Really?" He glanced over at her.

"That's right. He said if we were going to get an influx of visitors he wanted to have something that would light up at night."

"Well, it's about time he upgraded his sign, whether this stunt works or not."

Her fingers wrapped around his arm. "It's going to work. We're going to have so much business people will wonder why we didn't do this years ago."

"I hope you're right." He looked out the window and caught a glimpse of the sign outside Ortega's. "'Congratulations Bodie and Lacey'?"

She bounced on the seat next to him. "Isn't that sweet? I told you everyone's excited."

His heart squeezed in his chest. Like someone had put it in a vise and was slowly tightening the jaws.

"Look. Suzy put up a sign, too." She pointed to the taxidermy shop. There in the window someone had written PROUD VENDOR OF THE PHILLIPS WEDDING in neon marker.

"Do you think this is getting a little out of control?" He took a hand from the wheel and reached for hers.

"Of course not. I think we finally found a way to bring everyone together. After the warehouse closed most folks around here thought they'd have to move if they wanted to find another job. But now we're poised to bring a whole bunch of business to town."

Guilt pressed down on him. "If I'd have known things were that bad with my dad and—"

"Stop." Lacey squeezed his hand. "What's done is done. Now it's up to us to move forward."

Moving forward. Is that what they were doing? He didn't feel like he was moving at all, not forward, backward, or even sideways. If anything, he felt stuck. Like he'd been caught up in a web of some sort and had no idea how to cut himself loose. He pulled into an empty spot at the Burger Bonanza. Lacey let him open her door and even tucked her hand into the crook of his arm as they made their way inside.

Jojo met them at the hostess stand. "Ah, it's the lovebirds. How many more days until the wedding?"

"Next Saturday," Lacey said. "You'd better have it on the calendar. You're doing the cake."

Jojo grabbed two menus. "Don't worry about that. I already started on it. I'm thinking about opening up a little business of my own and doing cakes on the side. I figure someone's going to need to help all those brides we'll be bringing in."

"I think that's a great idea." Lacey shot him an *I told you so* grin as she slid into the corner booth.

Bodie took a seat on the vinyl bench and waited for Jojo to drop the menus and move away. "People are opening up businesses? This better work."

"Stop worrying. Now that we've secured the article in the *Texas Times* there's nothing standing in our way." She sidled up next to him. "Why don't you put your arm around me? Callan Hiller's keeping an eye on us and I want to give him a good show."

Bodie obliged, snugging his arm around Lacey's shoulders and pulling her tight against him. She smelled like summer and sun and something citrusy. It was enough to tighten that vise to the point where it felt like his heart was going to be crushed. He wanted to tell her how he felt, to lay it all out there and see how she'd respond.

Before he could say a word, a clinking noise came from the table behind them. Several other diners lifted their flatware and began to tap their utensils against their water glasses. A chorus of clinks surrounded them.

Lacey turned to face him, her mouth a mere inch or so from his. "I've only ever seen this done at wedding receptions, but I think they want us to kiss."

He glanced around the cozy interior of the restaurant. Callan stood. "Kiss, kiss, kiss," he chanted.

Bodie didn't need further encouragement. He cradled her head in his hands and lowered his mouth to hers. As their lips touched, the vise loosened.

Lacey gasped as Bodie deepened the kiss. She felt herself falling, head over heels, her heart so full it nearly burst out of her chest. A round of enthusiastic applause pulled her back to her senses. She broke the kiss, her lungs burning for air.

Bodie opened his eyes and focused on hers. "That ought to keep them satisfied for a while."

"Mmm-hmm." She didn't want to waste any breath on making words. As she gathered her scattered bearings about her, she reminded herself it was just a show. Even though her pulse rocketed, her cheeks tingled, and her toes curled so tight she felt a foot cramp coming on, it was all pretend.

Bodie cleared his throat. "You want a burger basket or should we go all out and get a dinner platter?"

"Oh, I'm not very hungry. I think I'll just get a salad tonight."

His brow furrowed. "You sure?"

"Yeah." Her stomach was so tied in knots she couldn't imagine forcing food into it.

Dinner passed without any other strange requests. Bodie downed his entire burger platter and still managed to finish off her salad. Jojo came by to check on them one more time.

As she approached the table, she pulled her phone out of her apron. "Y'all don't mind if I snap a picture real quick, do you? Helmut wants me to put it up on our social media. He thinks people will want to eat at the same place BoLa had their last date night before the big day."

"BoLa?" Bodie asked.

"It's a mash-up of your names. Bodie plus Lacey equals BoLa, get it? All the celeb couples do it."

"But we're not famous," Lacey protested.

"After that article comes out you will be." Jojo snapped a few photos. "Thanks. And Helmut says dinner's on him."

"You sure about that?" Lacey asked. "I've worked here off and on for years and I've never heard of him comping someone a meal."

Jojo shrugged. "I guess there's a first time for everything."

Bodie slid a ten under his plate for a tip. "Ready to get going?"

"I sure am." Maybe Bodie was right. Things might be getting a little out of control. But with the wedding only a week away, their time in the spotlight was almost up. Which reminded her, they still had one big detail to work out. As they neared his truck, she pulled on his hand. "You know, we still haven't figured out how we're going to break up."

"We haven't even gotten married yet and you already want to leave me?" he joked.

"I'm serious. The wedding won't be real but people will think it is. We'll need a good reason to separate after. Something believable."

"Irreconcilable differences?" he suggested.

She shook her head. "That sounds complicated. Maybe you could cheat on me."

"No." Bodie stopped in his tracks, letting her hand drop.

She'd continued moving forward so she turned to face him. "Why not? It's just pretend."

"I'm not going to be the cheater. If you want out, you cheat on me." His jaw set, a hint of anger or hurt flickered in his eyes.

"I can't cheat on you. I'm the mayor." What kind of mayor would she be if she cheated on her brand-new husband?

"Well, I'm a deputy sheriff. Cheating's off the table. Pick something else."

"Fine. Um, how about we just say that we moved too fast? That we need a little space to catch our breath? Everyone will be so busy keeping up with all of the new business in town they won't even think about us."

"Fine. We'll say we moved too fast."

"That it was a rash decision to get married." She nodded. "If I come up with something better between now and then I'll let you know. Does that sound okay?"

"Whatever you think."

Lacey cast a nervous glance his way. She'd been concerned only about getting the media coverage, hadn't really thought about what might come next. They rode back to his apartment in silence, the only sound coming from the stereo speakers playing the local country station.

He pulled into the spot next to her truck and cut the engine. "You want to come in?"

Oh, she wanted to come in, all right. She wanted to come in and stay a good long while. All of this pretending had made her realize just how empty her shell of a life had become. On the outside it seemed like she had it all together: the adoring fiancé, the high-profile job, the big plans to save her hometown. But she'd been empty on the inside for a long time. Until her forced time with Bodie had lit her up like the fireworks finale on the Fourth of July.

Her fake engagement had been the best thing to happen to her since . . . she tried but she couldn't think of anything better. As much as she wanted to continue the facade, to keep up pretending that she and Bodie were going to tie the knot for real, time was running out and she needed to untangle her heart from his before she was too far gone.

"I'd better not. I still have so much to do."

He nodded. "Yeah, I figured."

She took her time getting out of his truck and switching over to hers, all the while what-ifs and why-nots swirled around in her head, almost making her see stars. Better to leave things like this. If she went inside there was a good chance she'd give in to the feelings all of this pretending with Bodie had stirred up inside. That would only make things harder in the long run.

"So I'll see you on Saturday?" she asked.

"I'll be the one in the penguin suit." He smiled, the kind of smile that made her want to throw her arms around his neck and kiss that smirk right off his lips.

Instead, she responded with a grin of her own. Then she threw the truck in gear and gunned it out of the parking lot before she did something she'd regret. Like fall a little more in love with the man of her dreams. The man she'd convinced to pose as her fake fiancé.

forty-five

A bead of sweat formed on his upper lip. Bodie swabbed at it with the handkerchief Lacey's dad had given him. He shouldn't be nervous. This wasn't real. It would all be over within the next eight to ten hours. It was like the play he did in fifth grade. He'd stand up on the stage, say his lines, and tomorrow he'd go back to normal life. Whatever the new normal was.

"You ready for this?" Jonah came into the room in a matching rented tux. With his dad and pops in jail, Bodie didn't have anyone else to ask to be his best man. At least he wouldn't have to stand out there alone, even if it was only Jonah at his side.

"Can't wait." Bodie tried to squash the anxiety blooming in his chest.

"It's okay to be nervous, man. I puked ten minutes before Amelia walked down the aisle." Jonah clapped him on the back.

"No shit?" For some reason that made Bodie feel just slightly better.

Jonah shook his head. "Yeah. But then I saw her coming toward me and everything faded away. It was like it was just her and me and we were the only two people in the world."

"That's beautiful, man."

"You think so?" Jonah asked.

"Sure. You should put that in a love song or something." Bodie cracked a grin.

"Don't try giving me shit. I've seen the way you look at Lacey."

Bodie's stomach clenched. "Oh yeah, how's that?"

"Like she's it for you, dude. And you're it for her." Jonah adjusted his bow tie, winking at himself in the mirror.

More like she's the sun and the stars and the moon all rolled into one, Bodie thought. But he didn't say that. He hardly wanted to acknowledge those feelings to himself, much less let anyone else know what kind of fucked-up feelings he was having about his bride.

His bride.

He was marrying Lacey Cherish today. Even though it didn't count, even though they were both pretending, a part of him couldn't believe his good luck. Even though it would last only for an evening.

"Is she ready?" Bodie asked. Jonah had gone to check on things while he sweated it out, waiting for some signal that he should make his way to the garden.

"Just about." Jonah fidgeted with Bodie's tie. "And damn, she looks fine."

"I'm sure she does," Bodie said. He didn't need Jonah to drive the point home. Lacey would have looked fine in a potato sack. She sure as hell looked fine in nothing at all. As he remembered the last time he'd had his hands on her, his pulse ticked up.

"I mean, really fine. Like if I weren't already married, I'd give you a run for your money for her."

Bodie swatted Jonah's hands away. "Are you seriously

telling me on my wedding day that you want to make a play for my almost-wife?"

"What? Nah. Just saying she looks fantastic. You're going to be one lucky bastard later on tonight, know what I mean?"

Bodie closed his eyes for a beat, wishing for half a second that Luke was here with him, not this messed-up stand-in. When he got married for real, he'd want Luke by his side.

"You do know what I mean, right?" Jonah flung an elbow out, catching Bodie in the side.

"Yes," Bodie ground out between clenched teeth. He didn't need to be reminded of what ought to be happening on his wedding night. If this were a real wedding. And if Lacey were a real bride. And if he'd had the balls to tell her how he really felt. So many ifs.

Jojo knocked then cracked the door open a hair. "We're ready for you, gentlemen."

"Showtime." Jonah clapped him on the back, having no idea just how accurate his words were.

Bodie moved down the hall, casting a long look at the closed door to the bridal dressing room. What was Lacey thinking right now? Knowing her, she'd probably processed through today's events and was already making plans for how to handle it when the article came out. With a final glance at the door, he headed down the steps and out into the bright May afternoon.

Lacey straightened her veil. "Are you sure this looks okay?" she asked.

"You look absolutely stunning." Zina stepped behind her, meeting her gaze in the mirror. "Bodie's going to eat his heart out."

Lacey let her eyes drift closed, imagining what it

would feel like if she were about to walk down the aisle and marry Bodie Phillips for real.

"You sure you want to do this?" Zina asked.

Lacey's eyes opened wide. "Of course. We're in the homestretch now."

"What about tomorrow?" Zina slid a hairpin behind Lacey's ear, capturing an errant wave.

"Tomorrow's a whole day away."

Zina checked her watch. "Tomorrow's less than ten hours away. What's going to happen tomorrow when you wake up and realize you had the chance to tell Bodie how you really feel and missed it?"

"Don't be silly. I'm not going to mess anything up right now by telling him how I really feel."

"So you do love him?" Zina jumped, clapping her hands together.

"Love?" Lacey whirled around and gave her friend a teasing grin. "I've always loved Bodie. He's like the extra brother I never wanted."

"Honey, you can keep telling yourself that if you want, but I know the truth." Zina pinched Lacey's cheeks together. "You want to marry that man and make beautiful babies together. Admit it."

"I will not."

"If you don't tell him, I will."

"You wouldn't."

"You wanna bet?" Zina clamped her hands on her hips. Arguing with her was pointless—Lacey had learned that the hard way many times over.

"Not tonight. Tonight has to be perfect. Let's just get through the ceremony and I promise I'll talk to him about it."

"Tomorrow?" Zina asked.

Lacey nodded. "Or the day after that."

"Tomorrow or else I'm telling that man the truth." Zina held out her hand.

"Fine." Lacey took Zina's hand in hers.

"Girl, your hands are like ice cubes. You're going to give him the chills if you don't warm up." Zina rubbed Lacey's hands between hers.

"I don't know what's wrong with me today."

"You're in love with the man you're about to marry." Zina blew on their hands then rubbed even faster. "There's nothing wrong with you."

Lacey pondered that for a moment. She'd never come right out and admit it to Zina, but her friend was right. She did love Bodie. Loved him with a fierceness that scared the crap out of her. Everyone and everything she'd ever given her heart to had left her. She couldn't bear to tell Bodie how she felt and have him walk away. Losing her mom had been tragic—no one saw it coming and there'd been no way to protect herself from going through the pain. But if she told Bodie she loved him and he didn't say it back . . . well, she'd be setting herself up, risking her heart, her very soul. She wasn't sure she could put herself through that. Definitely not today, maybe not ever.

Jojo knocked at the door. "They're ready for you, Lacey."

Zina squeezed her hands. "Let's do this."

"Okay." Lacey nodded. She'd get through today and play tomorrow by ear. That's the best she could do, the most Zina could ask of her.

forty-six

Bodie stood next to the wooden arbor, waiting for his first glimpse of Lacey. Shotgun waddled down the aisle, a heart-shaped pillow attached to her collar. The fake rings nestled in the middle, tied on with thin satin ribbons. Lacey had balked when he suggested they involve Shotgun in the wedding. She'd argued that the poor dog would probably be so uncomfortable by then she might not make it down the aisle. Then she'd almost had a heart attack when he wanted to tie the rings to the pillow. Luckily he'd realized she was right. The giant fake diamond ring and the thin gold band that went along with it were safe and sound in Jonah's front pocket.

Bodie patted his thigh and Shotgun plopped down next to him, letting out a blast of gas as her bum hit the ground. He stifled a laugh. Poor dog.

Zina came next, taking long confident strides down the aisle. The orange dress—coral, he reminded himself—looked fabulous against her tanned skin. She made it to the front of the aisle and gave him a wink before stepping to the side and turning around to wait for Lacey.

A trumpet sounded, a pair of mariachis began to shake. The band he'd found at the last minute down at Ortega's Taqueria launched into a shaky rendition of "Here Comes the Bride."

Zina gave him one of her looks. The kind that made him squirm. He lifted his shoulders in a slight shrug. The friend he thought he could count on for the music was playing a gig up in Fort Worth tonight. At least they had something.

The blood rushed to his head, making him feel slightly dizzy as he caught his first look at Lacey. Like an angel, she floated down the aisle. The dress, her mama's dress, reached all the way to the ground and billowed out behind her. His gaze roamed over the dip at her waist, the obnoxious bouquet Suzy had created, then moved higher. Her smile dazzled him. Like looking right into the sun. She was so bright, so stunning, he had to look away before his emotions got the best of him.

After what seemed like eternity but also much too soon, she reached for him with one hand while she passed her flowers to Zina with the other. He took both of her hands in his and met her gaze. What he saw there was like looking at a reflection of himself. The fear, the uncertainty, it was right there in front of him. But more than that, he recognized love. A pure, shining love that flowed right through him, lighting him up inside until he felt like he could do anything as long as he had Lacey by his side.

The minister they'd found online leaned toward them. "You have the rings?" he whispered.

"Yes," Bodie said. "Jonah's got them." He didn't want to tear his eyes away from Lacey. Her smile told him she felt the same way. Once again, he wished he could pause time. Take a quick break to tell her he didn't want to pretend anymore. He wanted to marry her for real if she'd have him.

But before he could, Shotgun rolled to her side with a groan. He glanced down. Jonah put a hand on his shoulder. "She's fine, keep going."

Bodie looked up again, his heart in his throat as his eyes met Lacey's. Just looking at her hurt like hell.

The minister launched into the ceremony. "We're gathered here today to celebrate the union of Bodie and Lacey as they declare their love before each other and all of you."

Risking a quick look at the crowd, Bodie caught sight of Jay working the perimeter, snapping pictures with a giant camera. Samantha sat in the third row, dabbing at her eyes with a tissue. Good. Lacey would get her pictures and the article that would hopefully catapult her new venture to success. Jojo and Helmut sat on Lacey's side of the aisle. Lacey had asked Jojo to put her dad on video chat for the ceremony so he'd feel like he was part of it. Everyone who'd pitched in on the house renovation was there; their excitement and hope seemed to fill the air.

Then the mood shifted. Tension crackled through the crowd. Bodie tore his gaze away from Lacey's as a shadow fell over them. He looked up, just in time to catch a fist. A fist that connected with his jaw, sending him crashing into the wooden arbor. The sound of splitting wood flooded his ears.

He turned toward the attacker, ready for a fight. Was it someone sent by Buck? Was this his way of getting revenge?

Lacey launched herself onto the man's back. "Stop! Just stop." Her hands slid from his forehead down to cover his eyes.

The man spun one way, then the other, trying to dislodge her. He stumbled through the butterfly garden they'd just planted, crushing the young plants under heavy boots. Military boots.

"Get off me, Lacey. I've got a score to settle and I don't want you getting hurt."

Luke. Bodie hadn't seen his friend in years. The buzz cut threw him, but there was no denying the blond giant in front of him was Lacey's brother.

"Let me explain," Lacey shouted.

Luke grappled with her arms, trying to get a grip so he could slip her off his back. She slid to one side and he reached back, gently lowering her to the ground. She made a grab for his leg, trying to hold him back but it was too late.

Bodie stood his ground, his palms out in front of him. "I don't want to fight. Let's talk about this."

"No talking necessary," Luke growled. His fist connected with Bodie's arm. Pain radiated out from where the punch landed.

Bodie scrambled up the steps to the house. "Cut it out. Give me a chance to explain."

Luke flung the door open, sending it crashing into the plaster wall.

Bodie tried again. "It's not what you think, man."

"I think you took advantage of my sister." Luke reached out, shoving Bodie against the buffet table. Chafing dishes went flying. Barbecue sauce splattered the curtains. A Sterno can landed on the carpet. The flame licked at the tablecloth.

Bodie stomped out the fire and backed toward the door. He needed to get Luke out of there before he ruined the whole place. "Stop. You don't know what you're talking about."

Luke advanced, fury making his blue eyes burn bright. "I'm talking about you using her."

"I'd never do that." The fact Luke could even accuse him of something like that sparked a rage in his gut.

"Stop it, both of you." Lacey hiked her dress up and climbed the steps to the porch. "You're ruining everything. Luke, what are you doing here? You weren't supposed to find out about this until it was over and Bodie and I had gone our separate ways."

Bodie put a hand to his head. "Lacey, stop. You don't have to do this."

The look she gave him told him she didn't believe him. She thought he was still playing his part. "It's okay, Bodie. This is all my fault."

"How's it your fault?" Luke asked. "He's the one who took advantage. He's the one who knocked you up."

"Knocked me up?" Lacey turned her anger on her brother, her voice rising. "Who on earth told you that? I made Bodie pretend to be engaged to me so we could get an article in a magazine to promote the wedding venue. No one's knocked up. No one's really getting married. It's all fake."

Bodie reached for her hand, his heart breaking for her, for him, for everything real that had happened between them. "Lacey, I do love you."

She swatted his hand away. "Enough. It's over."

She didn't believe him. Either that or she didn't care. For her it had all been a means to an end. He'd underestimated her and her willingness to do whatever it would take to reach her goals. With a gaping hole in his chest where his heart had once beaten for her, he took one last look at the house then turned his back and walked away.

forty-seven

"It's ruined. Everything is ruined and it's all my fault."
Lacey sat on the grass next to Luke, wishing Bodie were
there to hold her hand. But she'd gone and ruined that,
too, and she couldn't even find him to apologize. He'd
rushed poor Shotgun to the vet. She'd gone into labor
while Luke had been chasing Bodie around the grounds
of the house, crushing everything in his path. At least the
fire hadn't spread. Bodie's quick thinking had prevented
any major damage to the house.

"I'm sorry." Luke slung his arm around her.

She appreciated the effort but his hug lacked the comfort of Bodie's. A new wave of tears threatened to over-
whelm her. She'd probably never have another chance to
feel Bodie's arms around her. He told her he loved her.
She'd waited her whole life to hear those words from him.
And she blew him off, dismissed him like he'd offered her
a piece of trash, not a piece of his heart.

"Where did you ever get the idea I was pregnant?"

Lacey flipped around to look at her brother. Despite the circumstances, it was good to see him.

Luke sighed. "It was an e-mail from Adeline. She said you and Bodie had been messing around and she overheard you saying you were pregnant. I couldn't believe it. But then she said you were getting married this weekend so I put in for emergency leave. I didn't want you to make a mistake."

"Adeline." Lacey's hands clenched into fists. "She was jealous because the reporter decided to cover my wedding in the magazine instead of hers. And she's probably still mad at me for getting arrested during her bachelorette party and ruining her weekend."

"What?" Luke eyed her from under the brim of his cap.

"Long story. Bottom line is, she'll go to any lengths to get what she wants."

Luke scoffed. "Sounds like someone else I know."

That truth hit a little too close to home. "I'm like that, too, aren't I? No wonder I scared Bodie away."

She let that thought settle over her, suffocating her, making it almost impossible to breathe.

"There you are." Samantha stopped in front of her, somehow untouched by the fight and the chaos that had taken its toll on everyone else. "I'm sure you realize we can't feature the wedding in *Texas Times* next month."

Lacey nodded. "I understand. I'm sorry I lied about the wedding."

Samantha planted a hand on her hip. "I don't know why you felt like you had to. This place is magical. You don't need the media coverage to make it into a success."

Jay grimaced and offered a pseudo salute. Lacey lifted her hand in a wave as they picked their way through the remains of her wedding day, heading toward the parking lot.

"When do you have to head back?" Lacey rested her head on Luke's shoulder.

"Next Friday."

"But that's barely a week. Why so soon?" He'd probably spend more time on airplanes than he would on the ground.

"That's emergency leave. I ought to get a few more weeks sometime this summer. We can have a longer visit then." He pushed up, pulling her to her feet next to him. "An uneventful visit, okay?"

"Okay. We should probably get you home so Dad can see you. How did you even get here?"

"Rented a car. Need a ride?"

"No. I'm going to stay here and see what I can do to help."

He pressed a kiss to her forehead. "Don't be so hard on yourself, okay?"

"Easier said than done." She pulled her brother in for a hug before letting him go. Then she climbed the steps, ready to do what she could to clean up the mess she'd made.

"Haven't you already done enough?" Jojo was the first one to notice her. "Go on home, Lacey. We don't need your help."

"But . . ." She glanced around, looking for a friendly face. Or at least a face that didn't look so angry. Helmut, Jojo, even Suzy, glared at her.

"Come on, Lacey, let's get you home." Zina put her hands on Lacey's shoulders, turning her toward the door.

"I want to help—"

"Trust me, now's not the time," Zina said.

Lacey let her friend lead her down the steps and across the lawn, where people folded up chairs, packed up the food that had been salvaged from the kitchen, and removed all evidence that this was supposed to have been the happiest day of her life.

With her heart shattering into a million pieces, Lacey turned her back on what she thought would be her future. There was no one to blame but herself. She'd let everyone down: her friends, her family, her town. But most of all, Bodie. He'd never be able to forgive her.

forty-eight

Someone knocked at the door. Bodie rolled over in bed, pulling a pillow over his head. There was no one he wanted to see, no one he wanted to hear from. Not now.

The knock came again, louder this time. He checked his phone for a message from the vet. She'd promised she'd call if anything happened with Shotgun. When he'd left at four this morning, the pup had been nursing her litter of eight. Seven girls and a boy. Poor little bastard didn't know what he was in for. Girls sucked.

"Bodie, open up. I'm not going away," Luke threatened.

The last person he expected at his door this morning was Luke Cherish. Okay, the second-to-last person. The very last person he expected to see was Lacey. Not after the way she'd dismissed him last night. He snagged the other pillow and pressed that one down on his head, too. The knocking stopped. Finally.

A minute later the sliding glass door to the patio opened. Luke let himself into the bedroom, standing like a hulk at the end of the bed. "Get up, we need to talk."

"What the hell, Luke? How did you get in here?"

"You should be more careful," Luke said with a smile. He held up a brown paper bag and a cup. "Brought you coffee and a breakfast taco from Ortega's."

Bodie wasn't up for chatting, but he'd missed out on dinner last night. His stomach growled. "Fine. You talk, I'll listen. But only until I finish my taco."

"Good thing I brought you two." Luke moved to the kitchen.

Bodie pulled a shirt on and followed. He took a seat on the opposite side of the table and reached for the bag.

Luke leaned back in his chair and sighed. "Lacey told me everything."

Everything? Bodie wondered if she told him about the night they spent in the hotel. Probably not or Luke would still be trying to kick his ass. He bit into the warm tortilla.

"I guess I owe you an apology." Luke looked away. Saying sorry had never come easy for him. "I know you were trying to do the right thing. I'm sorry I doubted your intentions."

His mouth full of the perfect blend of eggs and chorizo, Bodie just nodded.

"And for what it's worth, I've given it some thought and I think you and Lacey would be"—he scrubbed a hand over his chin—"Hell, I can't believe I'm saying this, but I think you might be good together."

Bodie's stomach churned. He dropped the little bit of his taco he hadn't finished yet. "We were good together. I didn't mean to let it get out of control. Went into it just trying to help. Well, that and your sister blackmailed me."

"She did?" Luke grinned.

Nodding, Bodie reached for the last bite of taco.

"Well, I'll be damned." Leaning forward, Luke dropped his voice a notch. "She feels bad about last night."

"I'm sure she'll get over it. She's probably already over

at the house, trying to figure out how to get everything fixed up again." That's what Lacey did.

"Nah. She's home. Won't come out of her room. I guess some folks told her off last night. They didn't appreciate being lied to."

"But she did it for them," Bodie said. "Everything she did, she did for the town. She put this wedding business above everything . . . her job, her own happiness."

"I guess it didn't work out. She's always been like that, you know that about her. She thinks if she can maintain control of things she won't get hurt."

Luke was right. All along Bodie thought Lacey was holding back because she didn't care. But she was scared. How had he not realized that before?

"I've got to go." Bodie scooted back from the table.

"But you haven't finished your taco."

"I don't have time for tacos. There's something I need to do."

"Something involving my sister?" Luke asked.

Bodie stepped into his boots then turned to face his best friend. "Something involving my future wife."

forty-nine

Lacey frowned as she licked the back of an envelope and pressed it closed. That ought to do it. She'd spent the last two days writing a personal apology note to each and every person who'd had anything to do with the renovation of the Phillips House. From the guy who trapped the armadillos to Bodie's friend who'd built the gorgeous arbor that had been smashed to pieces . . . she'd written *I'm sorry* so many times she'd practically had to hold her right hand still with her left to keep it from continuing to move.

They didn't want her help fixing things up and she didn't have another shift at the Burger Bonanza until next week. This was supposed to be her fake honeymoon where she and Bodie were going to hide out somewhere and let people think they were off celebrating their union as newlyweds. She didn't know where they were supposed to go—that was the one part of the weekend Bodie had kept as a surprise. He'd just told her to bring some casual clothes and toss in a swimsuit. For all she knew they'd be barricaded into his place for four days living on frozen pizza and beer.

Thinking about Bodie made her heart tighten. Especially when she recalled the look on his face the last time she'd seen him. Rejection. Confusion. Pain. She thought she'd been protecting herself by denying her feelings, but knowing she'd pushed him away hurt even worse than it would have if he'd left her.

So she'd ruined everything, not just Ido's chance to rebuild itself into a thriving destination-wedding community, but also any possibility of a relationship with the man she loved. The town would probably ask for her resignation. If what Bodie said was true and her dad was likely to get released from house arrest then she wouldn't have to stick around. She could go anywhere, make a fresh start, and keep a low profile for a change.

With a heavy heart at the thought of having to leave everything—and everyone—behind, she cracked open her bedroom door. She'd barely left her room in the past forty-eight hours.

"Dad, you got any stamps?" She padded down the hall toward the family room, the huge stack of envelopes in her hands.

"Hey, sweetheart." Dad met her in the hall. He'd shaved and had on a clean pair of khakis and a fresh shirt. Maybe he was starting to feel better now that she'd relieved him of the honor of being the most depressed person in the house. "Someone came by to see you."

"What?" Lacey blew a clump of hair away from her face. She hadn't bothered to take her updo down from the other night so her hair probably resembled a rat's nest. Or an armadillo burrow. Thinking about the lies she told about the rogue armadillo made her tear up again.

"Come here, sweetheart." Dad wrapped an arm around her and led her into the kitchen, where the table had been transformed. Tapered candles flickered and a black table-cloth stretched to the ground.

"What's this?" she asked, looking around.

Pointing to the table, her dad shrugged. A single plate sat in the center.

"Is that flan?" She set the envelopes down on the counter and moved closer. It was flan. She turned to look at her dad, but he was gone. "What's going on?"

Bodie entered the kitchen, looking absolutely edible in a pair of dark pants and a white button-down shirt. She took in a ragged breath, already wiping away the tears that threatened to spill over her lashes.

He took the plate from the table and held it out to her. A ring sat in the center of the flan, an emerald-cut yellow diamond, not nearly as big as the one he'd given her before.

"Lacey Cherish"—he got down on one knee—"I know we've had our ups and downs over the past few months, and I know the timing on this probably sucks . . ."

She nodded, not trusting herself to speak.

"But I need to let you know something. Our engagement started out fake but the feelings I have for you are very real."

Lacey shook out her hands, trying to quell the pinpricks of anxiety marching up and down her limbs.

"I'm going to ask you a question now and I want you to be totally honest with me, okay?"

She bit her lip and nodded.

"Will you do me the honor of—"

Lacey couldn't wait any longer. She ran to him, crashing into him, smothering his face with kisses, running her hands over his arms, his shoulders, his hair.

"Lacey. You didn't let me ask the question."

"It's yes. It's always been yes with you. Yes now, yes before, yes forever."

Bodie laughed. "I just wondered if you'd rather join me for flan or chocolate cake for dessert."

"I don't like flan." She kissed the edge of his mouth then trailed kisses to his ear.

"That's why I brought you the cake." He fell back to his butt, settling her on his lap. "But I also wanted to get your engagement story right."

"I'm so sorry." She ran her palms over his cheeks, wanting to make sure he was really here, in the flesh, not some figment of her imagination. "I just wanted everything to be perfect. But I screwed it up. And then you were there, and Luke, too."

Bodie ran a hand over her hair, trying to smooth it down. "I know. I'm sorry, too. I should have been up front with you about what was going on with my family."

"You were just trying to protect them." Like he'd tried to protect her. Like he protected everyone and everything. "I should have believed you when you said you weren't going to rig the election. You're not that kind of man."

"We both messed up." He touched his forehead to hers. "So you ready for the real question?"

She nodded.

"Will you marry me?"

In a split second those four words changed everything. "Yes! Of course I'll marry you. I've wanted to marry you my whole life."

"Good, let's go." Bodie slipped the ring on her finger and made a move to stand.

"What, now?" She ran a hand over her hair. "I can't marry you now, I'm a mess."

He pressed a kiss to her lips as he lifted her to her feet. "Don't worry, I lined up a little help."

fifty

♡

Bodie stood next to the repaired wooden arbor, waiting for his first glimpse of Lacey. There was no maid of honor, no best man. Shotgun was still at the vet taking care of her new brood so they didn't have a ring bearer, either. His gaze rested on each one of the folks who'd gathered under the gorgeous Texas sky to bear witness to him and Lacey pledging their love to each other.

Jojo gave him a thumbs-up then started the music he'd downloaded. Strains of "Here Comes the Bride" floated through the portable speakers. He tried to force a swallow past the lump in his throat. Her dad appeared first, his arm crooked at the elbow where Lacey had tucked her hand.

Bodie closed his eyes for a heartbeat. When he opened them again, she was there . . . a vision in white in the dress he'd driven into Houston to have dry-cleaned overnight. Escorted by her dad on one side and her brother on the other, she floated toward him.

Her lips curved into a tentative smile. The closer she came, the bigger her smile got until it stretched clear across her face. His cheeks hurt from beaming back at her but he couldn't help himself. He couldn't tear his eyes away from her any more than he could stop the world from turning or stop his heart from beating.

She paused in front of him and he waited while first her brother, then her dad, kissed her on the cheek and shook his hand. He was gaining so much more than a bride today, he was gaining a family. He'd always felt more a part of the Cherish family than his own but binding his heart to Lacey's for a lifetime would make it official.

Her dad took the small bouquet of wildflowers she'd been holding and handed them to Zina who sat in the front row. Lacey put both of her hands in Bodie's.

"Ladies and gentlemen, we're gathered here today to celebrate the union of Bodie and Lacey." Thank goodness the minister had been free. Bodie tried to listen but he could barely hear the man through the sound of blood whooshing through his ears.

"Do you, Bodie Phillips, take Lacey Cherish to be your lawfully wedded wife? Do you promise to love, honor, cherish, and protect her, in sickness and in health, for richer or for poorer, for as long as you both live?"

His heart pounded as he waited for the minister to finish speaking. "I do."

"Do you, Lacey Cherish, take Bodie Phillips to be your lawfully wedded husband? Do you promise to love, honor, cherish, and protect him, in sickness and in health, for richer or for poorer, for as long as you both live?"

Lacey's eyes shone. She nodded, smiling as she said the words, "I do."

Bodie let out a sigh as the minister led them through the exchange of rings. He couldn't tear his gaze away from Lacey, the most beautiful bride he'd ever seen. His bride. His wife.

As the two of them joined hands and turned to be introduced for the first time as husband and wife, he swept his gaze over those gathered. If Lacey thought she'd burned her bridges, she was wrong. The town had finally done what she'd been trying to get them to do all along. They'd come together to build something beautiful, something that would give them all hope for years to come.

The flash of a camera caught his attention and he blinked. There in the back, Jay crouched down in the center of the aisle and snapped picture after picture.

Whatever happened with Ido was out of his hands. He had what he needed—the woman next to him. No matter what came next, they'd face it together. As a couple, as a community, as a town.

epilogue

Lacey skipped up the steps to the sheriff's office. She'd been in the middle of a city council meeting when she'd gotten the call from Jojo, who'd talked to her sister in Houston, who'd been shopping at the local market and picked up a copy of *Texas Times*. Lacey had hopped in her truck and driven the ninety miles round-trip to Beaumont to grab her own copy, not willing to believe what she'd heard until she saw it with her own eyes.

"Is Bodie in?" She barely paused in the reception area before brushing past the sheriff's secretary's desk.

The woman pointed to Bodie's open door as Lacey whisked by.

"Hey, Sweets." He rounded the desk, greeting her with a kiss.

They'd been married only a month and she still couldn't believe this gorgeous, caring, wonderful man was hers. As his lips touched hers, heat blazed through her veins and she almost forgot the reason she had to barge into his office unannounced.

"Look! It's in here, all of it." She thrust the magazine at him.

"What's this?"

"I don't know what you said to them, but they sure came through. We've got a picture on the cover and they did a whole story inside."

He spread the issue out on his desk, flipping through the four-page spread Samantha and Jay had put together. The article didn't just cover the wedding venue, it went into detail about the people who came together to find a way to save their beloved town. There were pictures of the house, the grounds, and even one of Shotgun with her litter of puppies.

"Have you shown Shotgun yet?" he asked.

Lacey laughed. "No. But I will when I get home. Poor girl needs a break from those demanding puppies. They haven't let her have a moment's peace."

Bodie touched his nose to hers. "More like you need some cuddle time with the pups."

"Yeah, maybe I'll give her a break and let them crawl all over me for a while." She might joke, but she loved being around Shotgun and her puppies. "Have you decided which one we're going to keep?"

"If it were up to you, I think we'd end up with all of them."

Lacey grinned as she shrugged her shoulders. "When we get that place in the country you keep talking about, we'll have room."

"Well, we're for sure keeping the boy. I can't be the only male around."

Nodding, Lacey took his hands. "I figured you'd say that. Fine, the boy it is. And maybe one or two of his sisters?"

"We'll see."

"You sure you can't leave early today?" She wrapped an arm around his waist, snapping his hips to hers.

"I've got another lead on that dog-fighting ring. I told Suarez I'd follow up on it this afternoon."

"Good. But don't work too late. I'm making brisket for dinner." She arched a brow as he nuzzled her neck, whispering promises of what he'd do to her later.

Her phone buzzed in her purse, a number she didn't recognize. "Hold up a sec." Bodie pulled back as she answered. "Hello?"

"Hi, I saw the article in the *Texas Times* about your wedding venue. I'm wondering if you have any openings for this fall. I know it's short notice, but it sounds like exactly what my fiancé and I have in mind."

Lacey grinned up at Bodie. "Of course. Why don't you give me your name, phone number, and the date you're looking at? I'll need to check the calendar when I get back to the office but I'm pretty sure we can work something out."

Lacey jotted down the information on a receipt she found in her purse then disconnected.

"We did it." She held up the piece of paper, a proud grin making her cheeks feel like they were splitting in two.

"You did it, Sweets." Bodie pulled her in for a hug. "You were the one who had the vision, the drive, and the commitment to make it happen."

"Jojo's going to be thrilled. I've gotta go. I need to tell her." As she tucked her phone in her purse, it buzzed again. She glanced to Bodie. "What do I do?"

He laughed. "Answer it."

"Ido, Texas, providing homegrown happily ever afters. How can I help you?" Lacey's eyes widened as she listened to yet another bride inquire about booking the space.

While the woman carried on, Lacey ran her gaze over the man in front of her. He was just as responsible for this as she was, probably even more so. If he hadn't come back and forced her to face her feelings, she'd probably be waiting tables somewhere, afraid to set foot in Ido, Texas, ever again. She jotted down another number and disconnected.

"You were right, Bodie. It's happening." She stepped close, wrapping her arms around his waist.

He kissed her, slow and deep. Then pulled away, a grin on his face. "You know what you need to do now, don't you?"

"What's that?" If it was up to her, they'd go home, snuggle the new pups for a bit, then crawl into bed and not come up for air for hours.

"It's time for you to call a press conference."

"Oh no. The last time I did that, things didn't go so well." Her heart leapt into her throat as she thought about the last time she'd faced the town.

"Yeah, but this time you've got big news."

"And what exactly am I supposed to tell them?"

"That's easy, Sweets. You tell them Ido, Texas, is open for business."

acknowledgments

It takes a team to bring a book into the world. Huge thanks to everyone at Berkley for believing in this series and helping me bring Ido, Texas, to life. To my editor, Kristine Swartz, thanks for taking a chance on me and for making me look good! And to my agent, Jessica Watterson, I'm so glad we're in this together. Thanks for always having my back. To the members of Crushin' It Crew, my reader group, hugs and kisses for your continued support of my writing. Y'all have no idea how much joy it brings me to get to chat with you every day. And to my readers, thank you for reading my books and sharing them with your friends. You're the reason I get to tell stories and I'm so grateful for your support. To my critique partners and beta readers, especially Christina Hovland, Dawn Luedecke, Renee Ann Miller, and Serena Bell, thanks for catching my mistakes and typos before they made it onto the page. And to my family, especially my hubby and kiddos, thanks for your encouragement, your belief in me, and for sharing my books with your coworkers, friends, and sometimes even your teachers. So much for keeping this writing gig on the down low, huh? ;)

KEEP READING FOR AN EXCERPT FROM
DYLANN CRUSH'S NEXT
TYING THE KNOT IN TEXAS NOVEL . . .

her kind of cowboy

AVAILABLE IN PAPERBACK
JANUARY 2021 FROM JOVE!

♡

Zina Baxter kicked the covers off and let her foot drop to the ground. Her toes squished around in something unmistakably dog-related. Something unmistakably foul. She groaned. It had to be dog poop. She thought she'd housebroken the rescue pup she'd brought home from the shelter with her last night, but it looked like they still had a way to go.

Typically the sun would have risen by now but with the slew of thunderstorms that had settled over Ido, Texas, for the past several days, Zina couldn't make out more than a few hazy outlines in the early light of dawn.

"Dammit, Herbie. I thought we talked about this."

The pup hopped off the bed, the tags on his collar jangling, and appeared at her side. With a quick swipe of his tongue all of her anger dissipated. It wasn't his fault he wasn't housebroken yet. She'd been running the For Pitties' Sake pit bull rescue for a few years now. Even the most loving pups came with a ton of baggage. The thunder and lightning during last night's storm probably set him off.

She ran a hand over the back of his head. "It's okay, bud." Then she shifted her weight to her heels and waddled to the bathroom to clean off her foot. By the time she'd showered, cleaned up Herbie's mess, and driven the short distance to the shelter, the sky had lightened a few shades.

Staff would be in later, but she'd taken the morning shift today. That meant it was up to her to get the dogs fed and out for the morning. Herbie trotted alongside her as she unlocked the front door and let herself in to the crumbling building For Pitties' Sake had called home for the last several years. A puddle of liquid greeted her.

At first she thought one of the dozens of dogs at the rescue had broken out of its kennel and had an accident. But when she flipped on the light and looked toward the ceiling she immediately spotted the source of the leak. Her stomach twisted. Several tiles of the drop-down ceiling sagged. A line of rainwater dripped in a constant *plop-plop*, splashing onto her feet as she stood in shock.

Herbie plunged through the puddle, licking up the water and taking the opportunity to splash around.

"This isn't here to play with." Zina let out a sigh. She'd been working on an idea for a special event to increase awareness about the shelter. Now she'd have to shift all of her energy into raising enough funds to clean up this mess and make repairs. For a moment she wished she'd never taken on this project, had stayed in the military, and never come back to Ido, Texas.

A chorus of barks and yips sounded from the back of the building. The dogs. That's why she'd taken over. And that's why she'd stayed. As she made her way toward the back where the kennels were set up, her phone rang.

"Good morning, sunshine." Her best friend, Lacey, practically sang into the phone.

"What are you so happy about?"

"Gee, who crapped in your cereal this morning?"

"It wasn't my cereal. It was my bedroom floor and I put my foot in it."

"Oh, hon. Which lucky male did you take home with you last night?"

"Herbie."

"And that's the way he treated you?"

"Hey, I'm used to getting shit on by members of the opposite sex. Just look at my last attempt at a relationship." She should have known the last guy she tried dating was cheating on her. All the signs were there, she'd just been too busy to notice.

"We still on for lunch?"

"I've gotta cancel," Zina said. "There's a leak at the shelter and I've got to get it patched up before the rain starts again."

"Oh no. Are all of the dogs okay?" Lacey asked.

"Yeah, they seem to be. But I've got a few inches of water to sop up."

"My offer still stands, you know."

Zina shook her head. "I'm not going to pimp out my pups so you can bring in more crazy brides." Lacey had been after her to come up with some sort of puppy wedding package. Ever since she'd been elected mayor and revamped the tiny town of Idont, Texas, into Ido, she'd started billing it as the best place in Texas to tie the knot and had come up with all kinds of crackpot ideas.

"Just think about it, you bring over a couple of the dogs to take part in a few weddings and you'll earn enough to get the roof replaced in no time at all."

There had to be another way. Zina loved her bestie, they'd had each other's backs since they were in junior high together, but this latest obsession of Lacey's had her shaking her head. "I'll figure something out."

The muffled barks turned into an earsplitting chorus

as she pushed through the door from the front office to the back. "I'll have to call you later. I've got to get the dogs fed."

"I'll stop by with lunch around noon. Work for you?"

"Sure." One less thing to have to think about today. Although, holding Lacey at bay with her crazy ideas might take more effort than trying to figure out what to feed herself for lunch so it might not be an equal trade-off.

"See you in a bit."

Zina disconnected and slid her phone back into her pocket. As she let the first phase of pups out to the runs in back, she searched for more damage. Besides a few small drips and drops, the back of the building didn't seem to have any major issues. Thank goodness. She didn't think she could deal with another crisis.

Lacey might be embracing all things having to do with Ido, but Zina couldn't seem to get on board the crazy train idea of transforming their tiny town into a mecca for demanding brides. Ever since last spring when they'd had that article in *Texas Times*, the town had been bursting at the seams with weddings and the headaches that came with them.

Lacey was in hog heaven since her sole role as mayor was to force some breath of life back into the town. But Zina, along with quite a few other longtime residents, weren't so thrilled with having a slew of outsiders descend on their small corner of Texas every weekend. If anything, the wedding business had caused an increase in the number of pit bulls being abandoned to For Pitties' Sake. And that was something Zina vowed to fix.

"You really need to take care of this." Lacey stepped over the piles of towels Zina had used to sop up the water that continued to drip from the ceiling.

"I put a call in for someone to come take a look this

afternoon." Zina picked up the wet towels and traded them out for a fresh batch she'd just pulled out of the dryer. At this rate, she wouldn't be able to keep up. Unless she wanted to move into the shelter and work towel patrol all weekend, she needed to figure out a way to stop the water.

"I got you a taco dinner from Ortega's. That ought to lift your spirits." Lacey reached into the brown paper bag she'd brought with her and set the food on the counter.

Zina's stomach growled. She'd been so busy this morning the thought of breakfast hadn't even crossed her mind and now it was time for lunch. "Thanks. You're always looking out for me, aren't you?"

A grin spread across Lacey's face. "I sure am. That's why I think you need to take me up on my offer. It's easy money."

Zina shook her head. "No way. Pimping my pups out so you can make a buck off some bossy bride isn't going to help."

"I don't see how you can say that." Lacey clamped her hands to her hips. Her wedding ring caught the light from the fluorescent overheads and sent sparkles all over the walls.

"I know you think it would be helping, but I don't know how any of these dogs would react if we dumped them into one of your gussied-up wedding ordeals. With my luck some drunk bridesmaid would get bit and then I'd have liability issues in addition to the leak I've got going on now."

"But you could pick some of the most laid-back dogs. Like Buster." Lacey pointed to a square dog bed set up in the corner of the office.

A giant pit bull lifted his head at the mention of his name. His tail thumped against the linoleum, once, twice, before he let out a rush of gas.

"You want to clear the ceremony?" Zina asked as the stench of Buster's explosion wafted through the air. "Because if you're looking for a way to run off the wedding party, Buster's your dog."

Lacey wrinkled her nose then pinched it between her fingers. "Okay, so not Buster. But surely you've got another option. How many dogs do you have here right now?"

"Too many." Zina gathered the brown bag with one hand and waved the other in front of her face, trying to fan away Buster's stench. "Let's go sit out front."

"There have got to be a few sweet ones." Lacey followed her to the picnic table they'd set up in the shade of a giant live oak.

"I just don't feel comfortable with the idea." Zina shook her head before biting into her overflowing tortilla.

Or any of the ideas Lacey had been coming up with lately. Transforming the town into wedding central had been bad enough but Lacey kept trying to up the stakes. Zina had made multiple attempts to try to talk her down but Lacey was hell-bent on putting Ido on the map.

"Fine. I'll come up with another idea." Lacey bit into her taco with more force than necessary. The shell cracked dumping half of the contents onto the paper wrapper.

"Careful. Don't take out your aggression on the taco supreme." Zina grinned.

"Has anyone ever told you you're impossible?"

"You know you're the only person in town who thinks so."

"No one else knows you as well as I do." Lacey narrowed her eyes as she took another bite—a gentle bite.

Zina held back a response. Lacey might have a point, but holding her ground was the only thing that had ever worked for her. Until it hadn't. The one time she'd let someone else talk her into not listening to her gut she'd almost ended up with a hole in her head. Granted, life in Ido was much different than the time she spent on active duty in the Middle East. But still, she couldn't be too careful, especially not with the crazies who kept dumping pit bulls out there.

As if she could read her mind, Lacey finished a sip of her soda and turned to Zina. "You have any more incidents?"

"Hmm?" Zina tried to pretend she didn't know exactly what her friend meant.

"Vandalism. Bodie told me he was out at your place earlier this week."

"Nope. Nothing since then. They pretty much chalked it up to some kids with too much free time on their hands."

"Well if it happens again call Bodie first. He told me you called the sheriff's department and it took forever for them to send someone out."

Zina shrugged. "I don't want anyone to accuse me of taking special liberties."

"You're practically family. That's not taking special liberties, that's just what it is."

Practically family. The thought of Lacey with her blond hair and blue eyes fitting in with Zina's mix of Mexican, German, and Scottish heritage brought a grin to her face. Her friendship with Lacey was one of the only things holding her here in town. That and the dogs.

She'd been tempted to pick up and leave it all behind more than a time or two over the years. But something held her back. Maybe it was knowing Lacey would be lost without her. Maybe it was knowing she was actually making a difference in the lives of the dogs she was able to save. But if she were being honest with herself. Like, really, truly, gut-wrenchingly honest, she knew the main reason she stayed was that she was too afraid to leave.

"Hey, are you going to be out by the Phillips House anytime today?" Lacey asked.

"I can be. I need to pick up some more towels before I run out. What do you need?"

"I've got some linens I picked up from the dry cleaner from last weekend's wedding that need to be put away. Would you mind dropping them off for me?"

"Sure." It was the least she could do. Lacey wouldn't hesitate to do her a favor. All she ever had to do was ask.

Ready to find
your next great read?

Let us help.

Visit prh.com/nextread